Isla Gordon lives on the Jurassic Coast of England with her T. rex-sized Bernese mountain dog. Isla has been writing professionally since 2013 (and unprofessionally since she can remember). She also has five romantic comedies published under the name Lisa Dickenson.

Isla can't go a day without finding dog hair in her mouth.

A Snowfall
by the Sea

ISLA GORDON

SPHERE

SPHERE

First published in Great Britain in 2022 by Sphere

3 5 7 9 10 8 6 4

A CIP catalogue record for this book is available from the British Library.

ISBN 978-0-7515-8513-1

Typeset in Caslon by M Rules
Printed and bound in Great Britain by Clays Ltd, Elcograf S.p.A.

Papers used by Sphere are from well-managed forests and other responsible sources.

Sphere
An imprint of
Little, Brown Book Group
Carmelite House
50 Victoria Embankment
London
EC4Y 0DZ

An Hachette UK Company
www.hachette.co.uk

www.littlebrown.co.uk

Dedicated to
Paul, Laura, Beth & Rosie
See you at the seaside soon

Chapter 1

~ Now ~

October

Sometimes, wishing for change and wishing for things to stay the same could be as blended as sand in waves.

Cleo felt it all at once. The temperature of the seawater as it first washed over her bare feet (freezing). The exposure of standing there in her swimming costume for the first time in years (excruciating). How the expanse of ocean seemed before her (massive). The joy of being here on her own, without any interruptions, scratching against the concern that there was nobody else about, and what if something went wrong? How her soul was telling her it was time, while her brain was telling her maybe it wasn't.

The mid-October sun prickled at her skin even at this early hour of the morning, as if it didn't know autumn had started, as if it hadn't had the memo that the leaves were turning red and jumper dresses were being pulled out of the back of wardrobes to air out, ready for sweater weather. Even so, the same sun hadn't had a chance to heat the seawater yet today, and tiny, cold waves lapped at Cleo's ankles before dragging sand and small stones back past her toes.

She moved her feet, flexing the soles, and wrapped her arms around her, covering herself up a bit, a barrier between her and the ocean.

'Come on, then, you big chicken. It's only a bit of cold water. You could just get in, you know,' she muttered to herself, her words muffled by the seaside sounds, as soft as they were.

There was nobody on the beach at this time in the morning, at this time of year. She had total freedom to dip into the water, unwatched, unjudged. And she'd done the hardest thing, right? She was down here. When the alarm she'd been setting herself every day since the beginning of the month had gone off, she'd actually dragged herself out of bed, and come down here. All the other days she'd switched it off, too tired after an evening shift. Or she'd got as far as checking the sea conditions via Wavebreak Bay's beach webcams and had changed her mind. Or she'd detected a cold wind in the air, one that surely would be tickling the shore by the time she'd walked down there from her flat.

But today she was here, and the sky was yellows and blues and the sea a swirl of crystal-clear topaz and mint, and there was no wind, and no reason she couldn't break this apathy she'd been living under. All she had to do was dive in.

Cleo took an extra step forward, an icy wave foaming over her shin, and she let out a little swear as a seagull swooped past and, probably, rolled its eyes at her. It *was* cold, though.

Had it always been this cold? Maybe she should come back down to the beach a bit later, when the water might have warmed up a bit.

A memory swam into Cleo's mind of being a kid, maybe aged seven, and coming onto this beach for the first time.

'Look at the water!' she'd cried to Gabriela, her twin sister, as they'd raced down the cliff path from the house their parents had just moved them into.

'This beach is *all ours*,' screeched Gabriela, not quite accurately, cartwheeling in the sand in a way Cleo never managed but always tried anyway. The girls, having only experienced beaches a handful of times on family holidays, couldn't believe their luck that they now lived right next to one.

'I'm going to play in the sea every day,' Cleo had declared, picked herself up and ran to the water's edge before she skid to a halt to watch tiny pools of foam swirl on the surface of the shallow tide.

Cleo – now – was looking down at the same thing before her eyes. Morning sun glinting off the same ocean.

Back then, that first day, Gabriela hadn't wanted to get in the water. She'd shied away, unsure if it was safe, unsure if they should without their mum or dad to supervise. But Cleo could see their mum leaning over their garden fence on the cliff, overlooking the beach, waving at them.

'We can do this,' she'd told Gabriela. Cleo had taken her hand and the two had skipped and splashed a little way into the water, keeping within sight of their mum, close to the shore, only staying in the sea for a couple of minutes.

A couple of minutes was all it had taken for them to transform into water babies, beginning a love of the ocean for the twins that hadn't faded for years. Gabriela's interest had waned when she'd moved away to Cambridge University. Cleo's had remained up until a few years ago, when she'd begun to push aside her joy, saving it for a rainy day. Now it just seemed ... easier ... to stay on dry land.

Perhaps if she just ran into the ocean again, like she had as a little girl, it would all come back and she would be fixed—

Behind her, a little further along the beach, came the sound of someone stepping down from the esplanade and onto the big, round pebbles, the stones knocking against each other as they dislodged and shifted.

'Cleo!' called a voice, just as a chocolate brown Labrador pelted into her legs. 'Bloody hell, are you going in? You're brave!' It was Clarissa, from work, out for a morning walk with her dog, Plop.

'Yep. First swim of the season,' Cleo called back, not specifying which season, in which year. 'Wish me luck.'

Plop's wet tail was thwacking against her leg, while a tennis ball bobbed in the wave before her.

'You couldn't throw that ball for him, could you?' Clarissa asked, stepping closer, her pregnant belly visible through the slit in her jacket.

You know, maybe tomorrow *would* be a better day to swim. Cleo would be back down at the beach anyway, working the brunch shift at the restaurant – perhaps she could take a dip afterwards. Then the sun would have warmed swirls just below the surface, and it would be much more pleasant. She could even remember to bring her wetsuit (if it still fitted).

Besides, it would be good to give Clarissa a bit of company on her walk, especially since Plop kept dropping his ball in the ocean.

Yes, good idea. She wanted her first swim back in the sea, after years of feeling unmotivated, to be a gorgeous experience. Tomorrow.

Cleo turned back out of the ocean, having thrown Plop's ball, and slipped her shorts and sweater back on, pulling salt crystals up the lengths of her shins. After strolling the beach with her friend for half an hour, she made her way back up the pebbles and onto the esplanade, then began her walk home.

Opening the door to her studio flat, which sat on the top floor of an old Regency home overlooking the tennis courts, her foot stepped on the morning's post, already lying on the floor.

A bank statement, clothing catalogue, and ... Cleo smiled.

Dropping the other mail back on the floor, she looked at the picture on the front of the postcard. It showed a black-and-white photo of 'Machine Gun' Kelly (the gangster, not the musician) with a *Welcome to Alcatraz, San Francisco!* stamp across the lower half.

Cleo carried the postcard into her kitchen corner, where her fridge was covered in magnets holding up picture postcards from Northern California, and sat down on a stool to savour the words.

San Francisco, California
    1st October

Dear Cleo,
    Get ready, because it's nearly time! That sounds a
bit threatening, especially on a postcard with Alcatraz
on the front.
    My San Fran summer has pretty much come to a
close again. One day you should join me. I know you
love Wavebreak Bay but the SF Bay is cool too,
I promise.
    Wish you were here, but not really, because I'm
about to come over there!
    Love, Eliot x

Eliot spent each summer away, and always took time to
send her postcards filled with cute and funny thoughts, tales
of the things he'd seen and the flavours he'd tasted and the
sights he'd visited. Cleo made sure to send him postcards
too, but hers always lacked a similar sense of adventure.

Nevertheless, forgetting about her failed mission to leap
into the sea, she smiled. He was finally coming home.

Chapter 2

The following day, Cleo was staring out of the window of her flat, down towards the deserted tennis courts below, waiting for her twin sister to call her back. She'd been waiting for so long, gazing out of that window, that she felt like a woman from an old novel waiting for her lover – Eliot – to come home from sea.

Her friend. Her *friend* Eliot.

Either way, he still wouldn't be back in the UK for another couple of weeks. Although, who knows, maybe she'd still be waiting on her sister even then?

Eliot was Cleo's best friend, if best-friendship was defined by the person who knew the real you better than anyone, and actually seemed to like you for it. Even though he left Wavebreak Bay every year to spend the six spring and summery months in San Francisco, it was always effortless to fall back into what they had every time he returned.

There was one thing he didn't know about Cleo, though. Quite a big thing.

Her phone began tinkling with an incoming FaceTime.

'Hey, sorry about that,' Gabriela said, her phone propped up on her recipe holder while she did something on her laptop.

'No problem at all!' Cleo said, just happy to be having a catch-up with her sister. 'I was just watching the hang-gliders over the beach.'

'Beach' was a stretch – from her flat she could see just a small snip of blue ocean. But even that was better than nothing. And she'd adored this flat the moment she'd stepped inside it.

'I will never understand how you can still stare at sea for hours on end.'

'Haha, I know, it's weird, isn't it?' Cleo replied. For Gabriela, this seaside town was too sleepy for her nowadays, *especially* during the off-season, and, though she'd once loved the sea nearly as much as her sister, she had never felt the pull to move back.

'Are you pleased "Cleo-Season" is back?' her twin asked, looking into the screen with an amused, but fond, smile on her face, referring to Wavebreak Bay's typically quieter winters.

When September ended, that, to Cleo, was the real end of summer in their seaside town on Devon's Jurassic coast. Sure, every year the August bank holiday was heaving, but in Wavebreak Bay, nearly as many visitors swarmed the town the month *after* the kids went back to school. Everybody else trying to catch that summer sun before it faded away for the winter. If you can imagine what the last day of a self-catering holiday feels like, when you're trying to fit in all the final activities, eat all the food, play in the sea one last time, that's what the last weekend in September always felt like, except on a whole-town scale.

The seafood restaurant that Cleo worked in, Coacean, which sat on stilts above one end of the long beach, brimmed with customers from sunrise to the final sunset of September, and that's when Cleo-Season (as Gabriela had referred to it since they were kids, with summer being 'Gabriela-Season') could begin.

'I am *so* pleased,' Cleo replied, already feeling like she had a little more breathing space.

'Mum said Eliot is coming home again soon?' Gabriela asked.

'Yeah, it should be really nice.'

'I wonder if he's bagged a hot American girlfriend yet. How would you feel about that?'

Cleo shrugged, feigning indifference. 'I mean, if he was happy ... '

Gabriela rolled her eyes. 'You can say you'd hate it, you know. But seriously, one day he's going to bring back some stunning, volleyball-playing, American girlfriend, who will also be absolutely lovely so you'll feel compelled to become her best friend and next thing you know, you'll be watching TikTok videos of their romantic city breaks across Europe. And you'll be all, *that could have been meeeeee.*'

'No, I wouldn't,' Cleo protested, though Gabriela was probably right.

'Or, he won't come back at all.'

The words floated in the air between them like particles of dust. Every winter she worried it would be Eliot's last coming back to Wavebreak Bay. Every year she swore she would admit her feelings for him, and then every year, without fail, time would drift by in a happy haze while he was here and then she'd be waving him goodbye again. Putting her life on hold, again.

And in fact, last winter he *had* come home with a hot American girlfriend. In a way. He'd started seeing somebody during the summer, early days, casual, he'd said, until she'd shown up here to surprise him in the New Year. She'd been none too pleased with the presence of Cleo, so Cleo had kept her distance until she'd gone, but when she'd spoken to Eliot during his first few days back in San Francisco again, he'd admitted they'd split up, and that she wasn't right for him. But maybe the next girl would be.

Gabriela spoke again. 'It's been years. He's thirty-one now. You're thirty. What are you waiting for?'

Cleo didn't have the answer. She was waiting for him to make a move? She was waiting for the right moment? She was afraid he was going to reject her and then she'd lose the him she held on to tightly, even from across an ocean? So she was waiting, because waiting was easier than knowing?

She changed the subject. 'How are you? How's Derek?'

Gabriela leaned away from the camera at that moment and said something to someone near her, presumably her fiancé. 'He's fine,' she answered, facing the screen again.

'He wanted to tell you to watch *Orphan: First Kill* because he thought you might like it.'

'Oh great, I'll check it out!' Cleo enthused, dying inside just a little. She'd accidentally got herself into a pattern of watching horror movies after listening, with perhaps a little too much interest, to Derek discuss one the first time she'd met him. Now he kept suggesting new ones and then wanting to get her thoughts, and she didn't really enjoy them, but didn't want to be rude or hurt his feelings, when they were clearly a big deal for him.

And let's face it, Derek wasn't often one for extolling the virtues of things. Or places. Or people.

Gabriela and Cleo talked a little longer, about Gabriela's wedding plans for next year, about their parents' semi-retirement, about the girl Cleo saw in the restaurant the other day who they both went to school with, and who was now speaking with a faux-Australian accent for some reason.

'Are you coming home any time before Christmas?' Cleo asked, just before they rang off.

'Maybe. I presume you'll be around the whole time if I do, as usual?'

'Yeah, probably, as usual. Miss you, sis!'

Cleo said goodbye and pressed the button to end the call, her flat falling into silence again. Maybe in a couple of weeks she could have Eliot over and they could have a big catch-up.

She soon found herself lost in a daydream of Eliot returning, walking across the beach, taking her in his arms, not saying a word, and sweeping her into the kiss she'd played out in her mind a hundred times or more.

That thing he didn't know about her was that she'd fallen for him, and that the spark she held had ignited long, long ago.

Chapter 3

~ Then ~

Summer 2007

The first time Cleo Clearwater saw Eliot Ambrose was over the low, moss-covered stone wall that separated her garden from the house next door. In the fifteen years she'd grown up on this cliff above Wavebreak Bay, she'd never seen anyone occupy the compact, square neighbouring garden other than the older couple who lived there, who seemed to have always been grey, and were often frowning.

But now, the woman was by her back door, a smile on her face that made her seem brighter, as a teenage boy stepped out past her into the sunshine.

Cleo swallowed, watching, and tried to silence her unremitting hay-fever-induced sniffles.

There was a warm, light breeze that day that flipped at the pages of the magazine she'd found on the bus, while she sat on the swinging seat overlooking the crowded beach below. The magazine had the words *SEXY TIME* emblazoned upon it in a large, purple font, something that both enthralled and embarrassed Cleo, and she kept it firmly face down whenever either of her parents came outside.

It was the first day of the school summer holidays, which meant, combined with today's low tide, the exposed sand was awash with hundreds-and-thousands sprinkles of beach umbrellas, bathing suits, body boards, towels and picnics. The sea winds that rose upwards were saturated with the sounds of laughter and chatting and lapping waves, but Cleo was glad to be up here, away from the crowd.

The boy next door walked to the end of the garden, his profile to Cleo, and looked out across the sea. He had mid-brown hair, the colour of hazelnut ice cream, which waved in the breeze, and she could tell by how the wall only came up to his hips that he must be a little taller than her. His turquoise T-shirt was billowing in the warm air, and his hands were in the pockets of his shorts, like he was trying to make himself small, but even from her seat she could see there was a smile on his face.

He was the most delicious thing she'd *ever seen* and he was *right there, practically in her garden*. Just the knowledge of that caused a blush to creep in under her freckles.

'Urgh, what are you reading?' screeched a voice from behind Cleo, making her jump and tip out of the swinging seat onto the grass.

Gabriela plucked the magazine from, which lay face down on the ground, and flipped it over to where it was open, spread-eagle, on a page about how to have an amazing time in bed.

'I didn't . . . I wasn't . . . the wind kept turning the pages.' Cleo scrabbled to her feet and tried to grab at the magazine, only succeeding in ripping off the cover.

'Get off,' her twin sister said, turning her back, now engrossed in the article. 'You shouldn't be reading about this stuff—'

At that moment, Gabriela raised her eyes towards the neighbouring garden and stopped.

Cleo, grassy knees, blushing face and clasping the mangled cover of her magazine, followed her sister's gaze.

The boy was still standing at the end of the garden, the older woman thankfully nowhere to be seen, but he was now looking behind him, over at the twins. He pulled a hand from his pocket and waved. 'Hiya,' he said.

'Hiya,' Cleo mimicked, unintentionally parroting the boy.

'Hello,' Gabriela said, with her head tilted to the side as she took him in.

Cleo glanced at her sister and despite the biggest grin she'd slapped on her face, the one she'd practised in the mirror that showed all her teeth and went up to her eyes, her heart sank. He'd been hers, her fantasy, for two tiny minutes, but if Gabriela locked her sights on him, Cleo knew she couldn't compete. There was just something about her sister, a quality she possessed that Cleo didn't, a self-confidence like she'd figured out her identity long ago and was completely comfortable with it, and it drew people to her.

While Cleo searched her vocabulary for something to say – 'my name is' would have been a perfectly acceptable start, if she'd thought about it – Gabriela asked outright, 'Who are you? Are you related to our neighbours?'

'Yeah,' added Cleo, as if she, too, had been on the brink of asking the same thing, rather than just following Gabriela. As usual.

The boy nodded. 'I'm their grandson. I'm Eliot.'

'I'm Gabriela; this is Cleo.'

'Hi,' he replied, then looked at Cleo directly and said it again. 'Hi.'

'Hi,' she answered, the blush returning. Maybe it never left.

Gabriela looked over at her twin now, clocking the blush, amusement at the corners of her lips. But thankfully, the one thing her sister never did was that mortifying squawk her friends were prone to of declaring loudly, '*You're blushing! She's totally blushing!*'

From Gabriela's fingertips still dangled the offending magazine like she was waving a flag. Just as Cleo tried to snatch it back, her sister turned on her heel and said, 'I'm telling Mum you've been reading this.'

Cleo watched Gabriela stalk back into the house, not wanting to make a scene in front of this boy, instead emitting a faux-chuckle, like it was all great larks. She and her sister had taken to having moments where they screamed at each other over things that, to most people, seemed insignificant. Other times they bickered for hours, grating at each other about why the other twin wasn't more like them. Gabriela usually won, and Cleo backed down to keep the peace. But as quickly as those arguments came, they could dissipate, and the twins would be back to huddling close on the sofa, limbs tangled, Gabriela asking Cleo to plait her silky hair while she mesmerised her sister with details of her new, blossoming, snog-filled love life.

'Um ... ' Cleo searched for something to say, now Eliot and she were alone, but all she could think was, *I'm alone with a really cute boy and what if he leans over the wall to kiss me and I'd totally let him.*

'Are you twins?' Eliot asked.

'Yep,' Cleo said, desperate to throw out a second syllable somewhere to show him she could. 'How did you know?'

The sisters were non-identical, so a lot of people didn't realise they were twins. But Cleo could see the gold of her auburn curls reflected in strands of her sister's chestnut hair. She could see the matching freckles on both of their noses. When they were out on the water together, even as little girls, Cleo could see a similar sense of happy contentment reflected in Gabriela.

But Eliot saw it too. At least, he saw something in her. However, he just shrugged, a little shyly, and said, 'I don't know. Lucky guess.'

'So, um, ' why are you here?' Cleo asked. She'd meant, *What brings you to Wavebreak Bay? Why haven't I seen you at your grandparents' house before?* But, as her mum liked to say, Cleo had a long-standing infliction of foot-in-mouth disease so she rarely seemed to find the right words.

But Eliot didn't seem offended, or even fazed. 'I'm spending the summer with my grandparents.'

'Oh.' She nodded. And he nodded. And just as she was

about to say something else – though she didn't know what yet – he turned and walked back towards the bungalow.

'OK, see you round.'

'See you round,' she parroted, again.

Finally, as the door closed to the bungalow next door, Cleo allowed herself to take a big, pollen-filled, snotty sniff, just as her own back door opened.

'Cleo,' her mother, Felicity, barked, holding up the remnants of her magazine. 'What are you doing reading about these things?'

'It's not mine!' Cleo protested. It was. 'I wasn't reading it; I don't even know what it means.'

Behind Felicity, Gabriela smothered a guffaw and ran away. Cleo sniffed again.

'Would you come inside?' Felicity asked. 'You know the pollen count's high today.'

'No, Mum, I'm fine.'

'Cleo—'

'I'm honestly completely fine.' She sneezed and wiped her nose on the shoulder of her T-shirt. 'I want to be in the garden.'

That summer, Cleo spent more time in the garden than anywhere else. She ate breakfast out there, she read book after book, she painted her toenails, she fixed her bike, she watched each and every sunset. In fact, pretty much the only time she left was when she went down to the beach, usually early morning before the crowds of holidaymakers arrived, and often with her sister; though Gabriela almost always needed coaxing to get into the chilly water. Usually, Cleo was the one who was prone to following Gabriela about. But Gabriela liked her hair to have that salty look so she almost always ended up agreeing, joining Cleo for a morning swim or to take their recently purchased kayaks out so she could soak up a few rays before heading out with her friends for the day.

Cleo liked being the one who encouraged Gabriela into the sea. In every other aspect of their dynamic, it seemed like her twin was doing everything first, or found it easier, or that it was Cleo who needed to be emboldened to step out of her comfort zone. But for Cleo, the sea *was* her comfort zone, and when she was there any self-doubt just ... dissipated into the saltwater.

Their parents had told them this was the last summer they were allowed to laze around, and, next year, when they'd both turned sixteen – their birthdays being in May – they'd be expected to work at the family restaurant, Coacean, down in the town, unless they found something elsewhere.

So this summer, Cleo was staying firmly where she was. Where she had the most chance of 'running into' her new neighbour Eliot.

Oh, the daydreams she had about the two of them, falling in love over the garden wall, him taking her hand and leading her into his garden where they would dance under the moonlight. And then maybe he'd be an amazing dancer, like they were in their own version of her favourite movie, *Step Up*, and the two of them would have sizzling chemistry and moves together (overlooking her own dance skills). As she lay on the grass, her hay fever eventually fading away with the lessening of the pollen, she imagined having her first kiss with him; she imagined him confessing that he'd got a crush on her too; she imagined holding his hand and then telling everyone at school in September that she'd had a summer boyfriend.

But those wishes never materialised. She saw Eliot from time to time, and they chatted a little, and she tried to make lots of eye contact like the magazines told her to, but mostly he seemed to spend his days away from the house.

'Eliot, from next door, has made friends with Celeste's brother and his mates from the year above,' Gabriela declared one day in August as they were helping tug each other out of their wetsuits. 'He's sixteen too, apparently, and they're teaching him to surf.'

Cleo nodded nonchalantly, like this was only mildly interesting information and she hadn't been watching him intently any time the waves were high enough for him and his friends to practise on the beach at Wavebreak Bay. Celeste's big brother was popular, sporty and clever, and was expected to have aced all of his GCSEs when the results came out later that month. Celeste was always grumbling about how much pressure it put on her, especially since she couldn't give a flying fudge brownie about school grades, and even less about sports.

Eliot was sixteen, the year above her. An older man. She wondered how he'd done in his GCSEs. Perhaps he could give her some tips as she entered her own Year Eleven this September. Perhaps he could privately tutor her, and then their fingers could brush as they both reached for a pencil, and then he could lean over—

'Earth to Cleo, hello?' Gabriela was knocking on Cleo's head. 'Are you coming?'

'Where?'

'To the beach this evening, for the barbecue.'

'Whose barbecue?'

'*Celeste's.*'

Cleo was torn. She liked Celeste enough, and she really liked barbecues, but she always felt uncomfortable in big groups if she had to make small talk.

'Eliot will probably be there ... ' Gabriela coaxed, and Cleo flared a fiery red shade.

'What – why would I care about that? What?' Cleo flustered.

But Gabriela just rolled her eyes, and Cleo started planning her outfit.

She went to the barbecue that night, but was too shy to leave the side of her best friend, Amelie. Instead, she watched Eliot out of the corner of her eye as the sun dipped beyond the red cliffs and the air cooled.

The summer days drifted by in their long, slow way. And it wasn't until the winter came that Eliot became more than Cleo's crush next door.

Chapter 4

~ Now ~

'Right, chop-chop.' Cleo pepped herself up, pulling away from the window of her flat. Thinking of Eliot, it was probably time she thinned out the postcards on her fridge a bit before he came back and thought she'd set up a shrine to him or something.

Her home was a tiny cove of sunshine, the studio in the old house at the very far end of Wavebreak Bay's high street having big skylights above her loft bed. She was about a fifteen-minute walk through the town to the beach, but far enough that she never heard any noise from late-night pubs or early morning deliveries.

Cleo had lived here since the winter after she'd returned to Wavebreak Bay following university. She'd been here nearly ten years now, and nothing had really changed, from the pink and cream walls, to the shabby chic surf décor. It was exactly the same cosy coastal hideaway as it had been when she had moved in with visions of trailing sand across the wooden flooring every day. She'd even measured to make sure there would be somewhere she could prop her kayak, but soon realised heaving it up three flights of stairs wasn't ideal, and so had temporarily left it in her parents' garage. It was still in there. Nothing had changed. Except, maybe, for Cleo.

Leaving her latest postcard from Eliot on the fridge, along with a few of her favourite ones that had arrived this summer – one of a sea lion, one of a wave breaking over a place called Ocean Beach, and a rainbow-print Pride post-card – she gathered the others in her hand and took them to her wardrobe, which doubled as her 'Cleo Cupboard'.

One half of the wardrobe was dedicated to clothes, mostly her work shirts, and cubbyholes full of leggings, shorts and sweaters. The other half, well, it was where Cleo stored the things she didn't want the outside world to see.

As Cleo crouched on the floor, she ran her hand over her bone-dry wetsuit on the way down. It used to hang on the coat rack by the door, a tray under it to catch the drips after she'd rinsed it out in the shower, but when people came over, they'd see it and ask, 'Oh, do you go in the sea a lot?'

When her answer went from, 'Yes' to 'Yes, but it's been a while, you know ... weather' to 'Sometimes' to 'I used to', she moved it into here.

Also in the wardrobe were old books from her teenage years that she still liked but that she worried people would laugh at, her soft toy zebra, her journals, the brochure for the local amateur dramatics group that she had once consid-ered joining but chickened out, a dusty yoga mat, and her memory box, a deep wicker basket, which she pulled out, an old kayak paddle falling and bopping her on her head as she did so.

Cleo smoothed her fingers over all of her other belongings, giving them a little love before she shut them away again.

She lifted the lid of her memory box, and inside were bundles upon bundles of postcards, every one that Eliot had sent over the past five summers. She slipped the latest ones in under the elastic band of the top collection, and a thought crept in that whispered, Gabriela's words haunting her, *How long can you keep doing this? What ARE you waiting for?*

But she pushed aside that thought, right back in the wardrobe with her memory box.

Standing up, she looked at a poster on the inside of her cupboard door, showing the female surfer Alexis Alexander crouching on a pink-and-white board as she rode through the tunnel of a sun-glistened turquoise wave in Hawaii. In the corner of the poster was a quote from Alexis.

'"Be you",' Cleo read out loud before closing the door. 'Well, that's easy for you to say, Alexis, you're the coolest person in the world.'

Cleo stepped out of the front door of the house and basked for a moment. The temperature had dropped overnight and now, with chilly air and sunshine, this really was the perfect of all the weathers.

The sky seemed bigger in October, sweeping above her in a vast, blue dome. There were colour pops of orange and red leaves on the grass banks around the edge of the tennis courts, blown over from the apple orchard that inclined up one of the two hills that watched over the valley that was Wavebreak Bay.

Cleo skirted the edge of the courts, one of which was now occupied by a white-clothed couple, and she jumped as a neon-yellow ball thwacked into the chicken-wire fence with a *prang*, right by her head.

'Sorry!' called out the player.

'It's totally fine!' Cleo called back.

'I didn't see you there,' they continued.

'I know, I did come out of nowhere,' she laughed. 'Sorry.'

'No problem,' they replied, and got back to their game.

Cleo made her way onto the pavement of the high street that wove through the centre of the valley, and followed it as the pearl-and-ivory-painted residential homes melded into pastel B&Bs and businesses, and then into the familiar markers of most typical British beach towns, at least down here. She strolled alongside ice-cream shops, past FatFace, Joules, White Stuff, in between cafés that boasted cream teas brimming with dollops of local clotted cream.

She took in tell-tale signs that the off-season had arrived in Wavebreak Bay. Though most shops and businesses stayed open in the winter, more than people tended to think, there were some that shuttered their windows and locked the doors ready for lick of paint and a spring awakening in the new year.

Cleo spotted Marilyn coming out of her bakery to wipe the salt spray off the glass windows, a regular coating they were all used to, living on the coast.

'Marilyn,' Cleo called out. 'I tried one of those new chocolate orange scones of yours the other day. They were delicious – my new favourites! I think I like them even more than your regular ones.'

Marilyn, who was extremely proud of her award-winning scones and now also her gleaming windows, gave a slightly less gleaming smile to Cleo. 'Thanks, but they were actually made by my friend who visited last weekend, so it's back to my ones from now on, I'm afraid.'

'Oh, your scones are spectacular, I just meant those were the best *chocolate orange* scones I'd ever had.' Cleo scuttled away, cringing and wishing she'd never opened her big gob.

She neared the seafront, the sunshine like a guiding light between the two cliffs that cupped the town.

On the top of the west hill sat the ginormous and stately Wavebreak Views Hotel, which felt like a cross between Newquay's Headland Hotel where they filmed *The Witches* and the perfect setting for a Daphne du Maurier novel – except this one was all painted oyster-white. Next to the hotel was the Oceanside Youth Hostel, which overflowed with international visitors, especially during the summer months. The hotel wished that the hostel wasn't sharing its clifftop, and vice versa. But Cleo, at the risk of sounding a hundred years old, thought the presence of the hostel gave the town a happy, youthful feel.

That said, in the summer, Wavebreak Bay could be *heaving*. Holidaymakers were everywhere, the beaches bursting, the sea sparkling with so many bathers it was like the opening scene of *Jaws*. Not in a bad 'bring on a whopping shark to chomp them all' kind of way – it was lovely to see – it was just a lot.

However, in the winter, when all those people had drifted away, when the sunshine relaxed and hung lower in the sky, when the beach became primarily inhabited by local surfers and dashing dogs, that's when Cleo really loved living here.

And the best part of every winter? Eliot came home.

On the top of the other cliff, on the east side of the bay, was a row of wonderful, windswept houses, all several hundred years old and passed down through generations of families. Cleo was lucky enough to have grown up in one of them, watching the Atlantic waves crashing as she grew from a kid to a teen. Her parents still lived up there now, and had filled the house with a collection of pets since she and her sister had moved out.

Cleo stepped onto the esplanade, which stood above Wavebreak Bay's long beach, with a string of beach huts like a candy necklace separating the two.

The beach, which arced deeper on the east, the side of the cliffs with the houses on, was covered in large, smooth pebbles in shades of rose gold, stormy grey and sunrise yellow. And when the tide was out, a wide strip of sand was revealed. It was a picture postcard. And Cleo got to work every day looking out at it.

Amelie, her old school friend, jogged past with the sun bouncing off the reflective strips on her long-sleeved running vest, as Cleo began to walk along beside the beach.

'Cleo, are you going to work?' Amelie asked, pausing and jogging on the spot.

'I am indeed,' Cleo replied.

'I was going to call,' Amelie panted. 'But since you're going anyway, could you pencil me in for a table for tonight? Four people, six p.m.?'

'No problem!'

In all honesty, it was better when people phoned when they wanted a table at the restaurant she worked in, rather than asked her off the cuff, because she preferred to take table preference (inside or outside) and allergy info over the phone where possible. But Cleo could always give her a ring back later.

Coacean was the best restaurant in the whole of Wavebreak Bay, if she did say so herself. Founded by her parents back in the late nineties, and named after a combination of the twins' favourite words as children ('coast' and 'ocean'), Cleo had worked there full time ever since she moved back to the town, straight after university. It served super-fresh seafood, mouth-watering cocktails, and crisp, chilled wine, and sat on the eastern edge of the town. Cleo could be working out on the decking, and look up the cliff to her childhood home.

She was nearing the restaurant now, ready to start her shift. Even when the winter season came, Coacean remained the social hub of the town, so the days never dragged. She liked it more especially when the days got shorter and the interior, and exterior, of the restaurant glowed with thousands of warm white fairy lights.

Just before reaching Coacean, some bright colours down on the beach caught her attention, and she followed the steps down onto the pebbles to get a closer look.

A woman and a teenage boy were lazing in one of the two dinghies that were permanent features near the stilts of the restaurant, bright paint peeling under constant sun, and flower pots having been added long ago so that daffodils, daisies and tulips bloomed up from the bows throughout the year. Scattered beside the dinghy was an array of surfboards, bodyboards, kayaks and beach towels. A sign, from a local surf shop, read, *End of Season Sale!*

From a distance, Cleo gazed at a pink-and-white kayak, smaller and sleeker than her bulky, years-old one in her parents' garage. It was coloured like swirled strawberry ice cream, similar to the surfboard Alexis Alexander rode in her poster back home. Was this a sign? Was it, finally, time for her to stop making excuses and go back in the water?

No, no. She couldn't splash out on a new piece of equipment; she had a perfectly good kayak gathering dust. If she was going to invest in a new one she should have got on and done it years ago, when she'd first moved back, rather than losing interest and the skills. Could she even remember *how* to kayak safely these days? She should have bought that campervan she'd dreamed of and made time to explore the coastline. But she never had. And she wouldn't even fit into that whole scene now.

She almost wished she had a big, dramatic reason for not wanting to go in the water. Something she could blame her reluctance on, like having floated out into the middle of the Channel for three days with only her kayak and half a sandwich. But she could only blame herself. Over the years, a combo of a lack of motivation, putting other people first, a few instances of bumped heads, a mild panic attack, and a whole lot of excuses meant it was she who kept pushing the things she loved aside, letting them fade into the horizon. It was just . . . easier to put herself last.

But . . . the surf shop woman looked kind. Perhaps she could just ask how much it was? Then think about it? Maybe this was the year to take the bait?

Cleo hesitated on the spot, rehearsing exactly what she was going to say. Then took a breath, and—

'Oh, Graham!' she said, spotting a dog walker, one of her parents' friends, on the beach. 'I've finished that book I was going to lend you, if you still want to read it?'

'Yes, I'd love to – I've just finished mine,' Graham said, his beagle snuffling at a seashell.

'I'll drop it over to you.'

'Are you sure? I can pick it up?'

'No, it's fine; I'm always out and about.'

Graham waved a goodbye and Cleo faced the dinghies again, but now a group of surfers, fresh out of the water and in their twenties, were crowding the table, all dripping hair and laughing faces.

Cleo left, back up the steps, and continued towards work without looking back.

Well, looking back a little.

Chapter 5

As she reached the entrance of Coacean, despite the sunshine, despite the watersports sale she'd just been ogling, Cleo was hit with a wave of unexpected festive feeling, a hint in the air of things to come. It was still two months until the big day, but there was something about the colder wind today that was fluttering the autumn leaves down like snow, the scent of orange spices emitting from the vents outside the kitchen, and the sight of the two people dangling out of a window above the seafront's small, picturesque department store, hanging the first of the town's Christmas lights.

All of a sudden, she thought, *It's coming. Christmas is on its way*. It drenched her from her head to her toes and a million images flooded her mind of the twinkling lights, the steam coming off mulled-wine urns outside pubs, shivering bodies with laughing faces wearing Santa hats as they dipped their feet into the sea. Her insecurities from moments before scuttled back away, like crabs in a rock pool.

'What are you doing for Christmas?' Cleo asked Rosa a little while later as they were restacking the glasses behind the bar, a family sharing hot chocolates and brownies being the only customers at this time in the late morning.

'Oh my gosh, you reminded me, thank you. I need to ask Lucy if I can take the whole holidays off and go to New Zealand.'

Rosa had arrived at the start of the summer season, days after Eliot had left and just in the nick of time to stop Cleo from falling into a self-pity pit. Rosa had marched straight from the hostel to the restaurant on the day she'd landed in town, declaring she would make their ideal summer season staffing addition, and asking when she could start.

Cleo felt like Gabriela had come home, but with a New Zealand twang and more enthusiasm.

The two of them had become firm friends, and Cleo had been chuffed to bits when Rosahad said she was going to stay and hang out for the winter season too.

'You're going to head home?'

'I hope so, if I'm allowed the time off. I haven't been back since I arrived in what, April? And my family is huge and we love Christmas and spend it all together, so I don't want miss out if I can help it.'

'How big is huge?' Cleo asked. Rosa had told her about her immediate family – two brothers, her mum, dad, her gran who lived with them.

'I can't even remember everyone off the top of my head,' she laughed. 'But it's a menagerie of aunts and nephews and great-uncles. How about you? What does Christmas look like in the Clearwater household?'

'I can't even remember.' Cleo laughed, then felt bad, because her family – her parents at least – were right there and Rosa's were all the way in another hemisphere, and she knew she missed them. Cleo could throw a rock from here and smash one of her parents' windows. If she was having a bad day or something. So she backtracked. 'That's not true, not really, I just mean that I've worked over the last few Christmases so it's not been, you know, the normal family-lying-in-front-of-the-TV kinda day.'

'Hey, what's normal at Christmas, right?'

'Right,' Cleo agreed, glad she hadn't upset her friend.

'So will you take this Christmas off?' Rosa asked.

Cleo looked out of the window, her eyes trailing the front of the red cliff until they landed on her childhood home sitting in the centre of the stretch of detached, wind-swept houses. It *would* be nice to have a proper Christmas, without working. Spending the night at her parents' on Christmas Eve. Dad would probably do stockings for her and her sister. Maybe Gabriela would even bring Derek, her wannabe-cheffy fiancé, down and he could cook them a big roast turkey and Cleo could be the Susan-Chef and help chop carrots and eat all the roasted chestnuts. Perhaps she could find some mistletoe, have Eliot and a few others over for Christmas drinks. Maybe a Christmas beach bar-becue. Maybe a Christmas swim, like that year her parents had bought her a new wetsuit when she was seventeen, of swirling pinks and oranges, and she'd begged them to come in the water with her that very afternoon.

Cleo smiled at the memory. How she'd rushed straight out of the room to tug on the suit. 'Please, please, *please* let's go in the sea,' she'd cajoled.

'Clee, sweetheart, it's the middle of December, we're not all as hardy as you,' her mum had laughed. But Cleo hadn't let up, and after they'd let their Christmas lunch go down, before the glorious winter sun dipped too low, she had them out there on the beach, hands wrapped around flasks, all wearing their wetsuits but hers bright and sparkling new.

'Come on, Dad, I promise it won't feel too cold if you just go for it,' Cleo said. Her dad had always been the least keen on sea swimming, unless it was a particularly baking day. He blamed it on the time he'd spent in California 'in his youth' and how the Pacific, rather than Atlantic, Ocean was what had his heart. But he came in, as did her mum, as did Gabriela, though she insisted on Cleo taking some pics of her in the water to show off that she actually did it.

It wasn't just the 4mm of sunset-coloured neoprene that warmed her soul that Christmas, it was sharing that moment with her family.

Turning back to Rosa, Cleo nodded. 'Yes, I think I will this year, if I can.'

Maybe she could even convince her family to come for a Christmas Day swim in the ocean with her, for old times' sake. If she could convince herself, first.

Yes. As the day progressed, Cleo let her thoughts dance. How lovely it would be to have a long, family Christmas. A proper break, time to think, time to be. Space to watch Christmas romcoms on Netflix and listen to her Christmas Crooners playlist and devour wonderfully wintery romantic novels. Chances to hang out with Eliot outside work, make the most of him being back for the winter, taking walks together and drinking hot cider in cosy pubs.

'Cleo, could I have a word when you have time?' Lucy asked as she balanced three wide platters of coconut shrimp on Cleo's arms for a table outside on the decking, where lunchtime customers were congregating under the sunny skies and complimentary blankets, despite today's strong sea breeze.

'Sure!' Cleo answered with a smile, wondering when she could carve out time for a word.

Lucy managed Coacean for her parents, now they were semi-retired. Cleo's mum and dad, Felicity and Bryce, had come up with the idea of transforming the old lifeboat station into a family-run seafood restaurant before they'd even moved here, before she and Gabriela had even been born, after they'd taken a holiday to the Northern California coast. As they'd travelled, they'd been inspired by the array of delicious seafood restaurants. That was partly why they'd agreed so readily when Eliot had come to them with an idea, a business proposal, five years ago.

He and his cousin, Chris, who he'd lived with out in San Francisco, briefly, after university, shared a goal of opening a restaurant together. Eliot, who at this point had been working as Coacean's assistant manager, was keen to move his career forward, and had the idea for the restaurant to be a US branch of Coacean. Somewhere he could co-manage with his cousin, and to ensure continuity between the branches, he'd split his time between the Devon branch and the California branch – winters here, summers there.

Cleo placed the plates of shrimp down on the large, round table, scuttling back and forth for a while fetching the diners' condiments, drink refills, extra napkins, bowls of water for their fingers, all the time anxious to know what Lucy wanted with her. She got the bill for another table, cleared a ketchup splat off a window, and ducked back outside to shoo away the seagulls who were lurking with a lazy creepiness beside a customer who'd stepped out to try and take a photo of a cloud of mist that had sauntered in to hang above the opposite clifftop.

Eventually, when the lunchtime rush had calmed to a lull, so much so that, just for a moment, there wasn't a customer in the restaurant, Cleo decided she could stop spiralling that she'd done something wrong and finally chat with Lucy.

'They've all gone!' Cleo sang out with gusto as she wiped her hands on her apron. 'Every last one—'

'Um ... ' Somebody cleared their throat behind her and she whirled to see a final, lingering customer – a man, red-faced with embarrassment and still adjusting his belt having run out of the loos after Rosa had walked in to check if they needed cleaning and toilet roll refreshing.

Cleo's own faced pooled with a bright pink that could rival the vibrancy of an autumn evening sky. 'I didn't mean you!' she stuttered, catching Rosa's eye as she scuttled past the bar trying to hide her snigger. 'No, I knew *you* were still here, obviously, I was talking about . . . the seagulls! Except, look at that, they came back again.'

On the restaurant's large outdoor decking, that protruded out over the beach upon its stilts and had steps that led straight down onto the pebbles below, the resident seagulls had returned to stare at them eerily and ravage any leftover chips. Right now, two of them were going head-to-head on half a dressed crab.

Mortified, Cleo apologised her head off and thrust a whole bag of Fox's Glacier Mints in the poor chap's paws as a parting gift. 'Thank you for dining with us at Coacean!' she called.

With a final, more thorough, glance around the restaurant's interior, Cleo deemed it now truly free of customers.

'Nice save.' Rosa tinkled with laughter, her New Zealand accent always popping more when she spoke with a smile.

'I swear I didn't know he was still in here,' Cleo replied, a small chuckle escaping. She checked her watch and looked around for Lucy, keen to talk with her before the end of her shift.

'Are you coming to the pub after work?' Rosa asked, straightening some chairs.

What Cleo wanted to do for the rest of the day was walk down to the very edge of the sea, past where the pebbles faded into a strip of sand, throw a stone into the ocean for good luck, and then walk home and do nothing but watch *Real Housewives* for three hours straight. Perhaps with some fish and chips. She couldn't wait.

Oh yeah, and she was supposed to be taking that swim today. She'd brought her swimmers down especially (though had forgotten her wetsuit again).

'Um . . . ' She dawdled.

'Come on, you've earned it. We'd miss you if you weren't there,' Rosa cajoled.

Cleo longed for the company of the Beverly Hills housewives, but she didn't want to seem stand-offish to the others, so she said, 'Sure. Just for a little bit. Lucy!'

'Cleo, how did everything go today?' Lucy was just heading from the kitchen to the office and beckoned her inside.

'Great!'

Lucy looked at her closely. 'Are you sure?'

'Yes, absolutely, I'm just . . . ' Cleo fluttered her hands in the air. 'Excited to be having a moment alone with you. I mean. No, never mind. What can I do for you?'

'I wanted to talk to you about Christmas,' Lucy said, grabbing her laptop and opening up a spreadsheet.

'Oh, me too, actually,' Cleo replied with relief.

'Rosa just asked if she could take the whole Christmas period off to go home to New Zealand.'

Cleo nodded. 'Yes, I hope she can go? It would be amazing for her to get home. If you need me to cover any of her shifts . . . ?'

'Actually, funny you should say that. It seems everyone is thinking about Christmas plans this week – Dan wants to spend Christmas with his girlfriend's family, Anwar is hoping to celebrate Hogmanay in Scotland this year and Clarissa's due date is mid-December so I have to assume she'll be out.'

'She's already nauseated every time she has to serve a bowl of chowder,' Cleo said, recalling how concerned a customer had looked the other evening as Clarissa gagged when placing the bowl in front of them.

'Right,' Lucy said, drawing out the 'i'. 'So we're going to be pretty low staffed at this rate.'

Cleo was beginning to see how this was going – she knew she should jump in there and give her preference, put her own case forward to take Christmas off this year, but instead what came out of her mouth was, 'I'm happy to help out any way I can. Christmas is so busy for us.'

'I know you get it. You've worked the last few Christmases, huh?'

'I have.' Cleo nodded. Actually, she seemed to work every Christmas. It was her business – her parents', at least – so it was her duty to help when no one else could. 'And it's great, but I can definitely see the appeal of taking the time off, hahaha.'

'What are your plans this year?' Lucy asked.

'Nothing really,' Cleo answered, carefully. 'Probably just spending Christmas with my folks.' She pointed up the cliff.

'Not going away?'

Gulp. 'No. Do you need me to work?'

'Could you? If you're not doing anything else?'

Cleo's heart sank a little, like a pebble dropped into a small wave as it crossed onto the shore.

Before she could reply, Lucy continued. 'You won't be on your own, of course. I'll be working, Eliot's obviously back again – this year – so I'll be asking him to help out, and we'll be bringing in the usual handful of seasonal workers for December, but you're so ... reliable.'

Cleo nodded. How could she say no? And stop all her friends from having the Christmases they craved? Lucy needed her. Therefore, her parents needed her. And it wasn't like she had any proper plans, not really. She could still spend the holidays at her mum and dad's, just ducking out for a few hours when her shifts were scheduled. It would be selfish to say no. Plus ... you know ... it *was* guaranteed Eliot time.

'Yes,' she answered, hiding her disappointment behind a big grin; there was no need to make Lucy feel bad. 'Sure I can.'

'So you can do the usual? Christmas Eve, Christmas Day and Boxing Day?'

'Are we closing up after brunch on Christmas Day again?'

Lucy nodded. That was something, at least. 'You'll be done by two. And only brunch on Boxing Day, also.'

Cleo glanced back towards Rosa who was laughing with a customer on the phone, her face lit up by the sunshine out over the beach, and thought of her arriving back in New Zealand for Christmas, and how happy it would make her, and her family. 'Sounds good,' she said, with a firm nod. So her Christmas wish wasn't quite coming true, but it was a small sacrifice.

Lucy paused before saying, 'You sure, Cleo? You didn't have plans?'

'Nope, I'm in. I love working Christmas – we almost always have happy customers. And it's always fun working with Eliot, so ... '

Lucy gave Cleo a small smile like she could read her not-so-subtle mind.

As Cleo walked away, though, what Lucy had said about Eliot being 'back again – this year' toyed with her, forming a worried ball in her stomach. Did Lucy envisage him not coming back one year? Staying in America permanently? It was a little too similar to what her sister had said to her earlier that same day.

The thought of her time with him running out, grains within a sand clock that she didn't even know had been turned over just trickling away, before anything had ever begun between them, made her heart ache.

She played it so safe, like she had all the time in the world. But what if it was already too late? What if he did come back, having met someone who this time was right for him? And if it wasn't too late, in the words of her twin, what the hell was she waiting for?

Chapter 6

~ Then ~

Winter 2007

Eliot hadn't told anyone he was staying in Wavebreak Bay for longer than that first summer. In a way, he never really believed he would be. He was sure that after two months his parents would realise the gap in their lives and come to take him home. But they never came.

In the late August of 2007, Eliot's grandfather had driven him back up to north Devon to get his GCSE results from his school. His *old* school, he should say. He thought his parents might have been there, waiting to surprise him, waiting to ask him to come home, but he didn't see them until they'd driven around to his house, his *old* house, and told them the news.

'That's fantastic,' his mum had said with a warm enthusiasm when he'd told them his results. He had to admit, she seemed happier, calmer, like maybe things were working out for her and his dad, after all. Perhaps it all really was worth it, and if he just gave them a couple more weeks, they'd be asking him to come back, and everything would be normal again.

His mum and dad had been bickering so much over the past year. In that sense, it was a relief to be living with his grandparents across the county, where the only sounds were the waves below the cliffs and the occasional arguments between the girls next door. But still. When they'd said they needed space to try and rebuild their relationship, he wished they'd not cut him out, like he wasn't even part of their relationship.

It sucked that they'd moved him away. It sucked that they didn't want him back. He'd cried all the way back to Wavebreak Bay that afternoon.

So, come the autumn, Eliot had started at a new school. Going into the sixth form, at least he'd been one of a dozen new faces rather than the only kid who hadn't known his way around. Still, he'd felt lonely, even when he'd been surrounded by the new friends who had kept him busy over the summer.

One Sunday morning in October, Eliot was in his room contemplating calling his mum, again, to ask when he could come home, when he looked out of his window.

In the garden next door, one of the twins, Cleo, was dragging two kayaks into the low sunshine and sitting down in front of them with a pile of thick black ropes. He watched for a moment as she began to undo the bungee cord on the kayaks and rethread new ones on, stopping every minute or two to push her red curls away from her face.

She looked so determined, so self-occupied, while he wallowed about up here like a lost puppy with nobody to entertain him.

'What are you doing?' Eliot asked, finding himself out in the cool air, perching on the stone wall between their gardens.

Cleo looked up at him, dropping the end of a cord that twanged backwards, snapping her on the arm. She cursed quietly and stood, rubbing her forearm. 'Just fixing up a couple of things on our kayaks,' she explained, motioning to them. He'd seen her and her sister take out from time to time.

'Why?' he asked. He didn't really know anything about water sports, despite spending a large amount of the summer this year on the beach, including a few surf lessons from his new friends. But that was over now, for the most part, as his group didn't seem to regard hanging around on a chilly British beach during dark winter evenings as appealing at this time of year.

'Look at the sea.' Cleo motioned over the edge of the cliff, where the ocean was a pale blue sheet of glass, barely a ripple on its surface. 'It's supposed to be like this all day so I wanted to get out while I could, before it gets choppier next week. The wind's supposed to pick up from Tuesday, so . . . '

She trailed off. He liked that she knew about this stuff. 'So you still go out in the winter?' As if she hadn't just answered that in her previous statement.

But Cleo just nodded, her happy smile sparkling across

her face in a way he hadn't noticed before. He saw that the freckles on her nose were standing strong, refusing to retreat, and maybe this was why.

'Do you … ' She hesitated, mid-sentence, as if she was trying to formulate the right words. 'Do you want to have a go?'

'At tying those string things?'

'No, sorry, I mean on the kayak. Sometime. Or today.'

Of course that had been what she'd meant. Eliot's gaze fell to the two kayaks, so alien to him, and then back to the sea. He'd spent almost every day of the summer in there, forgetting everything and just being in the moment, and he missed it. But … 'I've never been in a kayak before,' he said by way of an answer.

'I mean, if you want, we can go out together and I can, like, teach you or whatever.' She gulped, seeming shy all of a sudden. 'I mean, I'm going out anyway, and normally Gabriela would come with me but she's not been into the whole winter water thing, lately.'

'Is it cold?'

'Duh!' Cleo said, letting out a snort of laughter, which was followed with a rush of blush on her cheeks, and then a cough, as if it could cover up the word that had already left her mouth. 'Yeah, it is a bit.' She shrugged. 'But I like it. It's less crowded, both in the water and on the beach, and if you want time to think, or to stop thinking, it's the best place to go.'

Yes, that was exactly how he felt. And so Eliot agreed, following Cleo down to the beach and into the sea that day, and many other days over the course of the winter.

48

That first time she took him out on the kayak – he in hers, she in her sister's – was magical. For reasons he didn't even appreciate until he was back home, salty and sun-kissed and ... happy.

'Ready, Eliot?' she said, as he took a seat inside the kayak, wobbling a little, splashing seawater onto his legs.

'I think so,' he answered.

She smiled at him so kindly that for a moment he forgot he was supposed to leave the shoreline and paddle towards her, taken by the sight of her, red hair warm under the winter sun, back straight, a relaxed ease as she manoeuvred that he'd rarely seen in her on land.

'Put your paddle in the water like so,' she explained, re-showing him how to position the blades.

After a little while, Cleo surprised him again by gliding her kayak towards him and dangling her legs over the sides and into the water. 'You're very confident,' he said, the words – meant appreciatively – coming out sounding awkward to his ears. 'I mean, this just seems like your place, you know? Like you're in your element out here, I s'pose.'

'I s'pose I am,' Cleo replied, tilting her head back and laughing, raising her paddle horizontally in the air with both hands. 'Woooooo! I love it. Do you love it?'

She looked back at him with directness, as if searching, hoping, that he got it.

Eliot nodded. 'I'm pretty sure I'm going to ache tomorrow in some weird places, and I have a little way to go to say I *love* kayaking, but I can see it happening, sometime. For sure.' He looked away, eyes on the clear-cut horizon, licking the saltwater he'd flicked onto his lips, wondering if he had anything insightful he could add. 'It doesn't feel . . . '

'What?' Cleo prompted, pushing an escaped curl out of her eyes.

'It's nice living by the sea,' he said, trying to phrase what he was thinking without coming across as a massive doofus. 'I'm . . . do you reckon, um, do you feel like the ocean has this way of just welcoming you, no matter what? Or whatever?'

What he wanted to admit was that he was lonely, but even though he didn't say the words, she seemed to get what was swimming through his mind.

Sliding alongside him, the ripple created by her kayak nudging them both so they were looking back at Wavebreak Bay, Cleo said, 'I totally think like that. I feel a bit . . . out of place sometimes, but then I come out here and I feel like me again.' She chuckled, which came out as kind of a cute snort. 'I don't know, maybe I'm just out of place everywhere and I'm just kidding myself.'

'No.' He grinned. *You're actually great.*

They bonded after that, moving from stilted, shy conversation to something deeper, despite them being in two different years at school. He wouldn't tell her this, because he didn't know how she would take it, but it was thanks to Cleo that he made it through Christmas that year.

His parents had arrived on Christmas Eve and he'd given up his room, which was still referred to as 'the spare room', for them to stay in until they left on Boxing Day, but by the middle of Christmas Day his mum and dad had been arguing so much they decided to head back to North Devon.

Apparently being here – the subtext being that having their child around again – wasn't working for their fragile relationship.

Cleo saw him holding back tears on the edge of the cliff that Christmas afternoon, a pink sunset filling the enormous sky overhead, and she sat with him, throwing stones over and into the ocean.

'Don't spend your Christmas out here with me,' he'd said, the pinks reflected in the whites of his eyes.

Cleo had rested her head on his shoulder in a way he would never have imagined her doing a mere couple of months ago, and he caught the fragrance of sea salt mixed with coconut shampoo and he thought the word: *home*. He didn't know why – he was sixty miles from his house, in a town where he still went down the wrong street at times, going to a school where he didn't know all the names of his classmates, and with a girl he'd only recently really got to know. But he wondered if he would ever smell anything again that would give him such a strong sense of peace.

'You might be the best friend I have here,' he told her that day. He should have said 'ever' rather than 'here', but he couldn't quite bring himself to admit it.

'Well, you'd better stay then,' she answered, simply, and in that, she'd given him the reason he'd been hoping for.

There were times over that winter when Eliot wondered what it would be like if he was still here next year, and she would be in the sixth form with him. They'd be at the same parties together, friends mixing across the year groups more than they did now. He wondered if he would ever kiss her, or ask her out, once that happened. But they were just thoughts that floated by. For now, she had her own friends, her own life, outside these two neighbouring gardens, and so did he. But he loved that, aside all of that, they had each other.

Until, they didn't.

The spring of 2008 was just around the corner when his grandparents broke the news that they were moving. The bungalow they rented on the clifftop was having its rent increased, and though they'd asked Eliot's parents if they could help out with money, since they were boarding their son, his mum and dad had refused.

How could they act like that? Eliot didn't *want* to go home now – he didn't even think of North Devon as his home any more. He lived here, in Wavebreak Bay.

While Eliot's grandparents made preparations to move all three of them down the coast to a home on the outskirts of Lyme Regis, he asked Cleo's parents for a job at their restaurant. He would be seventeen in a matter of weeks, and he planned to use every penny he had to finance driving lessons and the cheapest car he could find, so he wouldn't need to move schools again, or leave Wavebreak, or Cleo, behind. And once he had those, he'd give his earnings to his grandparents. It was the least he could do.

The day came that the bungalow was emptied, and whereas Eliot had thought it would take them all day to pack up and move, it was over surprisingly quickly. The walls were bare of picture frames, the bedrooms stripped of beds, the home no longer a home, at least for them.

'Ready, Eliot?' his grandmother asked late in the morning,

as he stood at the edge of the garden, looking down the road that wound up the cliff for Cleo's parents' car. Her family was out this morning, due back sometime in the afternoon, and he'd thought he'd see her before he went. Sure, he'd run into her at the restaurant in no time – she was due to start working there this summer too, once the school term was over. But he'd wanted to say goodbye properly, here. He wanted to tell her what she meant to him, not that he quite knew what he'd say.

But she wasn't back, and his grandparents were itching to go. His grandmother especially was sad to be leaving this house much sooner than they'd hoped, and a thin layer of bitterness had settled over them, the kind that pushes you to make your exit.

Eliot fiddled with something in his pocket. It was a gift for Cleo, a silly thing really – a piece of seaglass with a hole in it, that he'd found and looped a black cord through to make a necklace. It was a thank you. She'd probably think he was a huge dork for even making it. Nevertheless, he wanted her to have it.

Eliot walked to the wall between the two gardens and placed the gift on a patch of moss, a small pebble holding it in place, and, with a final look at the swinging seat where he'd first laid eyes on Cleo, he turned and left.

Chapter 7

~ Now ~

Late in the afternoon, Cleo left work. She'd stayed longer than she'd intended, finishing things up from her shift and helping prep for the dinner crowd. Now, darkness was falling. She hesitated, looking at the sea, and wondering if there was still enough daylight to warrant dipping her toes in the ocean, just to help kick-start her return to the water this winter.

No, no, it would be silly to go in now. She had no towel with her so she'd have to walk all the way home in wet socks. Maybe tomorrow.

Instead, after agreeing to a quick drink in the pub with Rosa, who was very insistent, Cleo decided she'd better check in on her parents, and so climbed the hill to the family home.

The building, an old, four-bed farmhouse painted a pale, dawn blue and with wooden beams in every room, sat back from the cliff, behind the South West Coast Path, which ran along the front of the garden. Neither of her parents were keen green-fingered types, so the garden itself was a neat lawn with wildflowers around each edge, and a stone wall separating it from the neighbouring garden. A swing seat still overlooked the bay, and behind the house was a garage used for storage.

'Hello, you!' Her dad's voice came out of the dark as Cleo opened the rickety white gate.

'Dad? Where are you?'

'Over here, chopping some logs,' Bryce said, and emerged wielding an axe from the side of the house.

'In the dark? You look like you've been a-murdering.'

He laughed. 'I was just doing a few because we need some extra for the fire this evening.'

They walked through the door together, Cleo taking a couple of freshly hacked logs from his arms.

'Hi, Mum,' she called.

Felicity came out of the living room holding a glass of wine, slipper socks on her feet, the starry PJ set Cleo had given her last Christmas snuggling her body, and her short, strawberry-blonde hair pulled into a mini ponytail. Her glasses were pushed onto her forehead and she held an unfolded map in one hand. 'Cleo.' She smiled as she said her daughter's name. 'I didn't know you were coming over this evening. Dad and I were just finishing up a few things and then were going to have a cosy night in front of the TV. Do you want to join us?'

'What's the map for?' Cleo asked, looking over her mum's shoulder as Felicity led them all back into the living room, Macaroni the double-cream-coloured golden retriever following her. Rhubarb, the Bernese mountain dog, who was draped across one end of the big corner sofa, lifted his head, yawned at Cleo, then stretched his toes out into the air. Blueberry the cat strolled past with a welcoming brush against her legs.

'Well . . . ' Felicity started, and looked at Bryce. 'Shall we tell her?'

'Yes, tell me!' Cleo enthused, as Bryce nodded. 'Are you going on holiday?'

'No, no, nothing like that. Although, actually, a trip over there wouldn't be a bad idea, come to think of it. If Lucy, or Cleo, could hold the fort.' Felicity was staring up at her husband as they had a silent conversation between them.

'What?' Cleo took a seat next to Rhubarb, tucking herself under his giant legs.

Felicity faced her daughter, an excited smile on her face. 'Your dad and I have been chatting and looking at some numbers, and Coacean is doing really well out in the States.'

'Eliot's a brilliant manager,' Cleo enthused, that always-present thrill rippling through her at saying his name out loud. She wondered if it would ever go away. Or would she always be like a teenager with a crush, even when they were old, married to other people, and she'd accepted it was never meant to be anything more? 'And his cousin Chris, of course.'

'Exactly,' said Bryce. 'Your mum and me were reminiscing about how exciting it was when we first opened the restaurant here in Wavebreak Bay. And then it was a real dream come true when the San Francisco branch opened.'

Felicity cut in, keen to be the one to tell the story. 'So, we were looking at a map of California and wondering whether it would be viable for Eliot to open a second branch out there.'

Cleo paused, looking between her parents. 'In San Francisco?'

'No, somewhere else. Maybe Monterey . . . San Diego . . . '

'But, why?' stuttered Cleo. 'I mean, that sounds brilliant, soooo exciting, but why not have a second UK branch?'

'We just think it's the right time for out there, and we can see Eliot doing what he does here, but over there. Splitting his time between the San Fran branch and this new one, at least for a couple of years while it gets set up.'

Cleo laughed, the same nervous laugh she'd always had when she wanted to cover a feeling of dread with a mask knitted of phrases like 'sounds AMAZING' and 'oh my God, WOW'. 'Just, not coming back here for winters at all any more?' she clarified.

Felicity continued. 'Well, we'd have to ask him, of course. He might have no interest at all in such a thing, but he's travelled back and forth for years now, moving every six months. He might be ready to stay put in one country. And if we went ahead with a second US branch, that could suit us very well.'

'Yeah, wow, it would be a great opportunity for him,' Cleo swallowed, 'and for the restaurant. Wow. But wouldn't a second UK branch be a good idea? No, sorry, you already said it was because of numbers and . . . something. Coooooool. You'll have to let me know when you come up with a plan. So, what were you about to watch?' She changed the subject,

58

pushing the nauseous feeling down into the bottom of her stomach, under the heaviness of Rhubarb's legs. *Shit shit shit shit shit.* Whyyyyy hadn't she done something about her thing for Eliot sooner?

Push down the thoughts, push them down, think about them later.

'Breaking Bad,' her mum said with tenderness, like she was telling her they were bingeing on *Last of the Summer Wine.*

Her dad took a seat and reached for the remote. 'How was work this evening?'

Cleo, grateful that they didn't pursue the subject, said, 'It was fine. Busy.'

'It always is,' Mum commented.

She nodded with agreement, then took a breath, forcing herself yet further away from gut-wrenching thoughts of Eliot no longer spending winters in Devon.

Cleo wasn't looking forward to breaking the news that she'd agreed to work over Christmas *again.* But it was OK, they'd understand. This Christmas would be different. This Christmas, she was going to make sure her parents, and her sister, still had the most festive, perfect Christmas possible. So she had to pop out and work, occasionally? She would make it up to them.

'Oh yeah, um. Just to let you know ... I'm really sorry,' she commenced with, then fumbled over her words, her brain trying to find ways to play down what she'd agreed to so it didn't disappoint them. She really *really* wanted to salvage what she could of Christmastime, those dreams of stockings and Netflix and Christmas books still fresh in her mind. 'Lucy asked me what my plans were for Christmas, and everyone else really wants to go away and have these big holiday shenanigans and I felt like I couldn't say no – you know I wouldn't have wanted to stop Rosa going to New Zealand for anything, and so I said … I could work. Over Christmas. Again. I'm really sorry. Do you mind?'

'Do we mind if you work over Christmas?' Felicity confirmed, with a glance at Bryce.

'Yes. I'm sorry, I know I was working last year, and the year before, well, every year really. But maybe we could have our Christmas dinner in the evening again? And I'm happy to do all of the cooking.' Cleo didn't quite know why she'd volunteered that; she'd never cooked a Christmas dinner in her life.

Her mum let out a small laugh. 'Actually, this works out quite well for us.'

'What do you mean?' Cleo frowned.

Her dad rested the remote on the arm of the chair and busied himself stacking the logs on the fire, and Felicity continued. 'We had Gabriela on the phone this evening, and she asked if Dad and I would spend Christmas with her and Derek this year.'

'So, they'd be here too?'

'Actually, no, they invited us to spend Christmas *with* them, up in Cambridge. Hosting their first Christmas together, isn't that lovely?'

'*So* lovely. Dammit.' Cleo felt the nervous-nausea return. 'OK. I can go back to Lucy and see if she has anyone else she could ask. I'm sure Eliot will work all he can. What day would you want us to travel up? Or is it a bit early to know exact details yet?'

When they hesitated, meeting each other's eyes, the fog lifted. Cleo's sister had invited her parents. Not Cleo.

'Don't worry about changing anything,' her mum said in a gentle voice. 'I think Gabriela assumed you'd be working over Christmas again, to be honest, since you always do, so probably isn't expecting you to make the journey up.'

Cleo nodded, keen to not rock the boat or make anyone feel uncomfortable. 'Oh, of course.' *But were they that grown apart these days that Gabriela wouldn't even check to make sure?*

'We were thinking of asking you, since you'll be here anyway,' Felicity said, facing her straight on, her fingers tickling Blueberry's back, 'if you'd mind pet-sitting for us over the holidays, while we're away?'

Cleo hesitated for just a second before answering, realising this meant spending Christmas on her own.

The sense of loneliness left her cold, like a window had been left open. *Even her twin sister didn't want to be around her.*

Bryce heard the hesitation and said in a cheerful voice, 'Or I can stay with you?'

'No,' Cleo said, immediately waving him away. *Don't be so selfish*, she scolded herself. To both her parents, she said, 'You should spend Christmas together, and with Gabriela and Derek, this is a big first for them. Their first Christmas together! Brilliant. I'll be totally fine. And yes, I can pet-sit.'

'Are you sure, Clee?' Felicity probed. 'We can do lots of

FaceTiming on Christmas Day and you can have friends over if you want.'

'Within reason,' her dad half-joked. 'No big parties.'

'Of course I'm sure. Now, don't let me stop you watching *Breaking Bad*, I'll head home.'

Felicity stood up from her seat again, pasting a smile on her face. 'Why don't you stay over tonight, have some dinner with us?'

'No, it's fine, I should get home,' Cleo said, suddenly itching to just switch off in front of her TV and then climb into her own bed.

'Go on. I'll make us spag bol? No fish whatsoever.'

'All right then, sure,' Cleo laughed. If this would make her mum happy . . . After a little more insisting that she didn't mind them watching a TV show she hadn't seen, and that she didn't mind spending Christmas pet-sitting, her parents settled in for the evening, and Cleo sat on the other side of the sofa, stroking Rhubarb, and munching on her pasta, before excusing herself for the night, and heading up to her childhood bedroom.

A little while later, there was a knock.

'Clee? Can I come in?' Felicity asked through the bedroom door.

'Yeah, of course,' Cleo answered, putting down the book she was barely reading, and sitting up in bed, the old Kookai T-shirt she'd found in a drawer riding up over her tummy under the duvet.

Her mum stepped into the room and walked over to her

bed, perching on the end, a sleep mask propped on her fore-head now in place of the reading glasses. 'I've got to ask,' she stated.

Cleo blinked. 'Ask what?'

'Do you want me to not ask Eliot?'

'What do you mean?' asked Cleo, knowing exactly what she meant.

'Would you rather he didn't stay in America, permanently? Because that's what he would maybe do, visa-depending, if we offered him the second US branch.'

Permanently. No, she wasn't OK with him leaving perma-nently. Her heart felt filled with heavy stones just thinking about it. But if that was what he wanted, who was she to stop him? She wasn't his girlfriend.

She was never his girlfriend.

She was just a friend.

And if that was what her parents wanted for the business they'd grown from scratch, she couldn't stand in their way.

Before she could answer, her mother continued, 'It's just that I know, *we* know, he's your dear friend. Maybe more at one time.' She booped her daughter on the nose and Cleo squawked her awkward laugh. 'But nothing's really changed between the two of you for a long time. As far as I know? So I'm sort of . . . assuming . . . you don't see anything happening there? Any more?'

'Muuuuuuuum,' Cleo whined. She'd never been one to share romantic thoughts with her mum. Not like Gabriela who'd never shied from telling everyone who'd listen about her love quests. 'He's just a friend . . . and of course I would be sad for him to not come back to Wavebreak Bay for whole winters any more, but he still has family in Devon. He'd still come back. Sometimes. I don't own him.'

And he doesn't owe *me*, she wallowed.

'And you're sure you're OK about Christmas?'

'Yes, of course, it's fine.'

Blueberry batted the door open then and preened into the room, slinking onto the bed covers and curling herself into a ball up against Cleo's thighs.

Cleo bade her mum a goodnight, and went back to her book. Only, she didn't read a word of it.

Instead, visions of her Christmas were dissipating, being pushed away. She could hardly feign surprise though – didn't this happen every year? Didn't she *let* it happen every year?

She worked so hard to do the right thing, to be accommodating, to put others first. She always wanted to make sure other people were happy. But *still*, people kept leaving her. Living their lives without her.

It struck her like a tidal wave, one she couldn't avoid, she couldn't run away from because she was already caught in its clutches: when had she become such a people-pleaser that she'd waved goodbye to herself?

Chapter 8

Cleo did a cursory lunge. Everybody else seemed to be stretching in the early morning sunshine, blowing out clouds of cold breath, rolling shoulders, flexing joints, balancing on one another while they contorted their hamstrings.

Beside her, Rosa was pinning a number to the front of her Santa suit, cursing into her beard as the safety pin stabbed her in the chest.

To say Cleo hadn't done any training for the 5k Santa Run would have been an exaggeration. Fair, but an exaggeration. She'd been on three runs in the lead-up to the event . . . one in March, one in June and one last week. And she was on her feet all day, every day, at the restaurant, so that had to count for something.

Still though. Looking around her at the other participants, with their headbands and GPS watches and arm straps holding isotonic pouches, she felt a little out of her depth, and unsure why she'd ever agreed to do this.

'There we go,' Rosa said, looking up and putting her Santa hat back on her head. 'You look great!'

'I look like I don't realise it's only October,' Cleo replied. 'No offence,' she added to three similarly dressed runners stretching nearby.

At that point, somebody with a megaphone among the sea of red felt suits started giving instructions that Cleo couldn't quite make out, and then a horn honked, and she was swept into the flow of a hundred and fifty bobbing Santas.

The sun was glittering through the trees, the early morning frost crisping the mud on the coast-path trail, and Cleo was struggling to keep her felt trousers up around her waist. This was the first year she'd joined in with the annual Santa Run, and with every step she was remembering why.

Don't be a downer. Don't let Rosa see how you feel . . . Cleo repeated this mantra, even as tears began to spring into her eyes. It was a silly reaction; it wasn't like she was even doing anything that tough, but, what with her revelation the other day, she was deeply feeling the fact that a lot of her life was spent doing things other people wanted her to do, rather than her wanting to do them herself.

And although she wanted to resent Rosa for dragging her into this, the truth was, she could only be angry at herself. Rosa had asked if she'd be up for taking part in the 5k with her – she'd said yes. Even though she'd thought, *That sounds awful! No thanks!*, she'd still just smiled and said, 'Sure.'

So now, as she jogged along, panting, painfully aware of people overtaking her with every step, mentally calculating how long until she could say she was a quarter done, then a half done, Cleo could only be angry at herself.

Her chest was burning by the time they rounded the corner near the restaurant and burst out into the morning light to run the length of the seafront. Something about seeing those gently lapping waves, still pink-tipped under the early sky, instantly soothed Cleo's soul somewhat, though she didn't know how the ocean had that effect on her, especially after she hadn't plunged into her for years.

So, what are you waiting for? Go after the run.

She would, but she'd probably be sweaty and in need of getting home and having a shower. And it would be silly to go in the sea *after* having washed her hair. Maybe tomorrow.

Cleo glanced at Rosa, who was pounding along, her forehead pink and sweating under the brim of the hot hat. 'I need to talk to you about something,' she stated, before she could change her mind.

Rosa turned her head to the side and pulled down her beard. 'Now?'

'Yeah, I think now.'

Another reason why Cleo would have benefitted from a bit of training: she hadn't realised she wasn't capable of chatting and running at the same time, and subsequently her words came out in wobbly half-sentences.

Nevertheless, swarmed by other Santas, she needed to get something off her chest. 'I have a confession.'

'I love it already,' Rosa replied. 'Spill.'

Cleo eyed the ocean for a minute, its power giving her power. 'I realised ... I'm a bit ... Stuck.'

'Stuck where?' Rosa asked. 'You mean you have a wedgie?'

Cleo shook her head, her hat falling over her eyes for a moment. 'No, in life.'

'Oh.'

The two of them jogged in silence for a minute, waving thanks to the well-wishers with their cosy coats and take-away coffees as they trudged past.

'Do you want to talk about it?' asked Rosa, swerving to dodge a child on a scooter who was careering along the centre of the esplanade like a salmon swimming upstream.

Nodding, then removing her Santa hat from her eyes again, Cleo panted, 'I just feel like ... I'm in ... Groundhog Year, you know?'

How could Rosa know, though? She'd moved to the UK back in the spring. She'd travelled across the whole world – this entire year had been a series of firsts for her. And before that, Cleo knew she'd moved jobs often. Things were always changing for Rosa, and good for her.

Nevertheless, Rosa called back a 'Yeah' from her position just in front as they had to move to single file to share the esplanade with a large St Bernard dog who was stretched across the tarmac on his side, having a snooze, despite the trample of feet jogging past.

'Every year,' Cleo continued. 'Every year is kind of the same and ... it's like I'm waiting for something but not ... not doing anything about it.'

'Like what?'

It had been several days since Cleo had been asked to spend Christmas working and pet-sitting, and had agreed.

And had practically told her parents that she'd be delighted if they'd offer Eliot a job that would stop him coming home. So she had been stewing on her situation. She hated that she'd become the person she was, where she found it easier to put everyone else first than face her own future. She hated that she was so afraid of what she could lose, or what people would think if she said no, that she never rocked the boat any more.

Every year, Cleo thought to herself, *This year I'll put myself first*. She'd do the things she loved. The things she'd been meaning to do. Then, the summer was invariably busy and she'd think, *This* winter, *when it's calmed down, when Eliot is back home*. Then they could go in the sea together, like the old days. She would tell him how she felt. She could get her kayak out again. She could have a good think about what she wanted and her future. Then, winter would roll around, and she would get caught up in the excitement of having her best friend home, snatching what she could of his time even though everyone wanted a piece of it, and catching up on chores left over from the busy summer holidays. And the sea seemed too choppy, or too cold, or it would be perfect out there and she'd still find an excuse. It was always tomorrow, tomorrow, tomorrow. Then, before she knew it, it was spring and he was gone again, and Cleo would think, This *summer I'll sort myself out, so that come winter I'll be in a better place.* Lather, rinse, repeat.

'I feel like a posh mug,' Cleo said.

'Like a rich knobhead?' Rosa asked.

'No, like an actual posh mug. Like, you know when you buy yourself – or someone gifts you – a really fancy mug, or bottle of body lotion, or diamond necklace.'

Rosa snorted. 'Yeah, I know it well. I'm laden down with diamonds over here.'

'You get the idea, though. And then you never use it because it's too nice and you're afraid of it breaking?'

'Yeah, I get what you're saying.'

'I feel like that. Like I'm not doing anything, I'm not living my life here, just keeping everything steady in case it breaks. I'm just on hold every year. Every year I think, "Next summer I'll do this, next winter I'll do that." Then everyday life takes over, and I lose the nerve.' And she was afraid of rocking the boat, and losing it all, she added to herself.

'Are you thinking of doing anything in particular?'

She was. Because if he was going to stop coming home, she might only have one shot left. She couldn't tread water any longer. 'What I need to do is start by being honest about something.'

Rosa fell back in line beside Cleo and peered at her, before sweat dripped in her eye. 'What are you not being honest about?'

Cleo's heart hammered in her chest, and her legs felt like jelly, and her hands were shaking. Was this a good idea? Once she admitted out loud how she felt then some-one would know, and then it was possible that Rosa would keep giving her *looks* whenever Cleo was around at the same time as Eliot.

'I have a crush on someone.'

Rosa thwacked her. 'Who?'

'No, it's not a crush. It's more than that. It's been so long . . . I don't know what I would call it.'

'*Who?*'

'Eliot.' There. She'd said it. It was out there now. Perhaps that was enough of a step forward and she could go home now? But she did feel a little lighter, a little brighter, a little like she might be able to finish the run after all.

But all Rosa did was laugh and say flatly, 'Oh.'

'Why, "oh"?'

'I've never even met the guy and even I know that's the most obvious confession on the planet.'

'What do you mean?'

'The way you talk about him. The postcards all over your kitchen. The fact you've been on cloud nine since the beginning of October, which just happens to be the month he's coming back. And the fact that Lucy and I talk about it all the time.'

'What?' Cleo cried, accepting a cup of water from a man in a high-vis vest and promptly dribbling it all over herself.

At that moment, the two of them rounded the end of the seafront and started back up the gentle incline towards the top of the town, where the run would end. Even at only a small degree of hill, Cleo needed her full lung capacity, so it wasn't until they *fiiiinally* reached the finish line that she could chat again with Rosa properly.

'We did it!' Rosa squealed, biting her participation medal like she was a winner at the Olympics.

Cleo, hunched over, her beard, hat and jacket beside her

while she tried not to throw up, murmured little more than a 'Yaaaay,' before collapsing onto the grass verge.

Rosa handed her half of her granola bar, which Cleo munched on, her face bright pink and pulsing. 'So, you're in love with Eliot, huh? And finally ready to admit it?'

Cleo felt her face pinken even further to the point she must be quite neon right now.

'*Are* you ready to admit it?' Rosa asked. 'Is that what you were trying to say?'

'Yes,' Cleo rasped, and took a long drink of water, followed by a deep breath. 'Something needs to change otherwise I'm just in this limbo of working and waiting and working and waiting and what am I waiting for? For him to make the first move?'

Rosa shrugged. 'Do you think he feels the same?'

'I don't know.' Falling silent, Cleo watched as some other exhausted runners pounded over the finish line, faces glowing but happy.

'OK, a different question. What about him makes you feel love?'

'What do I love about him?'

'No ... what is it about your relationship with Eliot, as things stand at the moment, which tells you you're in love with him?'

Cleo thought for a moment. 'Um. He's just ... we just ... '

'Can you be real with him?'

'I'm more real with him than I am with anyone else,' Cleo answered.

'What about me?' Rosa laughed.

'And you, of course,' Cleo replied, though she didn't quite mean it. She felt like she was always putting up some kind of front, putting on the costume of the close friend or caring sister, but something always held her back from being one hundred per cent at ease. But not with Eliot. Perhaps she was remembering the past with rose-tinted glasses, but she'd always felt herself around Eliot.

Chapter 9

~ Then ~

Summer 2008

While Cleo's classmates, and twin sister, were waking to the first morning of their summer holidays with the warm glow that came with a six-week stretch of freedom ahead of them, Cleo was waking with one person on her mind: Eliot.

She'd gone from seeing him every day to barely at all since he'd moved up the coast a couple of months before. With her head down revising for, and taking, her GCSEs (not to mention the fact she'd fallen into being Gabriela's personal exam-practice quizmaster, since her strong-minded sister had decided she wanted to get into Cambridge one day, come hell or high water), and Eliot now going straight from school to work or home, they'd done little more than pass each other in corridors or exchange endless text messages.

It didn't mean she hadn't noticed a change in him, though. A comfortableness as he settled into the school. His hair grew a little shaggier, the muscles on his arms a little more pronounced, his smile wider. He was always kinda gorgeous to her, but, with the shyness depleting and the salt breeze coating him, he was, dare she say it, a bit of a babe?

Gabriela thought so. She'd announced it a couple of weeks ago after their French exam, when she'd seen him playing rounders on the sports field outside the gym where the GCSEs were being held.

'Your friend Eliot is a massive hottie,' she declared, dumping her school bag on the kitchen table, spilling French revision notes onto the floor.

Cleo appreciated that she always called him 'your friend'. Really, he was a friend to both of them, but she felt it was her twin's way of saying, *Don't worry, I'm not interested like that.*

'No, he's not!' Cleo cried automatically, scooping up the paperwork. He totally was, though. He could have been on *The O.C.* It was a little intimidating, actually, and maybe that was why Cleo tended to steer clear at school.

But today, everything would change. Today she was due to start working at Coacean, alongside Eliot. Gabriela was to work there over the summer too, but had begged to start the following week so she could have a week of beach bumming with her friends to celebrate the end of a tough school year.

Gabriela couldn't understand that, for Cleo, spending time with Eliot again, even if she was working, was hanging out with one of *her* best friends.

Cleo was defo over her crush of the summer before – she and Eliot had moved to being really close friends, which was definitely way better. Definitely. Yes. The crush was a childish fantasy, she was soon to be entering the sixth form, where he was already, and they were just friends.

Nevertheless, her heart fluttered like the wings of a dragonfly as she dressed in the morning sunlight, her sister's snores emitting from the room next door, the seaglass necklace Eliot had left for her when he'd moved away glinting against her skin.

Cleo was sixteen now. She was more grown-up than she'd been last summer. More ready. Ready for the summers that sixteen-year-olds had in movies and on TV. A summer of fun, and trips to the beach, and kisses beside campfires, and ice creams melting down onto holding hands and late-night parties.

Yet, as grown out of her crush as she now was, she just couldn't picture anyone else she wanted to share those things with more than Eliot.

Cleo tied her curls back behind a pale blue headband, pulling a couple of tendrils loose around her face.

She tilted her head from side to side, then, with a sigh, tried to – unsuccessfully – stick the hair back into the band. Why did her hair have to be so ... so *unruly*? Why couldn't she just have inherited the shiny locks of her twin, which lay flat and smooth or with a perfect beachy wave, entirely depending on Gabriela's whim? Rather than fluffy curls that would succumb to nobody's will but their own?

A little twist of annoyance at herself contorted inside her, reminding her with a whisper that those sweet sixteen years from TV that she imagined wouldn't necessarily be a part of *her* reality.

She shook the tendrils loose again, defiance in her eyes. 'I think you're cool,' she whispered back.

Stepping into the corridor and then into her sister's bedroom, she lay down on the bed beside her.

'What d'you want?' Her sister huffed at being woken up.

'What are you doing today?' Cleo asked, swooping a clump of Gabriela's chestnut locks from dangling over her eyes.

'Mmm.' Gabriela cracked open an eye and peeped towards her window, which glowed a bright yellow square behind the curtains and signalled the sun was beaming, already high in the sky. 'I think I'm going to go to the beach. Suri wants us to try surfing with her since her mum got her and her brother boards for their birthdays. Do you want to come?'

Cleo would have loved to have tried surfing, but not today. 'I'm starting work today,' she said with a smile.

'Sucks to be you,' Gabriela murmured, pulling her hair back over her face. 'Say hi to lover boy from me, though.'

'What? Shut up.' Cleo blushed.

'Your hair looks cute. Give me a hug,' Gabriela whined, causing Cleo to laugh before bending down to embrace her warm, sleepy sister. Gabriela, as dry or snarky as she could be, always had a way of wanting her twin to look after her, almost mother her.

Leaving her sister to snooze, Cleo raced down the hill to the restaurant, to her first day of work.

Opening the entrance door that was nearly as familiar to her as her own home, she was hit with the aroma of baking fish and creamy coconut and bubbling chowders. And there he was.

'Eliot!' Cleo waved across the restaurant, before her dad appeared in front of her, an apron and a pen and paper in his hands.

'Welcome, sweetheart!' Bryce said, handing her his wares and then pulling a digital camera from his pocket and snapping a photo of the two of them. 'Your first day in the working world. How do you feel?'

'Excited,' Cleo answered, honestly, glancing to where Eliot had started laying cutlery on an empty table. He looked up, met her eyes, and a smile spread across his face.

Perhaps she wasn't entirely over her crush . . .

It was a long and languid summer, one that rolled from week to week as if there wasn't even any night-time breaking the days up. Cleo was content to work and steer clear of the beach until the tourists had drifted away again, and Eliot promised he'd make sure to keep coming over from Lyme Regis once they were back at school in the autumn, to take out the kayaks or swim in the ocean.

It tickled at Cleo like sand between her toes that maybe she needed to think carefully about whether her friendship with Eliot still meant something beyond that. But more than anything, she loved being around him. Sure, if he told her he liked her, or brushed against her fingers as they stood side by side out on the decking while she banged on about one day working on the water, or kissed her at a sixth-form party next year, she'd probably respond. But she didn't want to rock any boats, even when her feelings rose, a current hidden just under the surface.

Like that time they'd been clearing the outside deck at

the end of the day, the high tide lapping against the restaurant stilts, the late golden hour causing his brown hair to glow amber. The scent of seawater and kelp drifted by on a breeze and Cleo had closed her eyes for a moment to smell it, only to open them and find him there, in front of her.

'I . . . ' she'd begun, not knowing where her sentence was going, but something telling her she needed to part her lips.

'Your hair looks really cool in this light,' he stuttered, reaching out.

Normally, Cleo would refute him, tell him it didn't, ask him to shut up, but, as if Gabriela's confident genes took over for a second, she stepped forward, her only thought being, *Now, kiss him now, kiss him kiss him kiss himmmmmm.*

And then a wave had thudded against the stilts, sending a glittering splosh into the air and showering their feet and legs with cold water, causing them to jump back with a shriek.

Soggy, salty, and feeling self-conscious, Cleo laughed and picked up the last few dishes, shuffling inside quickly, and wondering if that kind of opportunity would ever come about again.

Chapter 10

~ Now ~

On the grass verge, sweaty from the Santa Run, Cleo pulled herself from her thoughts. Yes, she was always at ease with Eliot. Except ...

'Except I'm not real with him, am I?' she said to Rosa. 'There's this big secret I haven't told him, that I hold back, and I might tell him and he might feel angry, like I've been faking our friendship.'

'Have you?'

'No, not at all,' she answered. 'To me, my romantic feelings for Eliot lie on top of my friendship feelings. They're the icing on the cake. But if the icing can't be there, I still want the cake. The cake is still delicious.'

'Do you want to go and get some real cake?'

Standing, they peeled off the remainder of their Santa suits and pulled sweatshirts they'd stored in Rosa's rucksack over their running tops. Hobbling like cowboys heading to a saloon, the two of them made their way to the nearest café, a fairy-lit place with hundreds of hanging plants near the top of the town, and ordered three giant slices of cake between them, and two pots of tea.

'So,' said Rosa, through a mouthful of coconut sponge. 'What are you going to do about it?'

'I'm going to tell him. This winter. Before it's too late and I regret never knowing what might have been. I'll tell him. Somehow.'

'Wow.'

'Like I said, something has to change; I need to move forward, somehow, and, even if he doesn't like me in the same way, at least I'll know.'

'You'd be all right with that?'

'At least I would know,' Cleo repeated. At least she could then, maybe, start claiming back some of her life, rather than living entirely based around other people.

'And what if he does feel the same way?'

'What do you mean?'

'Would you want him to not go back to San Francisco at the end of the season?'

Cleo let out a sigh, sending crumbs scattering across the table. 'No, I'd want him to stay here with me. But I couldn't ask him to do that, so I guess I'd have to cross that bridge when I came to it.'

'What percentage sure are you that he likes you like that too?' Rosa asked.

'A hundred per cent,' Cleo joked, but behind her façade the question gnawed. It was the one she asked herself all the time, but never answered. Because she truly didn't know. Sometimes she thought maybe he felt more, sometimes she couldn't focus on anything other than the fact he saw her as his best friend.

'All right! I like that confidence. How are you going to tell him?'

'I don't know ... will you do it for me?' nudged Cleo.

Rosa laughed. 'No way. But I can help you plan for it.'

'OK, good, because I think you're more romantic than me.'

'What makes you think that?'

'Because I'm not romantic at all.' That wasn't entirely true. Cleo didn't know how to be *outwardly* romantic, but in her heart she was a romcom-watching, love-interest-swooning, audibly-cheers-when-TV-characters-kiss, romance-novel-devouring romantic old fool. But putting that into practice? She'd probably say something ridiculously inappropriate and then backtrack, and then apologise and run away.

Outside the window, the road that wove through this end of the town was quiet, save the odd local with shopping bags walking back towards their homes, and a few runners with the tell-tale shaking legs and sweat-spiked hair.

A guy strolled past, full wetsuit on, a surfboard under his arm despite the calm of the sea that day. Cleo watched as he waved to a passing car, which stopped, waited for him to cram his board inside, and then headed off, presumably to some other beach where there was a decent swell forming. She thought of Eliot living his dream in California, surfing beside the Golden Gate Bridge. Why would he ever want to stop that?

Once, she'd tried surfing, but it wasn't for her. That hadn't stopped her following Gabriela when she and her friends went on surf trips. Helping to carry boards, going on hot-chocolate runs, generally being the sidekick.

By telling Eliot how she felt, one way or another, it would mean one less thing in her life that she was sitting passively on the sidelines for. For her own sake, she needed to stop putting everything on hold waiting for him, or her sister, to come home.

Cleo turned back to look at Rosa. 'How shall I do this, then? How should I break the news to him?'

'"Break the news"? You aren't telling him something awful, remember. You're telling him you like him.'

'It is always nice to hear that someone likes you,' Cleo justified out loud.

'Do you want my advice?' Rosa asked, using her fork to split the slice of caramel coffee cake into two chunks.

'Absolutely.'

'It *is* a big deal. This guy is, what, your best friend?'

'Yes.' Cleo swallowed.

'I think you need to do it in a way that gives him space if he needs to think.'

'What would he need to think about? Surely if he needs to think, that means he doesn't like me in the same way.'

Rosa shook her head. 'Not necessarily. I was asked out by a girl last Christmas, and I really liked her, like, *really liked her*. I'm talking, "I still gaze at her Instagram posts" level of like. But when she asked me out, I needed to think, because I knew I was coming away, to here, and I didn't know how long for.'

'So what did you say?'

'I turned her down.'

Cleo's face fell. The thought of Eliot turning her down was like a kick in the ribs, but then so was the thought of waiting another year. And another. And another. Until the year he didn't come back at all.

Rosa scooped the rest of her cake onto Cleo's plate. 'You need this more than me,' she said. 'And listen, Eliot and I are totally different people. I'm guessing. I've never met the guy. But my point is, as far as we know, he's only back for the winter. It's possible he'd love to start something with you but thinks it could be too hard.'

'That does make sense ... '

'We don't know how he's going to feel, but either way I think you should do it in a very chill way. You know. Something really informal where you can just tell him and then, if necessary, leave him be for a couple of days. Give him some space. Like over a coffee date or something. Do you agree?'

'No, because I want to tell him and then kiss him and then keep hold of him until he goes back to California.' Cleo sighed. 'But that might be overkill, so yes, I agree.'

'When does he come back?'

Cleo checked the date on her phone. 'In a couple of days. I can't wait for you to meet him.'

'I hope I like him,' Rosa said. 'What if I think he's a dick?'

'What if he thinks you're a dick?'

Nodding, Rosa said, 'Fair point. So, what are your plans with him while he's back? Do you want to do this sooner rather than later, or give it a few weeks and see if anything happens naturally first, or ... ?'

Cleo pondered this. It would be good to see if the two of them could get together organically first, then she wouldn't need to do this big confession. But also, wasn't that just copping out? 'I want to have told him by Christmastime,' she declared, proud of herself for her decision. 'It's been nearly a decade since he and I moved back to the Bay, I won't let it get to the New Year without being honest. If you think that's a good timeline?'

'That's fine. All right, so sometime within the next eight weeks. That's extremely do-able. In fact, it's almost too long.'

'But then he wouldn't be leaving again until late March, so we'd still have plenty of time together, but not *too* long if I blow the whole thing and he finds it too awkward to be around me.'

'That's the spirit.'

Cleo was an idiot for leaving it so long and for wasting all of this time.

She was an idiot for getting herself into the situation where Eliot might hate her, accuse her of abusing his trust in their friendship when she had ulterior motives.

She was an idiot for not being honest sooner, but every year she'd told herself, *He's leaving soon. I can get over him this time.*

She groaned into her hands.

'What's wrong?' Rosa asked softly, placing a hand on Cleo's arm.

'There's something else, but you can't tell anyone I told you this.'

'Of course.' Rosa nodded. She was a good friend. Cleo

trusted that she really cared and wasn't just trying to lean into the gossip.

'My parents are thinking of asking him to open another branch out in the US, in California. And if he accepts, he might stop coming back here altogether. With the exception of the odd holiday, his life, every season, would become almost entirely based out there.'

'Oh . . . ' Rosa paused. 'That sucks. For you. Not for him.'

'That's exactly the problem. It's a great opportunity for him, and I don't want to stand in the way of that, or influence his decision. I don't know whether to tell him my thing before or after they've spoken to him. It's like . . . a chicken and egg situation.'

'Are you the chicken or the egg?'

'I think it's very clear I'm the chicken,' Cleo said, her chin in her hands.

Rosa shrugged her shoulders a little. 'I don't have the answers for you. I guess I'd just say the same as before – when you tell him how you feel, and when your folks have dropped their proposal too, give him space to think. Weigh up the options.'

'The outcome isn't important,' Cleo said, her voice subdued. 'His feelings for me can't be important; being honest and authentic is. I have to go into this with no expectations.'

'All right.' Rosa grinned. 'Well, that's a good thing.'

'What?'

'No expectations. If you don't go in there expecting a particular outcome, you can't fail.'

'That's true.'

'Promise me you won't be hard on yourself, Cleo? You and Eliot have a weird, intercontinental relationship with masses of time apart each year, and that's a tricky thing to navigate. So say "piss off" to the past and look ... look over there.'

Cleo looked up and followed the direction of Rosa's finger as she pointed out of the window to the sea in the distance. 'Look at what?'

'See that horizon? That's got your new beginnings sailing all over it.'

'You cheese ball,' Cleo laughed.

'You've got cheesy balls,' Rosa retorted, and put her Santa beard back on her face.

Cleo sat in the bath that night eating cupcakes and sipping on a can of Diet Coke. Her muscles had stiffened from the morning run, her legs ached, but she felt happy.

Change was coming.

Her life didn't revolve around Eliot and his coming and going, she wasn't stuck in her rut because of him, but he was part of it, and she was going to do something about it.

She bit down into the chocolate sponge, layering buttercream frosting on her nose.

It didn't matter what came next, whether he felt the same or she broke her own heart by baring it. Because, either way, change was coming.

Chapter 11

~ Then ~

Winter 2009

Eliot's last year of secondary school had finished before he'd barely registered it beginning. It was like a rip curl sweeping in and pulling his feet from under him. With university applications, mock exams, actual exams, parties, working in the restaurant and his eighteenth birthday, the year was a blur, and now he found himself on the brink of leaving Wavebreak Bay for University College Falmouth, down in Cornwall.

'All right, Gabriela, so you've done this a couple of times before, right?' Eliot asked. He and the twins were on the beach, white clouds blanketing overhead, and a tiny mist of rain drizzling down through the September breeze. With only a couple of weeks left in the bay, he was finally getting around to giving Cleo and Gabriela the surfing lesson he'd kept promising. Though why Cleo had wanted one from him, he had no idea. He'd only been surfing himself for a year or two, and they all knew people far better equipped. Still, though, she trusted him, he could repay her for teaching him to kayak, and he wanted to make this as fun as possible for her.

'A couple of times, yeah,' Gabriela said, distractedly glaring up at the sky. 'Can we hurry up and get in? It's cold today.'

'It'll probably feel warmer in the water because of it,' Cleo reasoned.

Eliot watched as Cleo practised the moves he had shown her, on the safety of the sand, and then led them into the water.

Immediately, the underside of Cleo's board slapped against an incoming wave and flipped out of her grasp, causing her to scamper back onto the beach to retrieve it.

'Sorry,' she called, this time securing the leash tighter.

'Don't worry about it,' said Eliot. 'Did it hit you, though? Are you OK?'

'No, I'm fine,' she laughed, striding back in. He liked that she wasn't one to easily give up on things at the first hurdle.

In the surf, Gabriela was a natural, standing up and only ever laughing if she fell off the board. It helped that this wasn't her first time. Cleo was putting on a brave face, but Eliot could sense it wasn't quite as fun for her.

When Gabriela went back up onto the beach to warm up, Eliot called across the water, 'What do you think, Cleo? Do you want to keep going?'

'We can't stop yet – I don't know how to surf. And I only have you for such a short amount of time more.' She smiled, and he didn't point out the little trail of salty snot dribbling down her face.

The two of them paddled out beyond the waves to where the sea was calm and neither of them could touch the bottom, then rested on the boards, with their feet dangling in the water.

'How are you doing?' Eliot asked.

Cleo contemplated the question. 'I really want to like surfing, but I don't think it's very me ... I'm sorry.'

'Why are you sorry?'

'I don't know. Maybe because I feel like I should like it? It's just ... when I see your face, when you're on a surfboard, I think you get the same feeling I do when I'm on a kayak, or just swimming. We both love the sea, right?'

'Right.' Thanks, in part, to her. Her fearlessness, her willingness to go out on the water even in the coldest of winters when nobody else wanted to, was part of what he liked so much about her. What he was so grateful for.

'Well, I think ... ' She tailed off, like she was trying to put it into words. 'I think maybe that, for you, it's the movement. For me, it's the still. But both give us a sense of happiness.'

She looked embarrassed then, like she'd given up on the sentence halfway through and felt a bit silly.

'I get what you mean,' he said, his eyes on her as the wind picked up the curls of her hair. She was so pretty. Even when she was drenched and windswept. Maybe especially then. 'Hey, um ... Thanks, Cleo,' he said, through salty lips. 'Thanks for being an awesome friend these past two years.'

For a moment they just looked at each other and although

he couldn't predict her feelings, to him it was the weight of *Would she let me kiss her?* that kept him in place.

'I think we might be friends for a lot longer than that,' Cleo replied.

'I think you're right,' said Eliot. 'I think we might be a part of each other's lives now.'

'No matter where we are. Even when you're surfing up a storm in California.'

'Agreed,' he laughed. He'd been talking all summer about how his older cousin Chris – who he looked up to more than he did his own dad – had met an American and fallen hard, and was setting up home in San Francisco.

There was something about the way Chris spoke about the place – like it was full of life, vibrancy, culture and cool. Plus, the beaches and the general lifestyle in California ... But more than anything, the fact he now had family out there meant that Eliot could feel San Francisco being a part of his future, somehow. He could just feel it.

But here in the present, Eliot's mind was on how he was going to miss Cleo so much. He should tell her, right now. He angled his board to face her, but she took that to mean they were going to attempt to catch a wave again, and she turned as well, facing away from him, looking over her other shoulder, ready to put in one last try.

'No, hang on, Cleo,' he called out, noticing the wave didn't look like a good one to chase, but his words were whipped away in the breeze. Perhaps muted under the drizzle. Either way, she didn't seem to hear him, and then it all happened so quickly.

One minute, Cleo was beside him, lying on her surfboard, red curls dangling into the water, arms beginning to paddle, then she was gone, her board flipping into the air, a flash of her wetsuit, a glimpse of her hair, a *thonk* of the edge of the board clapping down hard.

On the beach, Gabriela stood.

Eliot leapt into the sea, grabbing the safety leash and releasing himself from his own board, shoving it out of the way, and grasped for Cleo. He lifted her, spluttering, coughing, a small red cut on her forehead, which oozed diluted blood.

'Cleo? What the hell happened?' Gabriela cried, running into the shallow of the sea as Eliot helped her out.

'I'm fine, I'm totally fine, it was just a bomp,' she said, rubbing at her forehead. Then, her breath quickened, her skin paled, she whispered something about feeling faint, and she went limp, Gabriela and Eliot reaching to catch her before she fell.

Ten seconds. Maybe fifteen. Maybe even just five. She wasn't out for long but it felt like for ever to Eliot. And then she awoke, confused, crumpled, looking up at her sister and him with frightened eyes, the blood trickling down her forehead towards her ear.

'What . . . ' she started.

'It's OK. It's OK,' Eliot said, over and over. 'You fainted, shock probably.' His mum sometimes fainted if she hit a knee on a coffee table or stood up too fast from a hot bath, a host of reasons. But never because of something that was his fault, like this.

Eliot was shaking, trying to keep it together, but wanting nothing more than to wrap Cleo up in his arms and make sure she was OK. He should have been a better teacher. He was such an idiot. He never wanted to hurt her, not in any way.

'Sit down, let me have a look,' he said.

It was, as he thought, only a small injury, but enough for him to insist he took her to the local surgery for a check, still salty, still sandy, but he didn't care a bit.

She was, ultimately, cleared as fine. A little shaken, a little over the whole surfing experience, but, healthwise, fine.

The following weekend the weather was stunning. Calm seas, blue sky, it was as if it were the middle of June again and not late September. A group of them, including Gabriela, were going to drive up to the north coast where good waves had been forecast. When Cleo arrived with her twin, he was surprised, concerned, but pleased.

'You're coming surfing?' he asked.

'I'm coming to watch,' she corrected. 'I'm not sure I'm ready to throw myself back on a surfboard anytime soon. I'm a kayak girl, I think.'

'I like that that's your thing. Today looks perfect for kayaking, though.' He looked at the mirror-like water of Wavebreak Bay.

'I had been thinking of going out for a kayak ... ' She paused, looking out at the water with longing, before releasing a shrug. 'But Gab wanted me to come ... And besides, it means I get to spend time with you two, this way. Is that OK? Do you mind me being here?'

'Not at all,' he said, a little too quickly, a little too loudly. 'Do you want me to stay, do some kayaking with you?'

'No, God, don't let me hold you back,' she laughed.

All the drive up, he sat beside Cleo, their legs pressed against each other in the back of his friend's car, Gabriela on her other side. But he never managed to get her on her own that day. She was always playing sidekick to her sister, or he was being cajoled back into the sea with his friends.

Perhaps it was for the better. She was just starting her second year of sixth form – a tough year – and he was heading off to uni any minute now. What would he say to her anyway? *I like you, but we both have other things going on, so . . . never mind?* How lame would that be?

And then it was over, his time in Wavebreak Bay. It was his last Friday night and one of Eliot's best friends was hosting a goodbye party for his group before they went their separate ways. The house was heaving, Black Eyed Peas and David Guetta pumped from the iPod dock, and everyone Eliot loved was in one place, one last time.

Including Cleo.

He noticed her looking shy, standing with her own friends in one corner, Gabriela on the other side of the room, chatting up a storm. As he watched, Cleo took a sip from a plastic cup, a tendril of her hair dipping in and getting soaked, and he chuckled, swigging at his own rum and Coke.

An arm slung, heavy, over his shoulders, and a fog of alcohol filled the side of Eliot's face as the host, Aaron, leaned in close.

'Now's your last chance, man,' he said, pointing towards Cleo.

'It's not like that,' Eliot protested, though he couldn't keep the twinge of regret from his voice. He'd perhaps always wonder, secretly, if Cleo and he should have been more than friends. She already had a piece of his heart, after all.

'Well, don't waste tonight,' Aaron said, before strolling away.

Eliot pulled his gaze from Cleo. He was going to miss her, and this group so much. His friends in Wavebreak Bay had wrapped their arms around him when his parents had frozen him out from their own. They'd taught him to surf, they'd got him through his A levels, they'd helped him build back his confidence and he would miss every one of them.

Jessica, another of his good friends, danced into his line of vision as 'I Gotta Feeling' started playing. Jessica was fun and flirty and had a huge smile that lit up any room she went in. She was friendly, and she was about to go all the way up to a university in the north of England, and he might not see her again, so he danced with her when she asked. But when she came in for a boozy kiss, he disentangled himself under the guise of needing to say goodbye to some other people.

He ran straight into the other person he was thinking of.

'Hey,' said Cleo.

'Oh hey.' He gave her a hug, trying to not let his tipsiness be the reason he said anything stupid. Not that she'd care. They were always saying stupid things around each other, being themselves, but still. Perhaps not the impression he wanted to leave her with.

'Jessica looks nice this evening,' Cleo commented, and he hesitated. What did that mean? 'Now she's the type of cool surf girl I can just see you with.'

It didn't sound like Cleo. What was a 'cool surf girl' anyway? They all loved the sea around here in different ways; she had no need to separate herself.

'What?' he asked.

'You know, you clearly like her . . . '

He was confused. It sounded like she was reading a script and not being the usual Cleo. Why was she pushing him at Jessica? Perhaps she was trying to tell him something, in her kind way, before he said something and made a fool of himself . . .

Maybe it was him, maybe it was the drink. But maybe, especially since she seemed so keen on the idea of him and Jessica, maybe tonight was not the night to tell her who he actually liked.

In retrospect, it might have been the perfect time. But in that moment, instead, Eliot simply hugged her, touched the mark on her forehead where the surfboard had hit, kissed her cheek, and then focused on the present, his friends, the party, and riding the wave of nostalgia for good times that were about to become his past.

Besides, he thought, with the feel of the bump on her head a ghost on his fingertips, he'd said he didn't want to hurt Cleo. How could he take the risk of starting something with her, then leaving, and her hurting again, because of him? He'd seen enough hurt through his parents' relationship. He couldn't do it.

Chapter 12

~ Now ~

He was here. Eliot came home this morning, and was in Wavebreak Bay, now.

Cleo was lending an extra pair of hands for the brunch crowd, which she'd agreed to at the last minute when Lucy needed somebody to cover. And as usual, 'no' seemed to have escaped her vocabulary, even though she'd planned to meet Eliot at the train station that morning and bring him back, and had ended up arranging a taxi for him instead, despite his protests that he could sort it himself.

Now she was due to meet him on the beach, and she'd wanted to get there early to avoid missing a single second more.

Cleo checked the clock on the wall. She'd waited long enough, and the big table of customers had been given their bill quarter of an hour ago but had yet to show any signs of wanting to pay.

'Clarissa,' Cleo called upon one of her co-workers. 'I really need to go, I have somewhere to be—'

'Oh, right, Eliot is back today. Say hi from me! Tell him his baby can't wait to meet him.' She stroked her stomach and on seeing Cleo's jaw drop to the ground and plummet through the restaurant floorboards, hastily added, 'I'm joking, I'm joking.'

Removing her apron and pulling herself back together, Cleo said, 'Could you do me a huge favour and look after my big group for me? I'm just waiting for them to pay. You can keep any tips they leave.'

'Sure, go,' Clarissa said with a wave of her hand, still tittering at her joke.

Cleo raced out of the restaurant and down the steps onto the pebbles, surprised by the coolness of the air and the potential rain hanging heavy in the sky.

She hurried towards the centre of the beach, and exhaled with relief that she hadn't left him waiting. Not that he would have cared, but she didn't want to lose a single second.

The tide was out, leaving a wet, reddish strip of sand for the grey ocean to drift in and out over. On impulse – perhaps because she always felt more like her old self when he was near – Cleo pulled off her trainers and socks, yanked her leggings up around her calves, and went to the water's edge.

She stepped in, the wintry water encircling her ankles. A part of her, somewhere deep, itched to take the leap, plunge in, swim out of her depth, but she couldn't do it. She didn't have swimmers with her. Or a towel. And she was about to meet up with Eliot. And it really was quite a cold, grey day . . .

So after a moment she stepped back and settled into a seat on the chilly pebbles, feeling them shift underneath her, and retied her shoes while she watched the seafoam coming in and out, in and out.

She palmed some small stones and began tossing them into the waves, one by one.

He was her oldest and closest friend, no matter what happened over the course of this winter, even when they had five thousand miles between them, and she couldn't wait much longer to see him.

A memory of her and Eliot floated past, of them competing to see who could throw a pebble the furthest. Arms tangled together as they tried to knock the other off balance. Feet getting washed over with lapping waves. One of Cleo's flip-flops coming off and beginning to float away, and Eliot chasing it into the sea, then returning and kneeling down to put it back on her foot in a giggles-and-salt Cinderella moment.

Her heart missed him. Her soul missed him.

But she didn't have to wait long. From behind her, a pebble soared above her head and sploshed into the surf.

'I won.' His familiar voice rang out into the breeze, as soft, playful and warm as it always was.

Cleo scrambled to her feet, wobbling on the pebbles, and held herself in place for a moment – just a moment – to look at him.

There was Eliot, her Eliot, her long-time friend, her favourite person, her everything, who at the same time was no more than a possibility. He stood in front of Cleo, his hands in the pockets of his shorts, because of course he was in shorts even at the end of October. His brown hair was tinged with gold like it always was when he got back from a long summer in California, and she knew it would be back to the colour of firewood by the winter's end. His skin had a light tan and an airbrush of freckles, the kind you get from just being outside, as opposed to sunbathing. He smiled at her, a slow, familiar smile that raised up higher on the right side than the left, and caused his sea-grey eyes to twinkle.

He opened his arms wide, the sleeves of his teal hoodie slipping down over his forearms, something that never failed to make Cleo go weak at the knees without him even knowing.

She tried to say something but her words, as clumsy as they often were, refused to fall out of her mouth and instead she just stumbled towards him and accepted his strong, warm hold.

'And everything was right with the world,' Cleo breathed to herself, buried into his shoulder.

'Hmm?' he asked, and leant back a little so he could see her face.

They studied each other for a moment, his smile growing serious, his eyes on hers, and every other sound disappeared.

Was it going to be this easy? Could he possibly feel the same? Were they about to kiss? It felt completely right, and completely terrifying at the same time.

Then he swallowed, and the smile came back, and he said, 'Hello.'

'Hello,' Cleo replied, coming back down to earth like raining stars. 'Welcome home.'

He pulled her back in again and growled against her hair, 'It's good to be back, Cleo.'

She held on tight for a minute more, and it killed her that she'd have to let go eventually.

Maybe she should just tell him . . .

But now was not the time. He was probably jet-lagged and she probably smelt of vinegar and fish, which didn't scream 'kiss me quick'.

They broke apart and fell into a natural stroll side by side, following the shoreline's curve. They walked close together, shoulders bumping together as they navigated the tumbling pebbles under their feet, and as they chatted Cleo kept sneaking looks up at him.

'How was your journey?' she asked.

'Oh, fine, you know. I slept for a couple of hours but mainly was talking with an old couple who were coming over to visit his brother who he hadn't seen for seventeen years.'

'That's a long stretch.' *Scintillating contribution, Cleo.*

'And how was *your* journey . . . from Coacean to the beach?'

'It was fine, thanks,' she laughed.

The two of them fell silent until Eliot laughed and slung an arm over her shoulders. 'Why is it whenever we get back together, we're the most awkward people in the world for the first five minutes? Shall we just skip the small talk this time and go straight into the real catch-up? After I've chucked you in the sea, of course.'

'What? Oh my God!' With that, Eliot wrapped his arms around Cleo's waist and play-pulled her back into the waves, splashing salty foam up her leggings and drenching her trainers. She dragged at his hoodie, yanking him slingshot-style past her into the water.

'Wet crotch!' she yelled, then flushed for having made it so obvious she'd looked.

But he just laughed, standing in the surf, trailing his fingers and the ends of his sleeves in the water before bringing a wet, salty hand up and running it through his hair, tousling it. 'It's good to be back in this ocean again. Did you manage to go in over the summer?'

Cleo took a step backwards, casting her eyes down to the bubbles beside her feet. 'No.' She shook her head. 'Still avoiding the summertime crowds. I kept meaning to before the school holidays hit, but time got away from me.' How could she tell him that she saved going in the ocean until he came home, so they could go in together? Even though, in reality, it had been years since she'd been in now. How could she tell him that, when it was never something he'd asked her to put on hold for him?

'We always say this now, but we should make a pact to actually go in together this winter sometime,' he declared. 'Like we used to do. When we have more swimming-appropriate clothes on.'

'Yes, let's do that,' she said. And she was about to internally berate herself for saying yes to something just to appease someone else again, when she remembered that when she said yes to Eliot, she meant it.

Cleo signalled for him to come out of the water and they continued along the beach, heading in the direction of the coast path. 'Where do you want to go? What's the first thing you want to do now you're back?'

'I'm doing it – seeing you.'

'Come on, I'm serious.'

'So am I. You're what coming home is all about.' Eliot had a bouncy quality about him that day, like he was on cloud nine about being back in Wavebreak Bay. Cleo rationalised that it was most likely lack of sleep and hours on an aircraft followed by hours more on a train that had him acting like this.

'Do you think of San Francisco as your home now, too?' *Do you want to live there permanently?* That's what she really wanted to ask.

'Oh, for sure. But in a different way. One day you'll have to come out there. I'd love to show you … everything. I think you'd really like wiggly Lombard Street because it's like your hair.' He flicked one of her curls. 'And you'd love how creepy Alcatraz is. And there's this beautiful area across the bay called Sausalito that you can get to by boat. They have these floating homes that are incredible, and individual and unique. I can see you living in one of them.'

'It sounds amazing. I can't believe you ever come back.'

'There's nowhere like Wavebreak Bay,' he explained. 'Just look at this view.'

They'd started climbing the west hill and Eliot stopped and turned back to look at the town from this elevated position.

Cleo opened her mouth wide and stuck her tongue out.

'What are you doing?' he asked.

'Tasting the air.'

'OK.' He followed her lead and did the same. 'Tastes like ... salt.'

'And lip balm. But that might be me,' Cleo added.

'Are you this weird with anyone else?'

'Nope.' She shook her head and put her tongue away. 'I save it up for six months every year until you come back.'

'I consider myself lucky, then.'

They continued walking, talking, him telling her about his summer, his friends in California, the surf trips he'd taken to nearby states over the past months. She told him about work and how her family were doing and what the latest gossip was from Wavebreak Bay.

They kept talking and sharing right up until nightfall, sitting wrapped in duvets on the balcony of his tiny holiday cottage – he always rented it over the winter for a steal – until it was too cold, and Eliot couldn't contain his yawns any longer.

'I'm really not bored,' he explained. 'Just jet-lagged.'

Cleo gathered up her shoes and headed towards the door. 'It's completely fine. You're back now, we have plenty of time to hang out.'

They kissed each other on the cheek, and he lingered, squeezing her goodbye.

'Don't fall asleep on me,' she cackled, rather than just relax and enjoy the moment.

As she walked back towards her own home, Cleo knew there were moments she could have told him today. But also, she was encouraged to know their friendship was still solid. Hopefully, solid enough to withstand her feelings.

Usually, being sociable for a whole day, moulding herself to fit in, nodding, smiling, striving to be likeable and agreeable, would leave her exhausted. With Eliot she never felt that way. She felt the same relaxed serenity as if she'd taken a vacation.

Chapter 13

November

A week after Eliot came back to Wavebreak Bay, Cleo nearly
made her confession. So very nearly.

It was bonfire night, and Cleo had borrowed her mum's
car to drive everybody to a nearby manor house across the
border into Dorset, where a huge firework display and bonfire was held every year. It would be the first time Rosa was
meeting Eliot, and they were being joined by Clarissa from
work, and Levi, who'd done seasonal work in Coacean last
Christmas but had moved to working in the youth hostel
over the summer.

As Cleo navigated the field parking in the dark, with
Clarissa giving her unhelpful tips in the passenger seat like,
'Try and avoid the mud because you don't want to get stuck',
and, 'Since it's muddy everywhere, try and park near a four-by-
four', Eliot sat in the back getting a grilling on one side from
Rosa and having Levi trying to talk travelling on the other.

'Do you think you'll always split your time between
California and Devon?' Rosa was asking, and Cleo's ears

pricked. She tried to drown out Clarissa and listen to Eliot's response.

'I don't know about *always*,' he said. 'But it works well for now. I'm in a bit of a pattern with it all. I guess.'

'You don't sound sure?'

The car idled behind an SUV with ten million children spilling out, and Cleo waited while Eliot formed an answer.

Eventually, he spoke. 'It's been on my mind a lot this summer, actually. I think I'm ready for the next step, career-wise. Perhaps have a thing or a project that's *mine*. But I love my job still, and I really love being able to live in both places. So . . . ' He leant forward in his seat and spoke to Cleo. 'Don't say anything to your folks yet, Clee, it's just theoretical at the moment. I need to figure some stuff out.'

'Of course.' She gulped, her eyes on the brake lights ahead of her, thinking about her parents' looming request for him to stay in the US permanently. Would that be the career step he'd been waiting for?

'What would make you break the pattern?' Rosa asked. 'Or . . . who?'

'OK, we're here!' Cleo sang out, swinging the car into a spot between a Land Rover and a Porsche, and cutting off Rosa's questioning before she edged into obvious territory. She didn't want to think about him leaving now, not when he'd only just returned. But even more than that, she didn't want to be a roadblock that stood in the way of his dreams and opportunities. The thought of him wiping out his life adventures because of her was just . . . not something she wanted to think about now.

The five of them climbed out and skidded their way over the car-churned turf to join the throng of people heading into the estate.

Cleo clasped her hands together, pushing her woollen gloves on tighter from the cold.

'You OK?' asked Eliot, falling into step beside her.

'I know I say this to you every time you return, but I bet you wish you were back in California right now.'

'No,' he laughed. 'San Francisco can be chilly at times, too.'

'Scarf weather, though?' Cleo looked at his thick, woolly scarf of blues and indigoes, which sat atop his bulky jacket. 'Don't you ever consider staying out there over the winter?'

'I like being here in the winter,' he commented.

This was her in. *Say it, say it now, Cleo, do it, do it, do it.*

But of course she didn't, not even close. Instead, she called him a weirdo, then let out a strange, too-loud laugh, and then turned to ask Rosa if she was warm enough.

'*I approve,*' Rosa stage-whispered in response. 'He's scrumptious.'

A while later, the five of them stood a distance from the bonfire, the pumpkin-coloured flames warming their faces and casting a glow upon them all.

Cleo placed her paws on the rope separating the crowd from the fire, and inhaled the scent of smoke, listening to the crackle of the wood snapping under the flames.

Eliot's hand rested on hers for a second. 'Warmed up now?'

She turned and he held out a hot cider for her that he'd just bought from a stand on the grounds. As she brought it to her lips, the warm spices filled her nose, overtaking the smell of woodsmoke, and it reminded her of bonfire nights from the past, with Eliot, when there always seemed to be a flame that she was too afraid to fan.

Over the steam she connected with Rosa, and raised her eyebrows.

Should I tell him? she asked, without saying it aloud.

Rosa nodded her head. *Yes, bloody get on with it.*

'Eliot?' she said. He didn't hear her and for a moment she watched him staring towards the fire, the light flickering on his face. She longed to touch him, to rip the plaster so he could stop living in her thoughts all the time. 'Eliot?' she said, louder.

'Hey.' He turned with a smile, the fire flecking amber in the greys of his eyes, like when a sunset breaks through storm clouds.

She took his sleeve and angled him away from the others. 'Can I talk to you a minute?'

'Of course.'

Cleo never usually needed to rehearse what she was going to say to Eliot, but now she wished she had. She swallowed. 'Sorry, I think the smoke is making my throat dry.'

'Do you want some of my drink?' He offered his cup, and then looked down. 'Or, some of your own?'

She gulped at her cider, the sweet, hot liquid loosening her inhibitions. She could do this. She was a human being, capable of explaining something as simple as feelings.

OK. Let's go. 'Sometimes, over the past—'

A piercing squeal filled the air, followed by a *boom*, and

bright red and green sparkles exploded in the air above them, and the crowd exploded into the mandatory oohs and ahhs.

Eliot's attention was taken away and just as Cleo was about to speak again, the second firework whizzed, followed by a vivacious Catherine wheel, and then a further ten minutes of light display.

By the time it was finished, the crowd began to move and they were swept into a mass departure, and the moment had passed.

Chapter 14

Two weeks after Eliot flew back from California, Cleo would have blurted out the truth, if it wasn't for a tin of tomatoes.

'One crab cake burger, one smoked mackerel linguine, a side of garlic bread and some sharing fries,' Cleo read out to Coacean's chef, grabbing a sheet of paper towel to mop her forehead before she washed her hands and headed back out into the throng. The restaurant was like a second home to Cleo, somewhere she practically lived. She'd worked here for years, hosted birthdays, served Christmas dinners, manned the entrance during private events, and worked a hundred hot summer days. But it never failed to amaze her how a Saturday in the middle of November could still get such busy pockets that it felt like her feet weren't even stepping on the floor.

That was the last of the lunch orders, though. The tables were now clearing out, and she would have some space to breathe.

Eliot was overlapping his shift with hers today, as they often did in the winter, being two of the main full-time employees. Rosa was there today too, and when Cleo tried to walk back onto the restaurant floor, Rosa pulled her into the supplies pantry and closed the door.

'What are we doing in here?' Cleo laughed, knocking a gigantic tin of plum tomatoes with her elbow.

'Have you told him yet?' Rosa demanded.

'No, not yet,' Cleo hissed, giving the door a prod to make sure it was closed.

'You hang out with him every day. Do it soon otherwise you're going to waste the whole winter.'

'I told you, I'll do it by Christmas. I need time to think about exactly what I'm going to say.'

'"Eliot, I'm in love with you, what do you think?" There, how about that?'

Cleo rolled her eyes. 'Come on, though, you know as well as I do that I'd try and say that and all that would come out would be some comment about the weather and then I'd run away.'

Rosa shook her head and picked up a carrot. 'I thought you said you were always yourself around him? Why would you start acting like an idiot now?'

'Because ... the stakes are high.'

Cleo appreciated Rosa's advice, and she didn't want to seem like she was ignoring her when she was only trying to help, so she added, 'I will do it soon. I just need to find the right time.'

'Remember what I said.' Rosa waved her carrot at Cleo.

'Just rip the plaster off and make sure you can get out of there if you need to, to give him time to think.' Sensing Cleo's trepidation, she added, 'How about at the end of a shift? How about today?'

Cleo's eyebrows shot up and she checked the time on her phone. She was due to finish in ten minutes. She couldn't do it now, not when she was all seafoody and he would have to carry on working and making small talk with customers for the next four hours. But she found herself saying, 'OK, maybe,' to avoid having an argument.

'You will? You'll do it today?'

'I'll see.'

Rosa flung open the door to the store cupboard and called, 'Eliot!'

'What are you doing?' Cleo asked, her mouth suddenly getting that parched feeling again. 'Oh my God, I need some water.'

'Eliot, Cleo's in here with a headache, can you bring her some water?' Rosa turned back to her, eyes glittering, smile wide, and whispered, 'There you go – two birds, one stone and all that.' With that, she slipped out of the supply pantry, holding the door open for Eliot and then closing it behind him when he stepped inside.

In that small space, he stood close to her, his eyes laced with waves of concern, and held out a water. 'You have a headache?'

'No, not really,' she said, waving him off, but drank the water to stop her croaky voice.

'Do you want some fresh air?'

117

'Maybe,' Cleo replied.

Eliot turned in the small space to open the door. He gave it a rattle, then said, 'Hmm. It seems to be stuck.'

'Uh-oh, seven minutes in heaven!' Cleo contemplated opening the tin of tomatoes and drowning herself inside it.

He faced her again, that smile on his lips, and she gulped, a nervous laugh escaping. His laugh echoed hers, and he shrugged.

Two, maybe three seconds passed but, in those moments, Cleo studied his face – that she knew so well – one more time. That way, if he didn't want to see her any more after she told him, at least she could remember that smile.

There was a noise outside the door, and muffled voices. Rosa's was the clearest. 'No, I don't know, I don't think there's any in there.' Someone else spoke, and then Rosa continued, saying, 'OK, I'll go in and check.'

Eliot put his hand back on the door knob and rattled, and Cleo stepped closer to him. Was Rosa holding the door closed from the outside?

'Let me try.' The chef's voice came through clearer now, on the other side of the door.

'No, I've got it!' Rosa swung the door open. 'Oh, look at that, I fixed the problem. Hey, you two, since you've been doing inventory, are there any tins of tomatoes in there?'

Eliot reached onto the shelf and Rosa mouthed a sorry to Cleo, who stood, dazed, her hand around her empty water glass.

'That was weird,' said Eliot, guiding Cleo out of the

pantry when Rosa and the chef had got out of the way. 'How's your head?'

'It's really fine, just a little ... foggy.'

'You're finishing soon, right?'

Cleo nodded.

Eliot took her notepad and pen from her. 'Head off now, go home, drink some tea, rest up. I'll come by after my shift and see how you're doing.'

'No, Eliot, you don't have to do that—'

'It's fine.'

'No, really, I'll probably just have a good sleep. Thank you, though.'

'All right. Well, call me if you want me to come over.'

Cleo agreed that she would and it was only late that evening, when she was lying in bed, reading one of her favourite childhood books that she kept in her wardrobe, that realisation dropped the novel right onto her face.

Why oh why hadn't she accepted his offer to come over? That would have been the perfect opportunity. Now it was too late and, as usual, she would fall asleep to the tune of imagined futures that didn't know if they'd ever fly.

Chapter 15

Three weeks after Eliot came home, Cleo changed the course of her Christmas on the coast.

'You guys really have to leave now, I'm not joking. Look, you can glare at me all you want but I'm not leaving you alone with these chips.'

'Wow, look at this sunset!' Eliot stepped through the door to the restaurant decking, which was empty except for the face-off occurring between Cleo and the seagulls.

Cleo waved her tea towel in the air and the gulls reluctantly flew away, never taking their beady eyes off her, and settled on the beach below, their heads cocked in anticipation for the sound of the glass doors closing again.

Only now did Cleo look up and see the sight before her. It was one of those perfect November late afternoons. The sky was full of yellow as the sun lowered herself over the ocean, bathing the glacier-blue water in gold leaf. The sea itself was calm and hazy on the horizon, melting seamlessly into the skyline.

'Oh, look at that,' Cleo murmured, pointing out a group paddle-boarding, gliding effortlessly, the sun behind them.

'Shall we sack off work and go in?' Eliot was beside her now, the two of them leaning on the wooden railings, the golden hour glow on their faces, their arms almost touching.

'Inside?' she asked.

'In the sea?'

'God, yes please,' Cleo answered, only half joking. The water was liquid silk and her heart panged with a longing of missed opportunities and wasteful worries and wishes to dive right in.

It's all changing this year, she told herself. *Once Eliot knows, I'll be free of this rut.* If she could just have some quality, uninterrupted alone time with him . . .

With the feel of the wood ridges under her fingertips, and the salt-scented breeze blowing the warmth of the sun over her face, she began to relax and unfurl, like she always did near him. She couldn't stop the words from coming out of her mouth. 'I'm glad you're home to see this with me.'

'Me too,' Eliot replied.

'I know we've seen a thousand sunsets together but they never get old.'

'Unlike me.'

She laughed. 'Unlike *us*.'

After a moment, Eliot spoke again. 'You know what I read this morning?' Cleo tilted her head to the side and he continued. 'Apparently, we're forecast to have a white Christmas.'

She laughed; the sound being picked up by the slight, sunny breeze. 'I'm sure I hear that every year, and then we don't see a flake until sometime in January, and even then it's only on the top of the hills. Beast from the East aside,' she said, referencing the huge snowstorm a few years back that had wrapped a white duvet over their beach town.

'I don't know,' Eliot said. 'I think it could happen this year. I'd love to see the beach with snow on again.'

'Every day it's getting colder,' she agreed, nodding. 'Will you be heading to your grandparents for Christmas again? Or your mum and dad's?'

'Actually, not this year. My grandparents want to go to a hotel, like they did when they were younger. And Lucy wanted me to work, so I'm going to visit them, and maybe my folks, sometime after the big day.'

'You're staying around just to work?' Cleo faced him.

He shrugged. 'I don't mind. You'll be working too, right?'

'Well, yeah.' Her thoughts began to tumble into each other. 'Does that mean you'll be alone at Christmas?'

'Only when I go home from the restaurant.'

He didn't seem to mind; she guessed he was used to being independent. And actually, the more she'd got used to the idea of having some peace and quiet around Christmastime, some space and time by herself, the more she'd come around to the idea.

Still though ... She rushed to get her words out before they ran away. 'I'm on my own for Christmas too – Mum and Dad are spending the holidays with Gabriela and her fiancé.'

Cleo's heart pulsed. This was ... stupid. Or perfect. Or somewhere in between, which made it all the more tempting.

So, Eliot was going to be alone at Christmas. And so was she.

He raised his eyebrows a little, and a smile began a slow spread on both their faces. Without giving herself the chance to change her mind, Cleo asked the million-dollar question: 'Would you like to spend Christmas with me?'

'You asked him to *what*?' Rosa cried down the phone.

Cleo was walking back home, the wintery wind kissing the end of her phone in a way that meant she had to cup her hand over the receiver to be heard.

'I asked him to spend Christmas with me,' Cleo repeated. 'And he said yes. So that's when I'm going to do it – tell him how I feel.'

'At Christmas. In your home.'

'Exactly.' She felt on top of the world, so even when Rosa sighed down the line, Cleo cut her off with, 'What's a more magical time than Christmas? It's the perfect setting.' She and Eliot always had the most fun when they were alone, being natural with each other.

'But, now I hate to be *that person*, but what if he doesn't feel the same way?'

Her soaring heart swooped down a little. 'But what if he does?'

Rosa continued. 'It's just that Christmas is so ... loaded. It's a lot. And what if you tell him, and he rejects you, and then you're stuck talking about the weather over cold

Brussels sprouts and silently sobbing into your blanket in front of Christmas special reruns?'

'Wow, tell it like it is, Rosa. You paint quite the picture.'

'Look, I just don't want you to get hurt. I know this is a big deal for you. If this is how you want to do it, then it's your call. Obviously.'

Cleo hesitated, but that was quite true – it was her decision. Sure, she could take Rosa's advice and force herself to engineer a good time, in some snatched moment, prior to Christmas, but this felt right. It felt exciting. And she knew Eliot – even if he didn't feel the same, it wouldn't be awkward, he'd never let it be, and neither would she. So yes, despite what anyone (Rosa included) might think, she felt confident in her decision.

A part of her still itched, though, to just agree with Rosa and do what she suggested. She wished she didn't find it so much easier saying yes than no. But her answer was no. 'I'm going to tell him at Christmas. Sorry. This is too important to blurt out inside a pantry at work, or when we're in a crowd of other people. Sorry. I know you were trying to help.'

'All right, then,' said Rosa. 'Have you ever hosted a Christmas before?'

'I'm sure I can sling together a glorified Sunday roast and a few decorations,' Cleo replied, relieved that her opinion hadn't upset Rosa. She reached her house and ascended the steps to her flat.

Rosa laughed down the line. 'Well, if you need any help ... '

'Thank you, really.'

They rang off and Cleo entered her home. A tennis game was going on outside, and, though she usually ignored them, today she made a cup of tea and sat in her window seat to watch. In the distance she could glimpse the sea she'd just walked away from. With the sun now behind the cliffs, the sky was ice-cream colours of lilac melting to blush pink into vanilla yellow.

She hesitated, teetering on the edge of whether to put on her wetsuit and head down to the beach again. The old Cleo would have, she would have taken any opportunity she could have, especially in the off-season.

Cleo could almost imagine the cold water licking at the neck of her wetsuit, cooling her, calling her. She wanted to follow, to go back in, go back to *her*. But the thing about being stuck was, it wasn't so easy to just pull yourself out.

So Cleo told herself it wasn't worth heading out again now, getting all wet, then needing to wash her hair. Instead, she watched the two women on the courts outside. The tennis balls thwacked back and forth, and the sounds of laughter from the players drifted up to her window, reminding Cleo of when she and Gabriela used to come here as tweens, neither of them ever bothering to learn the rules of tennis, and instead just hurling the balls at each other as fast as they could.

Cleo didn't get up to check on her phone and what she might need to reply to. She didn't rush straight into doing chores so they didn't build up in case anyone needed her. She drank the whole cup, and watched the game, right up until the sky had faded to dark.

Chapter 16

~ Then ~

Winter 2010

'This doesn't feel right,' Cleo said, her voice catching, the tears in her eyes spilling over. A year previously she'd said goodbye to Eliot on this very spot, and now she and her twin were about to go their separate ways for university.

Last year, she and Eliot had hugged, wrapped in a towel together, here on the beach, after their attempt at surfing together. Pressed against his beating heart, her head pounding from being smacked with a surfboard, her mind still woozy and flooded from the embarrassment of passing out, she'd been sure he'd been thinking of kissing her, but nerves had got the better of her to do anything about it herself.

Tonight, she'd thought to herself the day of his leaving party; making a pact with herself that she would finally do something. Do what, she wasn't sure. Kiss him? Tell him about the feelings that were always a current under the surface of everything? She wasn't certain, but she had to do something before he left Wavebreak Bay.

And then it was too late, because he was practically kissing his friend Jessica.

'She's the type of cool surf girl I can just see you with,' Cleo had said to him, wishing she could push the words back into her mouth, wishing he would see they were only spilling out because they were pleading to be contradicted. She wanted him to say, *You're the girl I want to be with*. Her whole heart wanted him to never look at Jessica again and instead kiss her, because *she* was right for him, she knew it. But he didn't. And she didn't say anything either. Uggggghhhhh, that was a fine moment of self-sabotage, looking back, and she cringed at the memory of walking away, stepping back into the shadows.

Now, a year had passed and Cleo was pretty sure she would never get that closeness back with Eliot. She'd only seen him a handful of times since that night last September, when he returned from university for brief weekends.

When Cleo and Gabriela had finished their exams and left through the doors of their high school for the final time, they'd taken off to spend the summer in South America.

Three months of backpacking, of living in hostels, of opening their eyes to the world beyond Wavebreak Bay, and of sharing everything with each other from mosquito spray to memories. It had been the best summer, and Cleo wouldn't change a thing.

She and her twin had regained that closeness they'd had before their teenage years had them growing in different directions. Cleo had known all they needed was some quality time together. But now it was ending, it was really ending.

'I wish you were coming to live in Cambridge,' Gabriela sniffled. 'I don't know anyone there and it's so far away. And what do I know about linguistics, anyway?'

'Lots,' Cleo replied. 'You know you do; you've worked your butt cheeks off for this. I wish you were coming to Bath. You'll visit though, won't you?'

'Every weekend.' Gabriela squeezed her. 'Well, maybe every other weekend. And you have to come over to me as well.'

'Of course I will.'

Prior to their summer abroad, Gabriela had been positively itching to leave the safety and familiarity of Wavebreak Bay. It was like she'd spent the past few years picking at a seam until she was finally able to break free. But now, now that she wasn't just living out of a bag for a couple of months, but she was actually moving, she was scared, a neediness Gabriela rarely showed causing her to cling to Cleo.

'What am I going to do without you in the room next door?' Gabriela clutched her twin as the two of them sat on rocks on the beach, looking out towards the ocean, tears as salty as the sea spilling onto her face and being dragged sideways in the wind. 'I don't think I want to go, Clee. Maybe I could transfer to Bath and stay with you?'

It broke Cleo's heart, because if she could have one wish in this world, it would be to keep her twin by her side, especially now. It was, quite literally, like her other half was being taken away. But Gabriela had got into Cambridge

University – this was her dream – and so Cleo had to be the strong one here.

'No,' she said. 'You're going to be so successful, and brilliant and loved and Cambridge needs you there. You have to go. I'm so proud of you.'

'But—'

Cleo pulled Gabriela closer, their hair weaving together. 'We can do this. You can do this. And some of my DNA is right there in you so I'm never far, really.'

Gabriela wiped her snot on Cleo's sleeve, and the two of them sat in silence for a while, just the sound of the water lapping over the pebbles, moving them minutely into new places they'd never quite go back to, ever again.

'Can we come back?' Gabriela asked, looking up, her eyes meeting Cleo's. 'After uni, let's make a plan to come back here?' She shifted on the rock, a sparkle of energy returning, a faint smile on her lips, and she wiped at her tears.

'We'll be back before the end of uni,' Cleo said, confused. 'We'll come home at Christmas, if not before—'

'No, I mean, let's move back. Together. When we've both finished uni we could come back here and we could share a house ... or maybe live near each other, not in the same house because if you come back maybe you'll finally hook up with Eliot and you'll want to live with him.'

'No, Eliot's long gone ... ' Cleo said, blocking a wistful sound from creeping into her voice.

Gabriela scooted past her point. 'But we could come back and live here and Mum and Dad can give us the restaurant so we'd have something to do.'

Cleo laughed. It all sounded so easy. It all sounded, frankly, perfect. Because although she wanted to spread her wings, fly to Bath, learn everything there was to know on her natural sciences course, to her there was nowhere that felt more like home than Wavebreak Bay, and that was exactly where she wanted to spend her life. 'Sure,' she agreed, not expecting it to happen.

But what if it did? Wouldn't that be the best?

Chapter 17

~ Now ~

December

'Oof, sorry.' Cleo smiled at the other customer as they reached for a small cup of steaming mulled wine at the same time. 'After you.'

It was early December, and Wavebreak Bay was having its annual late night Christmas shopping evening, where local businesses kept their doors open until eight, put out moreish snacks and drinks and the staff usually adorned themselves in tinsel and festive jumpers. There was a cloud of merriment in the air, with Wham! and Mariah Carey bursting out of shop radios, and carol singers with charity boxes in huddles on the street, along with people holding out boxes of Quality Street for passers-by.

Cleo was shopping local for her gifts this year, and was already bumbling along with three large paper bags containing a white wooden photo frame for her sister, a scarf and gloves set for her dad and a slightly too pungent scented candle, which she'd planned to give to Rosa but the smell wasn't very appealing, to be honest. However, the sales assistant in the candle shop had been so lovely and Cleo had already eaten one of her mince pies so she felt she really should buy it. Perhaps Cleo would just keep this for herself and find something else for Rosa.

So, just her mum and Eliot to go, because if she was spending Christmas with Eliot, she had to give him a gift. And now something else for Rosa, she guessed. Cleo took her cup of mulled wine and moved aside, letting the cinnamon steam warm her face before she took a drink.

She was inside a gallery, one with glass sculptures and local photography and paintings of the Jurassic coast, and she turned her thoughts first to Eliot. Quelle surprise.

So what to buy your friend, who you were in love with, who, by Christmas Day, may love you back, or hate you for deceiving them for years? And what to buy somebody who spent half their lives moving continents and didn't typically keep a lot of stuff?

Then she spotted something she quite liked. It was a rectangular luggage tag made of wood, and one side was swirled blue and white resin covering three quarters of the tag, so it gave the appearance of sea on sand.

She picked it up and studied it. It was beautifully crafted, simple, beachy, and the colours were very Wavebreak Bay.

'Those are new in, but they sell fast,' said the salesperson.

'I bet, they're incredible. I'll take this one, please.' Then, in a rush of decisiveness, she selected a fused glass window hanging for her mum and a miniature painting of Wavebreak Bay for Rosa.

'No problem.' The assistant took the items. As he wrapped the luggage tag, window hanging and painting in tissue paper, he asked her, 'Do you have a nice Christmas planned?'

'I do, actually,' Cleo answered. 'A slightly different Christmas, but I'm looking forward to it. And you?'

'Oh yes, I can't wait. There you go.' He handed over the parcel inside a gift bag. 'Hope the recipients love them. Merry Christmas.'

'Merry Christmas.' Cleo grinned and hugged the parcel to her, pleased with her finds.

Stepping back out onto the street, Cleo accepted another mince pie from somebody dressed as a wise man outside a bank, even though she was actually a little full of mince pies now, if she was honest, this being her fourth. OK, fifth.

Above her, Wavebreak Bay's Christmas lights twinkled, strings of yellowy-white bulbs that were strung in zigzags between the rows of shops, culminating in a large Christmas tree right on the seafront, roped down with about eight guy-ropes so it didn't blow over in winter winds – like it had two years ago, right on top of somebody's open-top car, filling it with pine needles and bending the wing mirror. (Open-top in winter though?)

The sound of the waves rushing over the pebbles on the beach could be heard, even from back here, the constant reminder that the sea was still there in the dark, still doing its thing, no matter what any of the residents of Wavebreak Bay might be busying themselves with.

Cleo listened to the ocean for a minute, breathing in the near-freezing night air tinged with salt, until a brass band started up to her right, and she was brought back to the moment.

'Hark the Herald Angels Sing'. One of her favourites. Cleo watched them for a while, this group of five men and women, in matching red jackets and Santa hats, then popped a ten-pound note in their charity collection box.

She should make a new Christmas playlist. Something she could put on in the background at her parents' house over Christmas; something fun and cheesy and maybe a bit romantic, but not too much in case things didn't go in that direction.

It wasn't long to go now, and Cleo was putting in her time trying to orchestrate the perfect Christmas. Regardless of what she planned to say to Eliot, this was to be her first time hosting for the holidays, and it was her job to make sure she gave good memories.

But as for telling Eliot . . . she'd been stewing over Rosa's comments, how her big idea would result in not giving him any space to think. And she'd come up with a solution.

He was going to come to her parents' on the twenty-third. She'd let the two of them settle for twenty-four hours, relax into their environment, and then Cleo would spill her heart on Christmas Eve. She'd do it when they were both back from work – he was due to work the earlier brunch shift and she the overlapping lunchtime one, so they'd both be home by mid-afternoon – and afterwards she'd give him space in the house and take herself for a festive swim in the ocean.

Yep, she was doing it. A Christmas swim. Smashing two

things she'd been putting off in one go: a Christmas gift to herself and her wellbeing. Sure, it would be freezing cold, but once upon a time that would have never stopped her, and deep down she was still the same person who plunged into cold water and sought after a dreamy, salty, sandy life by the sea. Deep, deep down. It was time. It was so time.

This way, if Eliot said he didn't feel the same way, or worst-case, felt he'd been brought to her house for Christmas under false pretences and was angry, perhaps the awkwardness would be over by Christmas Day and they could go back to just friends?

The last of the mince pie went into her mouth but felt dry, her stomach churning. Hello, anxious thoughts.

Before she gave them a chance to fully form into the inevitable worries that had caused her to avoid rocking her boat as the years drifted by, Cleo took herself to the seafront and looked down at some actual boats, inhaling and exhaling with deep breaths that matched the incoming and outgoing waves.

'"Dear Gabriela and Derek,"' Cleo read aloud as she penned the Christmas card, sitting on the floor of her flat. Beside her, she'd just wrapped her sister's picture frame, in which she'd put a large print of her and her fiancé on the beach when they'd last come down to visit as a twosome, a month after they'd got engaged the year before.

Gabriela tended to like to vet her photos before they were printed or shown anywhere, but Cleo knew for a fact that she'd liked this one, having stated, 'Ooo, I look lovely, and he looks OK.' So, good enough. She could always change the picture if she wanted.

'"Have an amazing last Christmas as fiancée and fiancé and can't wait to celebrate the big day with you both next year. PS: don't let Mum have too much port on Christmas Eve, haha. Kiss kiss, Cleo".'

The wedding was set for next autumn. Set-ish. The two of them hadn't booked a date yet but both wanted a warm wedding somewhere near Cambridge, but not over the peak of summer, so 'September sometime' it was.

Cleo had always imagined she would be there when her twin sister got engaged. Not that she was entitled to be, she didn't know why she'd assumed she would, really, she just . . . had. They'd been together for all the big moments in each other's lives until then. Birthdays, Christmases, graduations, hospital trips. Even for things they hid from their parents, like when Gabriela first bought condoms or Cleo scraped such a massive gash into her car at uni, it was kinder to her wallet to scrap it than it was to repair it, they still shared with each other. So Cleo had just . . . assumed. But Derek had proposed in Cambridge – he rarely came down this way, something about it being too far to travel and the sea air giving him headaches – and Gabriela had told her over the phone.

Sometimes Cleo wondered if it was just her that was hanging on to the past for dear life.

Cleo put the card with the gift, and pushed them gently aside. She was going to give Gabriela's gift to her mum and dad to take up with them this year.

She flicked to the next Christmas track playing from her phone, choosing an upbeat Ariana Grande number. Fanning the Christmas cards out on the floor, she selected a nice one depicting a nativity play in a theatre to send to Uncle Stuart, his boyfriend Kaleb, and his son Charlie, since they were heading off on a Merry Murder Mystery weekend for Christmastime.

"'Merry Christmas, Stuart, Charlie and Kaleb, hope YULE get away with murder!'" Cleo chuckled at her joke and stuffed the card in the envelope.

She stood up and rolled her shoulders. That was the last of the Christmas cards – just in time too since December was already halfway gone. Now she needed to get up and do the next thing on her list before she remained hunched on the floor for evermore.

Cleo had done a neat job decorating her flat this year. She had a small tree on her window sill, some coloured lights around her window, and paper snowflakes that she'd chopped out of old newspaper. Usually, she went all out with the fairy lights in here, and then left them up for several months as she liked the ambient lighting, but she was planning to haul her box of them over to her parents' house to make it look even lovelier and warmer over Christmas.

Stepping over the cards and gifts towards her wardrobe, she took a breath.

Cleo took out the wetsuit, removing it from its hanger, where it had lived for the past few years. It felt light in her hands – there was a time it was always a bit heavy because it never fully dried before she used it again, but now there was no moisture. The granular sand that had once peppered the surface had long since dropped off, and when she held it to her face even the salty scent had disappeared. But it was still her suit, long arms and legs with bright turquoise flashes, and the body black and neon pink.

This was the first purchase she'd made when she'd moved back here, back when she'd had the idea that she'd start her mornings out in the ocean. And she had done that for a while, along with kayaking in her downtime.

But . . . she'd fallen out of the habit. It wasn't even that she didn't have time, as such, more that she used up her time – or perhaps her energy – on other people. Then one missed swim turned into two, which turned into her saying to people, 'Oh, I haven't been in for ages, I'll go this weekend, though, for sure, because the weather is going to be so nice.'

Cleo had dwelled on this too often; she wasn't going to do it again now. Instead, she stripped off to her undies and unzipped the suit, wanting to check it still fitted before she found herself in a situation right after telling Eliot she loved him of having to ask him to help roll her out of a badly fitting tube of neoprene.

She got her legs in, her bum in, her stomach in, and snapped it up over her arms without too much trouble, and, reaching behind her, hand flailing, found the pull-tab and managed to zip all the way to the top.

'Still a water baby,' Cleo whispered to herself. There was something about putting on her wetsuit that felt transformative, like she belonged. Like she wanted to streak her hair with sea salt and discuss rip currents with somebody.

Then she looked in the mirror, and her smile faded. It wasn't that the wetsuit didn't fit ... it fitted fine. A little snugger than it used to, but she didn't mind that. But it just didn't look *right*. She looked out of place and lacking and like she didn't belong among the salty-haired rip-curl-talkers, after all.

'We're not doing this,' she told herself in the mirror, tying her hair into a loose bun. 'Stop it.' Her thoughts stopped in their tracks, before trying one more needle. *No, but really, you won't be accepted*— 'Stop. It.' Then she added, in a whisper to herself, 'You're not that bad.'

Chapter 18

~ Then ~

Summer 2013

In one way, nothing had changed, but in so many others – everything had.

Cleo stepped out of her mum's car outside her childhood home at the top of the cliff, and let the sunny sea breeze wash over her. She could smell the ocean, feel its salt in the air, hear the pebbles rolling beneath the sea foam. She'd come home.

Three years of university were now behind her. Three years of new friends, hard work, exploring every corner of the city of Bath, and it had been amazing, but sometimes good things had to end to make room for the future.

And Wavebreak Bay was always going to be both her past, and her future.

'Shall I put your bags in your room?' Felicity asked, opening the car boot.

'I'll sort that, Mum.' Cleo snapped to attention, taking

her huge suitcase and dragging it through the house and up to her old bedroom, kissing her dad en route, who was busy putting the kettle on and slicing up a slab of her mum's 'welcome home' ginger cake.

By the end of the summer, Cleo hoped to have found somewhere of her own to live, perhaps a house share or a small flat. She wasn't really in any rush to move out of this big, beautiful house again, but she valued her own space now, as did her parents, she suspected.

She passed Gabriela's bedroom door and peeked inside. Just in case. But she knew her sister wouldn't be there, not really. She'd known from the start of their second year that her twin probably wouldn't be sticking to their promise of moving back to Wavebreak Bay when their degrees were completed. Gabriela was flourishing in Cambridge at the moment. Happy. Free.

Cleo would be here, should she ever change her mind, which Gabriela insisted she would do at some point, maybe in a year or so. For now, she'd have to just keep seeing Gabriela during holidays or for long weekends.

Back downstairs, Cleo took a cup of tea from her dad and walked through the back doors into their clifftop garden. Reaching the edge, she ran her free hand over the stones of the wall, warm from the early summer midday sun, and she thought of Eliot, a smile on her face at memories of how she used to gaze at him over this wall, that first year they met. She probably hadn't been as subtle as she'd thought she was.

Ahh, Eliot. Her first proper crush. It had been four years

since they'd been at school together, and worked together, and had hung out nearly every day. She'd seen him a few times in those years, but once she was at university too their paths crossed less and less often. Now he'd lived in California for the past year, after finishing his own degree, helping his cousin with a business in San Francisco. Sometimes they would text or Facebook message each other, and wow, he seemed happy. He was living his dream by being out there – hadn't he always talked about reuniting with Chris in California? So now, really, he was just a happy part of her history.

Still, though. The teenager she'd been would have liked to have had the opportunity to have kissed him, at least once.

Anyway, on the subject of kissing, she really needed to let Harry, her semi-serious boyfriend she'd got together with during her last year of university, know she'd arrived safely. Even if things with him were a little up in the air right now.

'How does it feel to be back?' Her dad's voice cut through her thoughts.

'It feels . . . ' Cleo paused, wanting to find the right word. Her emotions were colours right now – glittering turquoises, sunrise pinks, endless lemon yellows – but how to convey that? 'It feels . . . right.'

Right. And so, so exciting. Coming back to Wavebreak Bay felt like she was actually about to start living her real life. She was going to swim every day. She might even find a group to go swimming with, or maybe even start her own group! She was going to buy a campervan and take trips down the coast, catch fish, learn how to follow all of her parents' delicious seafood recipes. She was going to fall in love with someone – sadly, probably not Harry, if she was honest – and figure out who she was and do this 'yolo' thing people were always talking about.

While she did all this, she would work in the restaurant for a while until she found another job, maybe something freelance, maybe something to do with the water.

'And Coacean? Sure you're OK working there again, three years on?' Bryce smiled.

'Absolutely,' Cleo said. 'You know I always loved working there. Slightly wishing I'd thought about the timings a bit more and stayed in Bath until the summer holiday rush was over, but I'm here now and I'm ready to go.'

Felicity, who had also stepped into the sunlight and now stood with an arm around her husband, exchanged a smile with him.

'What?' Cleo asked, looking between the two.

'We're just pleased to have you back,' Felicity answered.

As the sun began a slow dip later that afternoon, Cleo got herself dressed in the familiar Coacean uniform of a blue-striped short-sleeved shirt and blue shorts, adding the new conch-shell-embroidered apron her parents had given her. She tied her hair back in a blue band, pulling out a curly strand, as she always did, applied a little coral-tinted lip balm, and made her way down the hill towards the restaurant for her first shift. Butterflies surprised her by waking up and dancing in her stomach.

'There's a surprise waiting for you down there,' Bryce had said before she left the house. Cleo assumed it was a bottle of fizz or maybe some of those coconut shrimps she'd insisted they never take off the menu because they were her favourite.

She wasn't expecting an entirely different kind of favourite to be leaning against the weathered wall outside the front entrance, and it stopped her in her tracks.

'What are you doing here?' Cleo asked before she'd even reached the bottom of the hill, placing a hand on her heart, her words being carried away from her in the warm air.

Eliot stood up straight, looking like the same Eliot from four years ago in his Coacean uniform, but a little taller, a little broader, a little stubblier, his hair a little longer and wavier. His skin had been kissed with a tan from California. He looked *good*, and, with a bunch of sunflowers dangling from one hand, he held his arms wide for her.

'Oh my God,' Cleo shrieked, legging it towards him, and they laughed in unison as they embraced.

'Cleo, you look amazing,' Eliot said, pulling away and holding her at arm's length, his grey eyes warm.

'So do you! Why aren't you in California right now?' She wondered if she was blushing, considering she'd only earlier been wishing she'd kissed him. 'I was just thinking about you!' she blurted. *Damn you, brain, stop betraying me!*

'I came home. Last week.'

'And you're working here again?'

'For the summer, at least. I told your parents not to say anything; I wanted to surprise you.'

Eliot looked bashful for a moment, and Cleo was lost for words, taking him in. 'Who are those for?' she asked, glancing at the sunflowers.

'For you,' he said, passing them to her with a bashful smile. 'I just saw them, and they were like sunshine, which is like you, and, I don't know. I'm being really lame.'

'You aren't, you doofus, they're gorge,' she laughed, taking them, her mind whirling with thoughts of why he was here, gazing at her like this, giving her flowers. Flowers were such un-Eliot-like things that the whole interaction made her feel on edge. But in a good way. Like a not-quite-forgotten wish was about to be whispered.

'Cleo, I know it's been a long time, but I wanted to talk to you about something, before you're surrounded by everyone else welcoming you home.'

'What is it?' Her heart was thudding.

Eliot paused, his eyes on her face, moving to her lips, his own lips curving into the smallest of smiles, and though a part of her mind was screaming to her mouth to not say a word, another part, some bloody annoying sensible part, told her to put a stop to it before it was too late. Before he said something that would change their friendship forever. Because if they remained friends, if nothing changed, then nothing could break, right?

And so she filled his hesitation with a seemingly harmless curve-ball by saying, 'I can't wait for you to meet my boyfriend.'

It was out there now. Eliot leant back, such a small movement they could both pretend it never happened, and, with a blink, he curved that smile into a larger, but less convincing one. 'A boyfriend? I'd love to.'

'His name is Harry. We met at uni. We've been together

a few months now and I don't know what's going to happen now term's over – no plans to be shacking up together any-time soon or anything, hahaha.' She was babbling, filling her awkwardness with more awkwardness. 'I don't know what'll happen, we'll see, but . . . yeah. Harry.'

'Harry.'

In truth, Harry had no plans to move to Devon nor had she to move back to Bath, where he was staying. They were giving longish-distance a go. But she felt his heart wasn't all-in, and she knew hers wasn't either.

Even more so, now.

'So . . . we're going to be working together again?' she asked.

He nodded, and with one more second's hesitation she stepped back into his arms.

'This is the best news ever. I've missed you, pal.'

'I've missed you too,' he said into her hair, and the breath near her neck reignited that flame deep within her.

It was a busy summer in Wavebreak Bay, without a lot of breaks, and one, probably overdue, break-up where she bid Harry goodbye when he visited in August. Come the autumn time, she and Eliot were solidly back in their old ways, only better. Their friendship had rebuilt itself, bigger, stronger, and they were as close as two platonic pals could be. But he'd not stepped forward again with Harry out of the picture, and, when the summer season closed, he moved to an office job in Exeter, wanting to put the creative skills he'd learned on his advertising course at uni to some use. And so Cleo had convinced herself that she didn't need to revert back to her teenage crush of longing gazes and wishful thinking, and instead focused on settling back into life beside the seaside.

Over the winter months, Cleo stuck to her plan, somewhat. She swam in the sea every day. She found a small studio flat on the outskirts of town. She took a steady income at the restaurant, and, just like she had at sixteen, really enjoyed working there.

As did Eliot, who, by the time spring started to creep back around, had accepted he was ill-suited to office life, and had found himself back in Wavebreak Bay, going for a supervisor role at the restaurant, talking about branding and advertising and how he wanted to work in management one day. He was regularly chatting to his entrepreneur cousin back in California, who was his mentor, in a way, especially since he still rarely saw his parents.

With the approach of another summer, the esplanade began to noticeably fill with more visitors than it had held the day before, and then more again, and the ice-cream shops reopened, and the hotels had been given a lick of paint, Cleo couldn't quite believe that nearly a year had gone by. Time flies when you're having fun, they said.

Chapter 19

~ Now ~

'I love this, thanks, mate!' Rosa screeched on opening her Christmas present.

'It's just a silly little thing, really,' Cleo said, looking over her shoulder at the tiny oil painting of their beach. 'I just thought you might like it.'

'I do, I love it.' Rosa reached over and gave her a hug. 'I got you something too, but open it at Christmas when I'm gone.'

'I can't open it now?' Cleo said, holding the book-shaped gift Rosa had just plonked in her hand. It was the twenty-first of December and Rosa was about to fly back to New Zealand, surely this was close enough to the big day?

'No, because I want you to have it at Christmas, and also, because we have to go.'

Cleo checked the time. 'Ooo crap, you're right.'

While Rosa put her painting carefully on the desk in her bedroom and turned out the lights, Cleo put her coat and gloves back on and waited by Rosa's front door.

'I think my flatmate won't be home until dark so I'll leave the hall light on for her, otherwise, let's go!'

Cleo took her holdall while Rosa bashed her huge suitcase down the stairs, out the door, and into Felicity's car, that Cleo had borrowed to take Rosa to the train station.

'Thank your mum for me, won't you?' Rosa said, as she jammed her suitcase in the boot, huffing into the icy air.

'Of course.' As they pulled away, heading towards Exeter St Davids station, Cleo asked, 'Are you excited to be seeing your family again?'

'Hell yeah,' she said. 'I can't wait, it feels like it's been for ever. And guess what?'

'What?'

'Remember that girl I told you about, who asked me out just before I came over here?'

'Yes . . . ?'

Rosa was practically wriggling in her seat. 'I'm going to meet up with her again. Just to see how we're both feeling.'

'You are?' Cleo grinned, the romantic in her swooning.

'Inspired by you and your determination to find love even when oceans divide you.' Rosa smiled. 'Speaking of, how are you feeling?'

'I'm nervous about hosting my first Christmas.' Cleo laughed.

'That's what you're most nervous about?'

'I wouldn't say *most* nervous, but it's one of the many upcoming things unnerving me and it's the one I'm choosing to focus on right now.'

'Well, Merry Christmas to you.'

Cleo was quiet for a bit, her eyes on the afternoon gloom of the road ahead of her. 'You know how, in American movies, people sing Christmas carols around pianos? Should I organise something like that, as the host?'

'Ah, I see, you're hosting Christmas in the golden era of Hollywood. I'm sorry, I didn't realise.' Rosa rummaged in her holdall to check she'd got her passport, which she had. 'No, you don't need to do that. You also don't need to coddle the guy and make him hot chocolate and canapés every five seconds. Just enjoy yourselves, hang out, be friends, have a root in front of the fireplace and then, come Boxing Day, see you later.'

'Oh my God, that's not going to happen,' Cleo insisted, knowing full well what Rosa was suggesting.

'It could happen . . . ' she insisted.

'You're right. You are right. I'm going to be so chilled, like *snow* chilled.'

'No, you dork,' Rosa said, checking her passport again. 'Just be you.'

'Merry Christmas!'

The following day, on December the twenty-second, Cleo bumped her bags through the front door of her childhood home, bonking her head against the wreath on the way in.

Macaroni stopped her in her tracks, pushing his nose against her knees, tail thwacking, while Blueberry took a leap for freedom through the open door before she'd closed it.

'Merry Christmas, Clee,' her mum said, appearing at the

end of the corner, threading a giant holly-leaf earring into one of her lobes, before coming towards her daughter with outstretched arms.

Cleo plonked her bags on the floor. It's possible she'd overpacked, considering she only lived a twenty-minute walk away, but she didn't know how these next few days were going to pan out so wanted to make sure she had everything from cute-and-slightly-sexy festive clothing, to warm and comforting heartbreak PJs, and everything in between. Plus, she'd brought her absolute favourite hoodie – one she'd stolen from Eliot three Christmases before when they'd spent New Year's on the beach, after the restaurant had closed, with friends. The fire had gone out before midnight, so he'd lent her his jumper and she'd never given it back. Because she had puked from too much Prosecco. Because she'd been nervous about the mere thought of finally kissing him at midnight.

As Macaroni inspected the contents of her holdall, which she hadn't managed to zip closed, Cleo hugged her mum.

'Are you sure you don't mind us going?' Felicity checked for the millionth time since she'd broken the news back in October.

'No, of course not,' Cleo said. 'I'll be working most of the time anyway; I'd only feel bad about making you wait around for me to open gifts and things.'

Cleo hadn't exactly told her folks that Eliot was coming to stay over the holidays. And by 'exactly' ... she hadn't mentioned it at all.

She was well aware that she was not, in fact, in high school but even though she was a solid thirty years old, she still found the idea of telling her mum and dad that she wanted to have a crush over to spend the night completely cringe. Because Felicity and Bryce absolutely knew that Eliot was Cleo's crush. They'd always known it.

Besides, if it didn't work out how she hoped it would, Cleo really wanted to avoid having to answer too many questions, from too many people, on precisely what it was about her that meant he didn't love her back.

Cleo shook away those thoughts. She couldn't think like that, not now that she was getting her game-face on. Thinking like that was what had held her back for years as it was, so desperate to not hurt herself, not make Eliot feel uncomfortable, not to rock that boat.

'Are you and Dad all packed?' she asked, following Felicity into the kitchen, where she had a half-packed shopping bag with bottles and treats poking out.

'Pretty much,' her mum said, picking up a bag of carrots. 'Will you eat these if I leave them?'

Beside Cleo, Rhubarb had wandered in and was salivating at the carrots. 'Yes, he and I will get through them.'

'You will be making yourself a nice Christmas lunch, won't you?' Felicity's voice was tinged with worry topped with a dash of guilt.

'Yes, Mum, I'll be just fine, I promise.' There was *really* no need for her mum to feel guilty – especially as Cleo was really quite looking forward to her cosy Christmas alone with Eliot, so she piled it on thick. 'I have a Tesco order being delivered later, a big stack of Christmas romcoms to watch, the restaurant is always fun to work in at this time of year and I'm even . . . ' Cleo took a breath, thinking of what she'd packed into the bottom of her holdall. 'I'm even thinking of taking a Christmas Day swim.'

'In the sea?' her dad asked in surprise, entering the kitchen with his electric toothbrush in one hand and a pair of walking socks in the other.

'Yes,' she said, with a firm nod of the head.

'Well, that's brilliant. It doesn't feel right not to see you out there, splashing about, these days. It's about time,' he commented.

'Excuse me, when did you last go in?'

'This September.'

'Oh.'

'But I'll be honest, it was easier to go in when we used to have you banging on about it every five minutes.'

Cleo laughed. 'What do you mean, banging on? I never forced you to go in the water!'

'Forced, no. Nagged, perhaps a little. You just wanted to share it with us. You always liked having company in the water. Remember that Christmas we all went in together because you wanted to try out your new wetsuit?'

'I remember.' She nodded. 'Anyway, Merry Christmas, Dad!'

He leant down to hug Cleo because Rhubarb had wandered over while they had been chatting and was now lying across her feet and snoring.

'Is Rosa on her way now?' Felicity asked, handing Bryce a cheese grater, which he swapped with her for the walking socks. Cleo had no idea what their packing method was, but she was staying out of it.

'Yes, she went up to the airport yesterday. Her flight was last night.'

'So she'll arrive on . . . ?'

'I think it's the morning of the twenty-third, tomorrow, New Zealand time, which is . . . ' she did a quick calculation, 'later tonight, I think.'

'And what's Eliot doing over Christmas?' Bryce asked, and Cleo saw her mum glance up and smile at him.

She pretended to not clock that they'd clearly talked before she came over and agreed that one of them should ask her that.

'He's spending time with his grandparents,' Cleo lied. 'They still live just over in Lyme Regis, so . . . '

Of course, Eliot wasn't planning to spend any of the holidays with his grandparents, and she knew he was a little relieved about the fact. They weren't the easiest to get on with, and over the years they'd decided Christmas was 'a load of old clap-trap'. Imagine if Scrooge had never changed and Marley hadn't died and was actually a woman with a thick Bristol accent , and the two of them got married. Nevertheless, to Cleo's benefit, this year they'd declined his offer to come to stay in his flat for Christmas, because they'd booked themselves into a hotel for a Christmas package, somewhere along the coast.

Yes, the super-Christmassy hotel Christmas packages. They did those kind of things at the Wavebreak Views Hotel and Cleo knew full well how gorgeously festive they were.

Anyway, he would see them at *some* point over the holiday period, so she wasn't entirely lying.

'You won't be seeing him?' her dad needled.

'Probably at work. I'll say a Merry Christmas from you,' Cleo teased. 'Is there anything I can do to help you pack?'

Felicity stuffed the walking socks in the food bag and then sent Bryce off to put the bag of Christmas presents in the car. 'I think we're nearly all set, but would you like your pressie from your dad and me?'

'Yes please!'

'All right,' Felicity said, fishing out of a drawer two gifts in white wrapping and handing one to her daughter. 'It's just something silly.'

Cleo opened the gift – a festive jumper with a huge light-up Christmas tree on the front. 'I love it! I'll wear it a lot over the next few days.'

'We thought it was very *you*,' her dad said, giving her a kiss on the head.

Cleo stood beside the car, the frosty wind whipping strands of her red hair around her pink cheeks. It seemed to have turned bitterly cold, and the weather further up the country was reporting snow and ice. After another quick hug, she wrapped her arms back around herself and her parents climbed in. 'Drive safe'.

Her mum immediately wound down the window. 'You will have time for a FaceTime on Christmas Day, won't you, Clee?'

'Of course, Mum. Go, enjoy being the guests instead of the hosts for a change.'

Cleo's dad put the car in reverse and turned it around so it faced the road that would take them alongside the sea, before they navigated off inland for the motorway. At the last minute, Felicity unbuckled and leapt out of the car again, pulling Cleo into her arms.

'Merry Christmas, my girl. I'll miss you this year.'

A lump bobbed in Cleo's throat. Her first Christmas without her family – it was like it had just hit them both. But she wanted her mum to think everything was fine so she said, 'Me too, but I can't wait. Go and have a brilliant time and don't let Gabriela boss you around.'

Felicity stroked Cleo's hair, who leant against her hand for a second, before waving them off as they drove away, pausing at the end of the lane to open the car door and let Blueberry out. The cat skittered back to the house and in through the ajar front door.

Skittering back inside herself, Cleo was surrounded by the silence left by collective thoughts and voices, and footsteps having slipped away.

'Thank you so much,' Cleo said to Mr Tesco Delivery when she'd unloaded and he was heading back to his van with his empty crates. 'And Merry Christmas!'

Shuffling the animals back into the house, she began putting away her shop. 'Yesss,' she whispered out loud at the enormous pepperoni pizza she'd bought for herself for tonight. She was going to watch all the *Princess Switch* movies on Netflix and try not to overthink the next couple of days.

Of course, she overthought for the rest of the evening. But although she was still nervous about hosting her first Christmas, and about her big confession, she meant what she'd said to Rosa all those weeks ago. It didn't matter what Eliot said, at the end of the day. Of course, she wanted him to feel the same way, but, either way, she couldn't be stuck any more in this limbo of waiting for something to change without her doing anything about it.

And if all went to plan, in forty-eight hours' time, she'd be out of limbo. Maybe she'd be celebrating on the other side, cocktail in hand, or maybe she would have fallen flat.

Tick, tock.

Chapter 20

Cleo waltzed out of work the next day, the day before Christmas Eve, as if she were officially driving home for Christmas. Which, in a way, she kind of was. Minus the driving.

Instead, she bid a farewell to Lucy, with a promise that she'd be back tomorrow for her Christmas Eve shift, and practically skipped up the hill to her parents' home. Her home for Christmas.

'Hello, you lot!' she said to the variety of wagging tails and soggy noses and warm leans that greeted her when she entered the house. After letting out whoever needed to go for a wee, and taking a comfort break herself, she made a whopping hot chocolate and sat on the sofa for a moment of silence.

Sipping on the sweet, steaming cocoa, her eyes trailed the second hand on the clock. Eliot would be here in less than an hour, at just about the time the sun would start to dip.

'Listen, Macaroni,' Cleo said to the golden retriever, who'd sat up beside her on the sofa and was staring down at her hot chocolate. 'Don't let me chicken out of this, will you? One way or another, by the end of Christmas, I'll be moving forward.'

He looked at her with his gigantic hazelnut eyes and raised a paw, which Cleo shook.

'Deal. OK, he'll be here soon, is there anything else we need to do?' Macaroni tilted his head to the side. 'You remember Eliot, right? He's the one with the big heart and nice smile. Not unlike you, actually, but more my type, no offence.'

Cleo downed the rest of her hot chocolate and got to work, feeling like Kevin in *Home Alone* when the countdown was on before the burglars arrived. Only, she wasn't planning on lobbing paint cans at Eliot.

She walked about the house, flicking on all her fairy lights until the house positively glowed with firefly romanticism to the point she could almost hear Sebastian from *The Little Mermaid* singing 'Kiss the Girl'.

She paused to inspect her work, and to wonder if she'd been watching too many movies lately.

Cleo's fingers hovered on the Bluetooth button on her phone, ready to connect it to her Echo. She'd spent yesterday evening making a playlist of all of her favourite Christmas songs, plus mixed in some songs she knew had meant something to her and Eliot over the years they'd known each other.

Although, thinking about it, the first thing they needed to do was take Rhubarb and Macaroni out for a walk. Perhaps, she thought, putting her phone back in her pocket, it would be better not to show all of her cards in one fell swoop.

The dogs heard him before Cleo did, the soft crunch of footsteps on the drive, breaking through the silence, and when Rhubarb and Macaroni started to lose their cool, Cleo's cool went scampering under the rugs too. Macaroni started howling, Rhubarb let out a single thunderous *woof* and Blueberry shifted position on the window sill to face away from this disturbance.

Cleo ran to the door, took a steadying breath, and then threw it open while Eliot was still a few steps away.

He stopped and smiled and something passed between them. Her on the threshold, him with the lemon-yellow sky and rolling ocean behind him. Her words disappeared into the frost-filled air. Was Cleo imagining that something felt different already?

'Merry Christmas,' he said, breaking the silence and holding up his bags. 'I come bearing Baileys, Quality Street, board games, some weird-sounding clementine liqueur from my grandparents, and a few gifts.'

'Well, come in,' Cleo laughed, but it sounded forced and while she stood out of the way so he could enter, she attempted to give herself a brief pep-talk on how to be a functioning person again. 'Are you OK giving me a hand walking the dogs before we crack into that lot?'

'Of course!' Eliot replied, already lost in the snuggly fur of Rhubarb's neck.

The two of them worked side by side unpacking his food and drink, and then Cleo showed him the guest room.

'I opened the window for you a little, but close it if you want, if you're cold, it's getting below freezing out there,' she babbled. 'And I left you some towels, and the bathroom is just down the corridor, and, um, my room is there.' Cleo pointed at her door, which was just ajar enough that he could probably see her framed *The Notebook* poster she'd never taken down. 'Um, and there's your bed.'

OH, FOR GOD'S SAKE, CLEO. *There's your bed*. She wished she could shut her mouth up sometimes.

'There it is.' He laughed and met her eye for a nanosecond.

'Dog walk!' Cleo clapped her hands together in the manner of a scout leader ready for the next activity, and raced off downstairs before he could see her blush.

Cleo knew why *she* was being weird, and she wondered if it was the same reason for Eliot. This was the first time the two of them had spent the night under the same roof, in all the years they'd been friends. Well, nearly. There'd been a winter wedding three years ago between two Coacean employees, and everyone from the restaurant had been invited. They'd all stayed over at a country pub out on Dartmoor. Cleo had been sharing a room, and bed, with a seasonal worker called Kim, and Eliot was in a single room. She remembered because he'd joked that Cleo could bunk in with him if Kim was still crying come bedtime (she'd drunk too much wine over the meal and had been sobbing about how romantic everything was ever since).

He'd just been joking, but it hadn't stopped Cleo thinking about it all night. She may have even been pointing out things to Kim, like the printed-out photos of the happy couple's parents and grandparents on their own wedding days, and the way they were singing into each other's ears during the first dance.

Actually ... there was another time, further back. They had to sleep on the floor of the restaurant together one winter, because there had been a party with a few customers who had then been in no state to drive home. Instead, the staff had simply got out some blankets and everybody had a snooze, right there, until the sun had come up.

Eliot and Cleo had slept beside each other. But she could remember that Asha had been working at the restaurant back then, and she'd had a thing for him (join the club) so had stuck pretty close to his side. Cleo didn't think anything ever happened between them, but still, she hadn't wanted to step on her toes, so she'd kept her distance, even when the two of them were only inches apart.

That was his first winter back since leaving for the summer. She'd missed him, and it had made her realise just how much.

But most of the time they were in different places, different parts of town, different continents. And now they were under one roof, sleeping just metres apart.

'You're lost in thought,' Eliot commented as they stepped outside with their bouncy crew and started around the cliff, following the coast path.

'I was thinking about sleeping next to you,' Cleo said before catching a laugh as it escaped, swallowing it down, and then mentally hurling herself off the edge of the cliff. 'I mean, that time we had the party at the restaurant and we slept on the floor. I don't know why it popped into my head.'

'That was probably the last time you and I had a sleepover,' he remarked, throwing a tennis ball inland for Macaroni who zoomed after it.

'Yeah,' Cleo agreed, then floundered for words again, instead letting out a nervous chuckle.

'What?' Eliot asked, glancing at her, the setting sun catching a flint of gold in his grey eyes and nearly igniting Cleo's soul right there on the clifftop.

'What?'

'You're being quiet this afternoon.'

'I am,' Cleo agreed. 'I don't know.'

Eliot put his hands in his pockets, a small smile on his face, and Cleo wondered if maybe everything that needed to be said didn't need words. Or maybe that was just her, forever wishful thinking. She sucked the cold air in between her lips.

They carried on walking and Cleo let her imagination roll like the tide. She imagined how this could be their future. Side by side, a few dogs, then her taking him home. Only, in that fantasy she'd be able to hold his hand, and he wouldn't be in a spare room. And he'd make sure her lips were never cold.

But with a glance at him, Cleo had to prepare herself that the idea in her mind could sink rather than swim. That he might go back to walking the beaches of San Francisco without her, and things might never be the same. She had to be ready for that to happen. Fall or fly, she still had to jump.

'How do you feel about your parents spending Christmas with your sister?' he asked as they looped around and began to walk back.

Cleo gazed out at the darkening sea for a minute to collect her thoughts. 'Honestly?'

'Of course.'

Of course. *I don't have to pretend with you, at least not about this.* 'I completely get it, and it's a difficult position for them to have to be in to decide which daughter to spend Christmas with. And I'm sure Gabriela is nervous and excited to host her first Christmas with her fiancé so I'm glad they'll be with her ... '

'But ... ?'

'But, to be honest, I was sad Gabriela didn't ask me. I know that sounds a little pathetic, but as far as she knew I would be alone at Christmas.'

'Did you tell her?'

'No, I didn't want to cause any upset. Besides, she probably just figured I'd be working, I don't blame her. She's just ... a bit of a dick sometimes.'

He laughed at that, a cloud of cold air escaping into the twilight air.

'How about you?' she said as they reached the house. 'How did you really feel about Christmas this year?'

'I feel like I'm spending Christmas with the best person possible.' He grinned and slung an arm over her as they entered the house, leaving the cold behind them.

Chapter 21

'I'm telling you, it's going to snow,' Eliot said, peering out into the darkness.

Cleo handed him a glass of red wine and stood to his right at the window. 'But look at the stars, there's not a cloud in the sky.'

They stood side by side, their breath fogging the glass of the window, the fairy lights behind them creating fire-fly reflection. Cleo's soft Christmas playlist playing in the background.

Her eyes refocused onto Eliot's reflection rather than the stars outside. *I think I love you.*

As if hearing her thoughts, she saw his gaze shift to her reflection too, and in that mirror of his face she searched for answers to how he felt.

In that moment, it felt to Cleo like they were on the brink. Finally. Like they'd both been on, and off, this trek for so long and were now about to reach the precipice. They were so close. Would they make it?

He held his wine in his left hand, and, as they stood there, he brought his right hand up and rested it on her back.

The warmth of his touch sent a current through her whole body. Was this it? Was he telling her that he thought about her, dreamt about her, loved her, the same way she did about him?

Eliot looked away from the window, and down to Cleo's face, a soft smile on his face.

She swallowed. *Kiss me. What are you waiting for?*

As if he was as full of anticipation as Cleo was, Macaroni began wagging his tail on the other side of the room, hard thwacks against the Christmas tree, causing a length of tinsel to attach itself to his tail.

Cleo dragged herself, and her heart, away from Eliot and the window, to untangle Macaroni.

'That dog.' She let out a wobbly chuckle. 'I'd better just refill their waters, one mo.'

In the kitchen, Cleo leaned her hands on the counter before filling two dog bowls with cold, fresh water. It was time to tell him, everything felt right about doing it now, but still, the thought – the worry – made her want to vom.

She ran her wrists under the cold tap for a moment. *Calm down.*

When she entered the living room again, Eliot was prodding at the fireplace with the poker, and he stood up, the iron bar falling from his hand. 'Oops.' He fumbled to pick it up. 'Dogs all watered?'

'Yep . . . '

They were silent, her mind blank of conversation, filling only with thoughts of how she felt, which threatened to spill out at any moment.

Eliot shifted, stooping to stroke a sleeping Rhubarb, before rising up and going to lean on the mantelpiece but missing and stumbling. 'Oops.' He laughed again.

Cleo's hand shook as she brought the wine to her lips and sipped, smoky spices crashing through her mouth like a wave.

'Why am I so nervous?' she murmured. 'Why are we both so nervous?'

She met his eyes and he held her gaze. The crackling firewood caused the glow on his features to flicker. He held his own glass in front of him with one hand, the other in his pocket.

Cleo's heart beat in her chest like the bass of the greatest love song as she waited for his answer.

Eliot raised his shoulders in a slow shrug, a small smile creeping onto the side of his mouth. He swallowed, like a thousand memories and thoughts were moving like waves through his mind. And then in a low voice, he answered, 'I think we both know why.'

She had time for one inhale, and one exhale. Just enough time to take his words in and lay them upon her heart like paper confetti.

A light from beyond the window crept through the crack in the curtains and swept like a search beam across the living room. A millisecond later the crunch of tyres on the ground cut through the low music.

Nooooooooooo!

Cleo and Eliot broke eye contact and looked towards the window, and the dogs leapt from their dozy positions on sofas and floors to scramble to the door. Rhubarb's tail swooshed side to side in recognition of the noise of that particular car.

Cleo swallowed and stumbled towards the curtains, like she'd woken in the middle of a really perfect dream.

She wanted to go back to sleep so badly.

Opening the curtain, she frowned to see her mum's car pulling to a stop, the headlights switching off, and then she, her dad, and – to her surprise – Gabriela, stepped out.

'They're home,' Cleo said, her voice croaking, and she swung around to look at Eliot. 'My parents, and my sister, are back. What day is it?' Maybe she'd miscalculated, missed Christmas, and it was actually Boxing Day already.

'Um.' Eliot swallowed and also seemed to snap into gear. 'The twenty-third. Aren't they supposed to . . . ?'

'Yes.' Cleo watched for a second longer as her sister wrapped her coat around herself tightly, a grumpy expression on her features, and her mum and dad reached into the boot and pulled out bags.

Oh my God, they're home!

Quick as lightning, Cleo blew out the candles and flicked on the light. She paused the music and wiped off her lipstick.

'Are you OK?' Eliot asked, standing in the centre of the room looking – rightfully – like he had no idea why Cleo was acting like a teenager caught having a house party. 'Are we not supposed to be here?'

'Um.' She faced him for the first time. '*You* aren't supposed to be.'

A laugh escaped him and, to his credit, rather than being mad or demanding answers right now, he jumped into action and grabbed his sweatshirt and wine glass and scampered to crouch behind the sofa.

'No, I mean, you can be here, Eliot, they just didn't *know* I was having you over. You can come out.'

He hovered in a half-squat. 'Are you sure?'

'Yes, I'm just . . . ' She searched for how to explain without having to explain. 'My sister, in particular, will just jump to conclusions.'

Cleo gestured her arms towards the wine and the candle smoke curling upwards, and they met each other's eyes again, and Eliot let out a small chuckle.

At that moment, the door flung open and her sister tornadoed in, a flurry of oversized puffer jackets and icy air. Macaroni and Rhubarb were beside themselves at seeing her in all her unexpected glory, and while she dropped to her knees to embrace them dramatically, Felicity and Bryce shuffled their way in behind her, laden with all the bags.

Cleo raced over to help, Eliot with her.

'Cleo,' Felicity said with a sigh.

'What happened, what's going on?'

'My life is in tatters, that's what's going on,' Gabriela declared, standing up straight and dropping her silver puffer to the ground, where Blueberry promptly sauntered over and curled up on top of it. At that moment, all three of them – her mum, dad and Gabriela – clocked Eliot who had seamlessly moved their bags into the house, closed the door, put the kettle on and was taking Bryce's coat before they realised he was there.

Gabriela cocked her head to the side and smiled, the smudged mascara under her eyes only making her look more alluring. 'Eliot Ambrose.' She spoke his name like it was butter in her lips. 'You just can't keep away from Devon, can you?'

'Hello, Eliot,' said Felicity, leaning in to give him a kiss on the cheek before meeting Cleo's eyes and raising her eyebrows.

'What did we interrupt?' Gabriela asked with a smirk.

Cleo ignored her question and fired back with, 'What happened, why are you all home? Is Derek with you?'

Gabriela's smile dropped and she huffed into the living room, flopping in the centre of the sofa. She let out a big sigh, and on the exhale seemed to collapse into herself, her face dropping into her hands. 'We broke up,' she said, her voice muffled.

'Oh my God!' Cleo looked to her mum and dad who nodded and took themselves towards the kitchen, angling Eliot to go with them. Embarrassingly, she also had the private thought, *Oh good, no more horror movies.*

She went to sit beside her sister on the sofa. 'Gabriela, I'm so sorry.'

Gabriela snuffled while Cleo stroked her hair. 'You know when you just know something isn't going to work out but you keep trying because on paper it really should?'

'Mmm-hmm.' Cleo nodded.

'I just didn't feel like I could be myself around him. Not

really. And I am awesome, so I don't think I should have to hide myself for anyone.'

'Quite,' Cleo agreed.

Gabriela peered at her for a moment, like she was weighing up whether or not Cleo was agreeing that she shouldn't hide herself, or agreeing that she'd not been herself around Derek.

Cleo contemplated saying nothing, then added, in a quiet voice, 'It's nice to see you again.'

Her sister fell silent for a few minutes, then, with a defiant sigh, asked, 'Were you and Eliot shagging?'

'What?' Cleo laughed, reflexively looking towards the door in case he was standing there.

'When we walked in? You turned the lights on and you've got red wine all over your lips.'

Cleo clamped her hand over her sister's mouth.

'No, and would you shut up?'

'Don't be mad at me, I'm heartbroken,' she protested, weaving her arms around Cleo's waist just like she used to do, and pouting. Gabriela could be unpleasant and/or sulky when she was in a huff, but Cleo had to give her a bit of a pass this time, she supposed.

'Sorry. But no, we weren't shagging,' Cleo said in a low voice. 'It just, he just, he was going to be spending Christmas alone too so we decided to, you know, split a turkey.'

Gabriela studied her for a moment with weeping eyes. 'So nothing is happening between you two?'

'No,' Cleo said, semi-truthfully.

Gabriela nodded, seeming relieved that her twin wasn't

shacked up and happy when she was going through a break-up.

Bryce poked his head into the living room and Cleo saw him clock the half-drunk wine and half-burned candles. 'Gabriela, do you want a cup of tea? And you of course, Clee?'

'I'll get them.' Cleo stood up. Finding Eliot in the kitchen studying the different mugs, she moved over and put a hand on his arm. 'I'm so sorry about this,' she whispered.

He smiled at her. 'It's no problem, it's their home. And your home. I'll make the teas and then I'll head back to my flat.'

'What? No!' she cried. 'You don't want to spend Christmas here any more ... with me?'

'Of course I do, but ... '

'Please stay.' Her words came out rushed. She didn't know how she was going to get her plan back on track exactly, but she had to try.

She had a flashback then of the first time she'd accepted her feelings for Eliot had bubbled back from friendship to more. It had been nearly five years ago, at his going away party, a beach barbecue that had lasted late into the evening after the sun had gone down. She'd not been able to drag herself away from him all night, and when he'd all of a sudden announced he was going home before he drank any more and missed his train in the morning, her hope had crashed. A hope she hadn't even known she'd been hanging on to, and all she'd wanted was for him to stay and not be about to move to the other side of the world.

Back then she hadn't even known he'd definitely be coming back at the end of the summer. She still didn't really know that for sure, year on year.

'You're sure?' he asked, squeezing a tea bag into the side of a Captain America (more specifically, Chris Evans) mug of her mum's.

'Yes,' she said. 'If you still want to?'

'Christmas with the Clearwaters ... All of them ... Why not?'

Cleo lay in her bed that night, knowing Eliot was one wall away, listening to the soft sound of snow against her window.

She was sure, *sure*, they were something to each other. More than friends.

Baring her soul, risking losing the things she held closest to her heart, those things scared her to her core. But something was happening.

Cleo drifted to sleep the night before Christmas Eve, and dreamt of fireflies illuminating new beginnings.

Chapter 22

~ Then ~

Spring 2018

The days were starting to get longer, the sea winds had less chill in them, the light held on for longer, bathing the beach pebbles of Wavebreak Bay in a rose-gold glow that lasted into the early evening.

This was all well and good, but Eliot was leaving. He was moving away, to a place that felt like the other side of the earth. Her Eliot, her best friend, confidant, playmate, her maybe-more, was about to be the one who got away.

'Are you happy for him?' Gabriela asked her down the phone line, as Cleo walked the dark, quiet high street, empty save for a few people milling towards one of the pubs or eateries. Some of them were probably going to Coacean. Some perhaps to the same place she was going.

'Of course! San Francisco ... I mean ... California ... you know ... wooooooo.' *So convincing.*

'Wow, so convincing,' Gabriela chortled, echoing her

179

thoughts. 'You can say, "Hell no, I want him to stay," if you want to.'

'No, I can't,' Cleo hissed, looking around her. 'And I am happy for him.'

Eliot's cousin Chris, his mentor, had been talking about opening a restaurant together ever since he'd lived out there. And the summer before, Eliot had confided in her, he'd started to put pressure on him, saying they had to do this together now, or Chris would do it alone. 'Let's do this together now, or I'm going to have to do it alone,' he'd said. For Eliot, it had been a pipe dream that had turned into a goal, which had become an ultimatum. Eliot had wanted to make it happen. In fact, the specifics – of not starting from scratch but of opening a branch of Coacean in the USA – had been his idea.

So he'd asked for a meeting with Coacean's owners, Cleo's mum and dad, and they'd met his ideas with more enthusiasm than Cleo could authentically muster up. Then, in a flurry of video calls and logistics that had swept through their lives like a tidal wave, the deal had been struck, and the US branch of Coacean would be opening. And for continuity between the branches, they'd wanted Eliot to co-manage the San Francisco branch each summer season, and be back in Wavebreak Bay to work here during the winter season.

He'd only be gone for half the year. Each year. His grandparents hadn't minded. His parents probably wouldn't even notice. And his best friend, Cleo, well, she'd been over the moon for him. Of course.

'OK, sure.' Gabriela unleashed another snicker. 'Hey, guess what?'

'What?'

'I met someone at work. A guy called Derek and he's a chef. Well, he wants to be, one day. Not seafood, though. And he's our age and he's as delish as his crème brûlées.'

'That's awesome.' Cleo stepped out onto the esplanade, spotting the glowing embers of the campfire on the opposite end of the beach. It was Eliot's final night in the bay, and his friends had thrown him a beach bonfire to say farewell.

'I'll bring him down at some point, though he doesn't get much time off and he's never been to Devon,' she tinkled with laughter.

'Never been to Devon? All the more reason!' answered Cleo, distracted by trying to pick Eliot out in the crowd.

'I think you'll like him, sis. He's really nice.'

Cleo stopped and huddled against the closed door of the sea-front ice-cream parlour, sheltering from the breeze. 'Nice? You never say a guy is nice. You once told me cream cheese is nice and that you'd never describe a man like that. What's going on?'

'I *know* I've said Eliot is nice before.'

'Exactly. You said, and I quote, "God, Eliot is so *nice*, he's like cream cheese and I want my dates to be more like jalapenos."'

Gabriela laughed. 'I don't remember that, but I was probably just pissed that he always liked you more than me. Anyway, Derek is like cream cheese combined with jalapenos.'

That did actually sound quite nice. Cleo was pleased for her sister.

181

It was getting late, that rose-gold light having faded to the navy blues of twilight, and now the stars were out overhead, as if to remind Cleo just how far Eliot would be flying away in the morning.

She was happy for him, of course. Good for him having a purpose and a dream and a goal and going for them all. If he was happy, he deserved it all.

But ... now she was going to lose him, it had hit her like a cliff fall just how much she'd been lying to herself about how she felt about him.

If only she hadn't let the years slip by, as if the two of them were indestructible, as if the flame she held for him – deep down and closely guarded – was perfectly safe. Sure, it had flickered from time to time, but nobody got her like Eliot did, and soon enough the flame held steady again. But now, time was up.

Down on the beach, the campfire crackled, the drinks raised high in the air, smiles and hugs and memories were being thrown and caught between all.

Cleo spent the evening in a fog of indecision. Should she confess, tell him she thought she was going to miss him, as more than a friend? Or would that be the most selfish thing she could do right now? How could that possibly be the thing he'd need to hear right now?

From across the campfire, Eliot stood and got everyone's attention by tapping a pebble against his beer bottle.

'I think I'd better leave,' he said, and as he met her eyes, Cleo's heart replied, *Don't leave.*

Eliot made the rounds, saying goodbye, swaying a little, a

happy, warm, merriment about him, which showed itself in the embraces and in that big grin of his. When he reached Cleo, he placed his hands on her shoulders and his forehead against hers, their lips only inches apart and said, 'Why am I leaving?'

'What?' she asked, not sure if this was a rhetorical question. 'Because you're an idiot, but an idiot with a dream?' she offered.

'Five years. I never meant to come back to here from San Fran for five years. But Wavebreak Bay . . . I'm telling you . . . there's something about it. It's a little like living in paradise. You know? So why would I leave?'

Cleo shrugged. 'Because you want the escape, the adventure, the thrill of living in two places? You've always been like that, ever since I first knew you, when you were just sixteen.'

'A young'un!' He laughed, and swayed a little, then brought his face back close to hers, steadying himself in her gaze. 'Ahhh, I'm a coward,' he whispered, so quiet she didn't quite hear the words.

'You what?'

'I should have . . . I've wasted . . . Now I'm going . . . '

'Eliot, what are you mumbling?'

'You deserve a much better friend than me,' he said, with a smile, his forehead against hers. 'I have to say goodbye. But it's only for now, Clee. It's only for now.'

Kiss him, she thought. *What are you waiting for?*

Instead, though, she heard herself say, 'You say that, but you'll find some amazing, cool, hip girl in San Francisco and after a while you won't want to come home to here again.'

Eliot pulled his head back and looked at her. 'Is that what you think?'

'Of course,' she answered, with a false cheeriness. 'You're a catch, Eliot Ambrose. I can't wait for you to make someone happy!'

Why did she have to say the wrong thing all the time? This wasn't how she felt at all. At least, she wanted him to make someone happy: her.

She felt the bond between them – the maybes, the closeness – fading like the embers of the fire, scattering into the night air, ashes of what might have been.

That night, after he'd left, she'd stood at the edge of the gentle waves, sighing in and out in the darkness, and let a few tears fall.

She didn't return into the water again until the winter.

Chapter 23

~ Now ~

Christmas Eve

Cleo woke up to the noise of woofing out in the garden, and for a moment panicked that she hadn't locked the door and that the dogs had got out in the night. But then the sound of her mum laughing floated up to her window and she remembered how her cosy Christmas alone with Eliot had become him joining her for a family Christmas instead, and she groaned into her pillow.

Grappling for her phone, she shot a message to Rosa.

> Morning from the UK! Hope your flight went well.
> Operation Christmas Snogs isn't going to plan
> so far . . . sister has split with fiancé and she and
> parents have reappeared for the holidays!

She saw that the message had been delivered to Rosa's phone, so she must have arrived safely. Cleo didn't wait for an answer though, because something made her sit up and open the curtains of the window behind the bed. That something being Eliot's voice outside with her mum.

And when she opened the curtains, Cleo gasped. Audibly. Like she was auditioning for *Bridgerton* or something.

Outside the window, the sky was a milky baby blue, wispy clouds overhead that were dropping tiny snowflakes onto the grass below. She craned her neck and saw it had left a thin layer across the cliffs, the rooftops down in the town, even the beach pebbles had a frosted topping. The town was transformed.

Cleo was squashing herself so much against the window that when she spotted Eliot playing with Rhubarb down below, the dog rolling with ecstatic happiness in the snow, she tumbled off the edge of the bed.

Quick as she could in her sleepy state, Cleo flung on some nearby clothes and thudded down the stairs, to the muffled sound of her sister growling, 'Shut. Up.' from inside her room.

Cleo opened the door and peeped in. 'You OK this morning?'

'Mmm,' Gabriela humphed, then, just before Cleo closed the door again, she added, in that childlike whine, 'Come in and give me a hug.'

Cleo did as she was asked, noticing the phone lying on Gabriela's pillow, as if she had slept with it beside her, just in case.

'It's all snowy outside,' said Cleo, softly.

'Great.' Gabriela released the hug and rolled over, closing her eyes again, and Cleo crept back out of her room.

Adding welly socks over her lilac leggings, and her dad's parka over her ancient, but favourite, Quiksilver hoodie with all the holes in, Cleo jammed her feet into her walking boots, laced them up loosely, and flung open the back door.

'Are we having a white Christmas after all?' she boomed a little too loudly before casting a sheepish look towards the neighbours' houses.

The air was a skin-tingling cold, like the feel of fine sea spray at dawn, and Cleo stuck her tongue out to taste an icy snowflake. Tiny drips could be heard all around her, in places that wouldn't usually drip, from snow melting off window sills and tree branches in the sunshine.

Macaroni zoomed over to her, all wiggling bottom and smiling face, and Rhubarb, too, leapt up, his dark fur now mottled with a frosty coating. Blueberry the cat sidled past, exiting the house behind Cleo and walking with distaste around the edge of the garden before disappearing under a bush.

Woomph. The world's tiniest snowball hit Cleo in the shoulder and sent sprinkles of cold down her arm and up onto her neck.

She looked at Eliot with surprise.

'Morning!' he called from where he was hiding behind her mum.

Dropping to the ground, Cleo scooped up her own, rather pathetic, clump of snow and swung her arm round and round like a baseball player.

'Don't you dare,' her mum warned, laughing, while Eliot continued to cower behind her.

Then, quick as a flash, Eliot yelled, 'Now!'

Felicity reached her hand behind her back, took something from Eliot who she was in cahoots with, and threw a snowball right at her daughter.

Only, it hit the wrong daughter.

'Mum!'

Standing by the back door, a couple of metres behind Cleo, who had just ducked out of the way of the flying snowball, was Gabriela. Dressed in nothing but slippers and a thick dressing gown over silky PJs, a sleep mask propped up on her head, and now icy water dripping from her face, she very much did not look like the image of Christmas spirit.

Cleo tried not to laugh.

'Mum, what the actual hell?' Gabriela wiped at her face with the sleeve.

'I was aiming for Cleo,' Felicity explained.

'Hey . . . ' protested Cleo.

'Honestly,' Gabriela huffed. 'You lot have no consideration for the fact my room is right above this garden. I've already been dumped and now I have to be snowballed as well.'

She'd always had a flair for drama, but, even so, Cleo could see her sister was visibly upset. 'I'll get you a towel. And how about a cup of tea?'

Gabriela pouted. 'Hot chocolate?'

'Sure.' Cleo began to lead her back inside when Eliot jogged over.

'I'll make it,' he offered. 'Sorry, Gabriela, that was my fault. Your mum and I were ganging up on Cleo.'

He led Gabriela inside but before closing the door turned to Cleo with that warm smile. 'I won that round, but it's only going to snow more. I have to go to work soon, but I'm sure you can get me back later.'

'I *will* get you back later,' Cleo clarified. 'But I'll make my sister the drink, you don't need to. You get ready for work.'

'It's fine, honestly. You go ahead and walk the dogs with your mum. We should catch up later.' The way he looked her directly in her eyes . . .

'Want to hit the coast path?' her mum called, when Eliot went inside.

Cleo watched through the light of the window for a moment, as Eliot moved with ease around her kitchen, Gabriela directing him towards cupboards, her frown melting to the point she even let out a laugh. Good to know she was still capable of laughing.

Rhubarb appeared, shoving his bulky body through her legs so she stood over him like a cowboy riding a very short Dartmoor pony.

'Walk time, then?' Cleo asked him, and left the window.

As they walked, the snow fell harder, creating flurries of icing sugar against rocks and filling in the gaps on the grass until the clifftop was covered in an inch of white.

'Look at the beach,' Cleo said to her mum as they rounded back towards the house.

Below them, the pebbles had become an expanse of snow-topped Christmas puddings, stretching all the way along the shore. The cliff opposite was white too, with the sky above now grown thick with bright clouds, the blues tucked away. The lights of the restaurant below their cliff were on, and Cleo could imagine Eliot and the other staff peering out of the windows in awe.

'I expect you'll still have quite a lot of diners today, even with all of this,' Felicity said, shielding her face from falling flakes. 'I remember one winter it snowed when you and Gabriela were very little and the restaurant was heaving.'

'I don't know,' Cleo answered. 'You're probably right. Christmas Eve is always busy, mostly with locals, and it's not like you can't walk in this. I think a lot of people will still want to come out specifically *because* they'll want to be somewhere warm and cosy with good food and those views.'

They walked on a little further, but before they reached the house, Cleo said, 'Is there anything I can go and pick up in town while I'm out? Anything any of you need?'

'I don't think so. We left Gabriela's in rather a rush, but I did bring that cool bag of food back with me.'

'And I'd already got loads to eat and drink because you know ... Christmas.' Cleo had bought a fairly small turkey for just her and Eliot, but she was sure it could stretch to five people, if everyone didn't mind having a modest portion. 'Do you think Gabriela will be OK?'

Her mum stopped at the garden gate and looked out to sea for a moment, and Rhubarb took the opportunity to stick his nose in the snow, so Macaroni had to do the same. 'I think she'll be just fine. To be honest ... ' She trailed off.

'What?'

'... I think their split was for the best. I don't think her heart was completely in it.'

'Her heart?' Cleo raised her eyebrows. 'I thought he split up with her?'

'He did. But she just didn't seem a hundred per cent happy.'

Cleo nodded. She agreed – not that she'd ever admitted that to her twin, because Gabriela was the one who had always been so sure about herself, her wants, her needs. She felt bad now. Maybe she should have said something?

She crunched across the grass, the dogs leading the way, and opened the door to the warm house. She could hear the TV on in the living room, and could see her sister lounging on the sofa, still in her PJs and dressing gown.

Cleo removed her boots and got to work feeding the zoo of animals before starting with her family.

'Gabriela, another hot chocolate?'

'Yes please,' Gabriela called, making no attempt to get up and bring her mug into the kitchen.

'What are you watching?' Cleo asked, coming into the living room and spotting her wine glass from last night beside the TV. She picked it up, then saw Eliot's on the coffee table, and wavered, remembering how close she'd come to telling him the truth. Last night he'd practically told her he was feeling the same, hadn't he? Or was her memory playing tricks on her? But that look between them, the pause, the way he'd said . . . was it, *I think we both know why*, when she'd made some remark about them both being nervous. That must have meant—

'Christmas reruns of *The Office*,' Gabriela replied. 'The American version. Dad tried to watch it with me but kept asking where David Brent was so I told him to go away.'

'Where is he now?'

'Either back in bed, or ... out getting logs, or ... ' Gabriela trailed off, snorting at something Mindy Kaling was saying on the TV.

'Morning, Clee, Merry Christmas Eve,' her dad said, entering the living room. 'I've been in the loft and brought down your favourite Christmas decoration!'

Bryce was holding an inflatable snowman in the air for his girls to see, and while Cleo, who had always hated the thing because she was convinced it was giving her the stink eye, made suitable 'Ooo, brilliant,' sounds, Gabriela turned the volume up on the TV.

'Who wants to help me blow this thing up?'

'We've got the pump in the garage, haven't we?' Felicity asked, mopping the snowy ends of her bobbed hair with a towel.

Cleo looked out the window. The snow had been falling, and blowing, right in towards the garage, causing a small drift to build up against the door. 'I'm not sure you'll get in there at the moment, unless you're quick.'

'I'm on it,' her dad said, heading towards the coat rack. It was kind of nice having her family back around at Christmas. Even if it did throw three human-shaped obstacles in the way of her time with Eliot, but Cleo could work around them, she wasn't going to give up that easily, not this time.

Cleo picked up her sister's mug and the two discarded wine glasses. 'So, another hot chocolate for you—'

'With marshmallows, please, and a candy cane.'

'Yes, ma'am. Nothing like a massive sugar hit to get over a broken heart.'

Gabriela dragged her eyes from the TV to cast a pained glance at her sister. 'I wasn't even thinking about my broken heart at that moment.'

'Oh. Sorry. Shall I make you some breakfast? How about a bacon sandwich?'

'How about eggs on toast?'

Did they have eggs? Yes, she'd got a carton of them in her Tesco order – she'd been planning to enlist Eliot to whip up a pre-work scrambled egg brekkie on Christmas morning for the two of them. 'No problem. Mum, tea? Brekkie?'

'Yes please.' Her mum yawned. 'Sorry, I'm a bit tired from the drive yesterday. Do you want a hand?'

'No, I've got it. What would you like? Gab's having eggs on toast.'

'I'd love some toast, if you don't mind. Your dad'll have the same, I'm sure.'

Cleo set to work, clearing up, making teas, cooking rounds of toast and poaching eggs for her sister. She popped some Christmas music on, kept an eye on the steady snow falling outside, and afterwards went to have a hot, steamy shower, her fingertips and toes now defrosted, and feeling happy.

A little later, Cleo, who would be heading out to work in a while, looked out the window to see the snow had picked up. Fat flakes now flurried down from above, obscuring her view across the beach. She dried her hair wearing her Christmas Eve ensemble: the new red sweater with a light-up Christmas tree on the front, her blue work shorts, and glittering tights.

Downstairs she could hear a lot of huffing coming from her dad.

'What's wrong?' she asked, descending the stairs to see him sitting in front of the flaccid snowman.

'I couldn't get into the garage so I'm having to blow this thing up by hand. Or mouth, as it were.'

'Bloody hell, Dad, give that to me. Gabriela and I will blow it up.'

An 'Ew' came from the direction of the living room.

So Cleo huffed and puffed on her own, at the bottom of the stairs, her face growing pink and her carefully dried hair sticking statically to the snowman as it bobbed in front of her, all the time peering at her with malice, she just knew it.

When the task was finally, nearly done, Felicity paused in the doorway of the living room. 'Oh, I have a missed call from your brother, Bryce.' She pressed the button to call him back but a minute later hung up again. 'No answer. Must have just been calling to wish us all a Merry Christmas.'

'Does he think you're still all up in Cambridge?' Cleo asked.

'Probably,' her dad answered. 'Looks like he called the landline too while I was outside and you were in the shower, Cleo.'

'I heard it ringing but thought Gabriela answered,' said Felicity.

'I couldn't be bothered to get up because the whole

194

concept of landlines these days is ridiculous,' Gabriela called from the sofa.

'You're ridiculous,' teased Bryce.

Cleo took her phone from her pocket. She hadn't checked it all morning but she saw that she too had a missed call from her uncle Stuart. Stuart was her dad's brother, but from her grandfather's second marriage, so at forty-five was a good fifteen years younger than her dad.

He lived up in Bath, and Cleo had always got on well with him, and had even stayed with him and Charlie for a term during uni, when her house-share had succumbed to damp. Now a teenager, Charlie had been just six then, dealing with his dad's splitting up, but the two of them had welcomed her into their home and they'd grown close.

She hadn't managed to see Stuart for a while though, and it panged at her that she hadn't even met his boyfriend, Kaleb, who he'd been together with for over a year now.

'He's heading on that murder mystery weekend today, isn't he?' Cleo asked her dad.

Bryce hung up the landline phone, it also having rung out on attempting to call Stuart back.

'Yes, a "Merry Murder Mystery" down in Cornwall with . . . well, I assume with Kaleb and Charlie.'

The noise of the gate clunking alerted Rhubarb and Macaroni first, who came pelting out of the living room and skidding past Cleo and the snowman. Macaroni walloped straight into it, one of his claws catching the rubber, and, with a high-pitched squeal emitting from the inflatable, popped a hole in it.

Cleo watched the air – her breath – escape and the snow-man relax back into a puddle. 'Ah, man,' she muttered.

'Is someone here?' Gabriela said, having risen from the sofa, her dressing gown draped over her shoulders. Her eyes were hopeful, like maybe it was Derek having driven down from Cambridge to tell of his regret in calling off their relationship, but Felicity, peering out of the window, saw their visitor first.

'It's Stuart!' she cried, watching a man exit the car, shielding the heavy snowfall from his eyes as he helped a tall woman in a large, felt hat with a feather in it out from the passenger seat. 'With some woman and with Charlie.'

'A woman?' Bryce asked. He went to the front door, and opened it, calling, 'Stu, what are you doing here?'

Cleo stood behind her dad inside the doorway, peering over his shoulder. Stuart looked stressed, Charlie looked miserable, and the woman, who appeared to be around her parents' age, if not a little older, looked like she'd just stepped out of the movie *Sunset Boulevard*.

Stuart looked over at Bryce, seeming defeated. 'I'm sorry. I did try and phone.'

'We just saw the missed calls,' Cleo said, holding up her phone as if providing evidence. 'Are you OK?'

'Can we come in?' Stuart asked.

'Of course,' said Bryce, ushering the three of them inside, where they were met with towels and offers to take bags or hold arms while they took their shoes off.

'I'm desperate for a wee, then I'll explain everything,' Stuart said, dashing into the downstairs cloakroom.

'Hello,' the woman said to Cleo, Gabriela, Felicity and Bryce, in turn. 'Hello. Hello. Hello.'

'Hello,' they chorused back. It felt rude to say, *Who are you and why are you here?* So instead, Cleo said, 'That's a nice coat.'

The woman brushed the snow off her floor-length, bright purple woollen jacket with purple faux-fur trim. 'Thank you. It's vintage.'

'Ooo,' Cleo replied, hoping that was the right noise to impart. She wasn't very clued up on 'vintage' unless you counted the low-rise jeans she still kept in the back of her drawers, just in case. 'Hi, Charlie, wow, you've grown!' Classic awkward comment.

'Hi, Cleo, hi, everyone.'

'Ahh, that's better,' Stuart said, re-emerging into the hall-way. 'Merry Christmas, all!'

'Merry Christmas,' everyone chorused in return.

'Now that's out of the way,' Stuart said, turning to Bryce. 'We have the hugest favour to ask.'

'What's wrong? Is it the car? Do you need a lift to Cornwall?' Cleo's dad asked.

'Not exactly,' Stuart replied. 'Because we can't go to Cornwall any more.'

There was a chorus of *whys* and *what happends*, and Gabriela said, 'Where's Kaleb? Did you break up?'

Cleo could detect the slight hope in her voice. Gabriela loved Stuart, and Cleo knew she'd met Kaleb at least once and had raved about him, but she guessed that right now misery would love some company.

Stuart faced her. 'No, absolutely not. Unfortunately, Kaleb had to pull out of the trip because of work, but Charlie, Gloria and me were all game to stick to having a good old Merry Murdering weekend. Oh, Gloria, this is my family, family, meet Gloria.'

'Charmed,' Gloria said.

'Charmed,' Cleo replied, still with no idea of who Gloria was.

Stuart continued. 'But halfway down to Cornwall, the snow got so bad that Charlie called the hotel for us to check we'd still be able to drive up there, only to find they'd had a frozen pipe burst and were in the process of calling around all the guests to cancel.'

'The roads are really bad,' Charlie added.

Gloria nodded sagely. 'Overnight ice and more compacted snow atop,' she declared. 'Much worse than here. Much, much worse.'

'Blimey,' Cleo's mum said.

'So in short,' Stuart continued, 'we were about level with the turnoff to Wavebreak Bay when we found this out, and roads are being locked down left, right and centre so we didn't think we could – and didn't fancy trying to – drive all the way back again right now. Soooo ... '

'Would you be darlings and let us stay?' Gloria asked, removing her coat and handing it to Cleo.

'Just until the snow's cleared a bit,' Stuart added. 'I'll keep an eye on the news today; it might even be all right this afternoon if the gritters are out.'

'Of course you can stay, it's Christmas,' Cleo found

herself saying. 'Come in, come in, let me make you all a cup of tea.'

In the kitchen, Cleo boiled a full kettle, washed up some mugs, found a packet of biscuits, and mentally ran through the number of people now in the house. Her and Eliot, her mum, dad and Gabriela, and now Stuart, Charlie and this behatted woman, Gloria. Eight people. OK, that was … manageable. She might have to rejig a few things.

Like when she was going to get some alone time with Eliot.

But this could be fun; the more the merrier.

She sighed.

'What's up?' Gabriela appeared in the door of the kitchen.

Cleo beckoned her over and said in a low voice, 'I don't think Stuart et al will be going anywhere today. It's getting a little crowded, so I think it makes sense for Eliot and me to head home.'

'Together?'

'Probably not, you know how tiny my flat is. I guess I'll go back to mine and he to his.'

'*No*,' Gabriela wailed. 'Don't leave, I want to have Christmas with you!'

'But there's not really enough space here any more, and I could come back over for Christmas Day. It just doesn't make sense to all try and stay.'

'Pleeeease, Cleo,' said Gabriela, taking the milk bottle out of her sister's hands and snaking her arms around her. 'My fiancé already left me, don't you leave me as well.'

How could she say no to that? Though it broke her heart to

know that Eliot would still probably leave to go back to his own home, her twin sister needed her. Even if she hadn't invited her along for her Christmas initially, she needed her now.

And wasn't that something Cleo had wished for?

'OK, I'll stay,' she replied. It would be fine.

She took out the teas, and the biscuits, and stood by the door of the living room while they all took seats and discussed the weather.

'The beach looks good, doesn't it?' Stuart said, after taking a long sip of his tea with his eyes closed.

'I'm going to go for a swim later today,' Cleo blurted out. 'Or tomorrow.' Sometime, at least. Hopefully straight after she'd had her talk with Eliot.

The room fell silent and they all looked at her.

'Bollocks you are,' Gabriela scoffed.

'You can't swim in this,' her mum said. 'You'll freeze.'

'I'd be safe,' Cleo protested. 'I have my wetsuit with me and everything.'

'That's cool,' Charlie said, grabbing another biscuit while the attention was on Cleo.

'You can come with me if you like!'

His hand froze on the way to his mouth.

She looked at the room. 'You all can! We could all have a Christmas Eve, or Christmas Day, swim together, you know, like they do in Exmouth.'

'And Budleigh Salterton,' Bryce piped up.

'Exactly,' Cleo said. 'Sidmouth has a Boxing Day swim. Plymouth has a New Year's swim. Maybe we could start a Wavebreak Bay tradition? Who's up for it?'

The room was so silent Cleo could hear the soft flakes patting against the window.

Eventually, Gabriela spoke. 'Well, it's a nope from me.' Shocker.

But Cleo ignored the comment, keen to drum up camaraderie. 'Stuart? You'd be up for it, surely?'

He chucked a biscuit in his mouth and signalled that he'd answer when he'd swallowed.

Gloria put down her mug and faced Cleo like she was about to launch into a monologue. 'My darling girl. Though I'm grateful for the recommendation, and though a wetsuit does show off my spectacular figure, I was rather expecting to spend the Christmas break in a situation closer to a hotel spa's jacuzzi than the icy licks of the Atlantic Ocean.'

'Well, think about it. It sounds like you must have swimming costumes with you, so ... ' Cleo checked the time on her phone. 'I have to dash out to work now, does anyone need anything from the shops while I'm in the town?'

'Perhaps some more bread,' said Bryce.

'Can you get me a magazine or something?' Gabriela asked.

'Nothing for me, thank you,' Charlie said.

'Your dad's right – bread would be good. And perhaps milk. Oh, and a Chocolate Orange would be nice, if they have one,' added Felicity.

'If I give you some money, could you get me a bottle of whisky, Cleo?' Stuart said, reaching for his wallet. 'I was so looking forward to having a dram by the fireplace in the hotel lounge.'

'Ah yes,' sighed Gloria. 'Now we won't be solving any

murders, I would so love a new mystery to read in front of the fireplace, should you find yourself near a bookshop.'

Cleo nodded, making a list on her phone. 'Right. Bread, milk, magazine, Choc Orange, whisky, murder mystery book.' She'd have to try three different stores to get that lot, so here's hoping they were all still open this Christmas Eve.

She pulled on her coat while her mum followed her into the hallway. 'Mum,' Cleo said. 'Uncle Stu said he'd keep an eye on the weather and the news today. Just in case they *don't* manage to head back up to Bath later, let me sort out the sleeping arrangements with regards to Eliot and the spare room when I'm home later, OK?' *If Eliot was even willing to stay.*

'All right, sweetheart,' her mum said. 'We'll figure it out once you're home. Two-ish?'

'Ish. Maybe two thirty by the time I've been to the shops.'

Felicity pulled Cleo into a hug and said quietly into her ear, 'Merry Christmas, Clee. I'm sorry we interrupted your time with Eliot.'

'You didn't, Mum—' Cleo began to protest. 'It's your house!'

'If you want us to all go out for a walk or to the pub or anything to get out of your way for a bit, just say the word.'

Cleo smiled a goodbye and opened the door, the force of the snow like a cold power shower. Her curls frizzed on impact, and the lights on her Christmas tree jumper flickered and extinguished. She had a feeling that by the time she got home, nobody would be going anywhere.

Chapter 24

The restaurant was, as expected, heaving. Full to the brim of mainly Wavebreak Bay residents, familiar faces, along with some who'd arrived for a Christmas break in one of the hotels or B&Bs, prior to the blizzard that was happening outside.

The window ledges were piling high with thick bands of snow, the chairs and tables out on the decking blanketed. The waves outside the windows were tickling up against snow-sprinkled pebbles, the salt rinsing them clean, only for a new layer to try and land again.

Although Cleo and Eliot's shifts crossed over by about an hour, she barely saw more than glimpses of him in the rush, and shortly after one o'clock, Cleo caught hold of Lucy.

'Is Eliot still here?'

'He just left,' Lucy replied over the sound of the Christmas music Coacean was playing loudly, then sped off into the kitchen.

'*Penises*,' Cleo cursed in a whisper, and quickly apologised to a passing old woman en route to the toilets.

She hightailed it outside onto the deck, pushing open the door, a blast of cold hitting her, and looked at the path up to the cliff, where Eliot was retreating. 'Eliot?' she called, hoping they couldn't hear her inside. But her words were whipped away on the wind, so she had to retreat back inside, shaking the plump snowflakes from her hair. *Surprise, Eliot!* She thought. *We're now spending Christmas with my extended family, too.*

'Cleo, could I grab another lemon wedge, when you have a mo?' asked Patrick, a nice guy and local fisherman who she'd gone to school with. He was there with his parents, and Isabelle, his girlfriend. Cleo expected he was sick to death of fish, but they, like others, were taking their time over their meals while they sat beside the window, looking out at the beautiful winter wonderland beyond.

'Sure,' Cleo said. 'You're not planning to go out any more today, are you?' The sea actually didn't look too choppy, just a bit of a swell. But either way, she wouldn't fancy being out on a fishing boat right now.

'No.' He grinned. 'I'm cosying up for Chrimbo, now. Actually, we're out tonight celebrating.'

'Celebrating what?'

'We're moving to France in the spring. Nothing to do with this weather.'

'Wow, permanently?'

'Yep, selling the house, the campervan, half our stuff, and we're out of here. It's just been made official.'

204

She fetched Patrick's lemon, impressed with their big move, and then passed another table. 'Crystal, is the shop closed?' Cleo asked the owner of the general store. Usually, Crystal worked over the three main Christmas days, giving the rest of the staff the days off.

'Hi, Cleo. Yep, all closed. The delivery lorry couldn't get down into the valley this morning so we shut up at lunchtime. We'll try and be open tomorrow though. Unless you're desperate now?' Crystal started to rise from her seat. 'I can head back and get you something, you can pay me later?'

'No, no, no, sit down and enjoy your meal, I don't need anything at all,' Cleo said.

Hmm, that was the milk, bread, Choc Orange and magazine out of the snow-covered door then. Perhaps she could raid Coacean's pantry for essentials, though she didn't want to leave the kitchen short if delivery lorries were getting themselves stuck in snowdrifts. Was it worth traipsing through this weather just for the whisky and the mystery novel?

No, it was not worth it, as she found out after leaving work that afternoon. With the snow prickling her face as it blew sideways, she covered her mouth with her scarf and pulled the hood of her coat tightly around her head, then trudged first to the off licence, which was dark and locked, then the bookshop, which, too, was dark and locked. What with the establishments that shut for the whole of winter, plus those that closed early on Christmas Eve anyway, the whole town was deserted. Barely any footsteps other than hers could be seen on the pavements, and they were swallowed up quickly. The grit that had been on the central road through town was even losing the battle, with snow setting above the slush, now.

Cleo made her way back up the coast path towards the house, her sturdy walking boots stopping her from slipping about too much, though she was panting with effort by the time she reached the top.

She caught her breath and looked back down at the sea. The beach did look spectacular with its white gown on, but realistically, she didn't think she'd be taking that first dip today.

There was a time she would have gone in come rain or shine, as long as it was safe to do so. That's how much the ocean had meant to her. Where had that girl gone?

In the driveway, Stuart's car still sat, now under its own snow duvet. A snowvet, perhaps. It was no surprise, really. But what did cause her to frown were the extra voices she heard when she opened the door. Who was that? Was Gloria putting on a show and doing a Bristolian accent?

'Hey.' Eliot appeared in front of her, helping her out of her coat.

'Eliot,' she breathed, reaching in for a hug, his warmth instantly feeling perfection against her cold and wet body. Didn't it always? Even when they used to come out of the sea together, he'd always warm up quicker than her, like he had an in-built radiator, and he'd pull her close, just like this. 'I'm so sorry, I didn't get a chance to tell you, you've probably now met our extra guests—'

'Eliot,' somebody barked. Cleo stepped back and looked

206

around him to see the frowning face of an older woman. 'Are you fetching my book or not?'

'One minute, Gran, my friend Cleo's just got home and I need to fill her in.'

'I'll just sit here and die of boredom then,' the woman grumbled, retreating to the living room.

'So, fun story,' Eliot said. 'You may remember my gran, she's really happy to be here. As is my grandad.'

'Shit!' arose the shout of an angry man whose voice Cleo realised she hadn't heard in years.

'Grandpa,' Eliot called back in a warning tone, before facing Cleo with raised eyebrows. 'Sorry, he's trying to find "something, bloody anything" to watch on the TV at the moment.'

'Erm.' Cleo blinked. 'Netflix has lots of sitcoms if that's his jam?'

'No,' barked Eliot's grandfather.

'He prefers true crime documentaries,' Eliot explained. 'And his hearing aid is turned right up so he can hear everything in all rooms, it feels like.'

Cleo nodded. 'All right then. We can find some true crime. Has he watched *The Tinder Swindler*?'

He ran a hand, damp from Cleo's coat when he'd hugged her, through his hair, transferring a snowflake from her to him and she watched it melt as he spoke. 'I called my gran just before I left work, to check they'd made it to their hotel. But Gran said they'd cancelled their trip because they couldn't get over there. Then she admitted the power had gone in their house, so I borrowed the Land Rover from your neighbours, the ones who moved in after my grandparents left, before I even came back into this house and went to get them. I was going to ask if you'd mind hugely if they stayed this weekend but, when I got back, I realised you already had extra guests, so I'll take them over to mine instead.'

'Wait, so you wouldn't be spending Christmas here?'

'I don't think I can,' Eliot said, his eyes on hers.

'No,' Cleo said.

'No?'

'No, I mean yes, I mean – just stay here, all of you. It'll be ... fun.'

'I don't think you have enough space here,' he replied.

Cleo thought fast. 'We can share.' Blush. 'All of us, I mean, we'll figure it out.'

He hesitated. 'I did already check and the Wavebreak Views is booked up over the holidays. And the place they had been booked into would have been too far a drive in these conditions, for my liking. But we'll be fine at my place.'

'No, just ... ' She didn't want him to go, not again. It was like the beach bonfire all those years ago when he suddenly left before she'd had the chance for anything to begin. 'How about we leave the rest of them here and you and I can just go back to my place?'

Tell him now.

'That's tempting,' Eliot said, and their eyes held each other again.

But she knew as well as he did it wouldn't be right. She'd promised her sister, and he couldn't leave his grandparents.

Cleo took a deep breath, stepped out of her boots and marched into the living room.

On the armchair that was one foot from the TV, Eliot's grandpa, who hadn't changed much over the years, was jabbing at the TV remote. His gran sat primly on a dining chair someone had put by the window, staring out with the forlornness of a Jane Austen character. Gloria was perusing the bookshelves, her legs in a wide stance like she was stretching out her hips. Charlie flicked through the *Radio Times*, sat on the floor. Stuart was texting on his phone, a smile on his face that told Cleo he must be conversing with Kaleb. Her mum and dad were on the sofa beside Stuart, trying to suggest suitable programmes for Eliot's grandpa. And Gabriela had taken up residence on the other armchair, her legs over the side, staring into space.

'Hi, everyone,' Cleo said. Then to the newcomers she said, 'Hello, I'm Cleo, I don't know if you remember me from when you lived next door?'

'Hello, Cleo, thank you for having us,' Eliot's gran said, her voice strained as she avoided the question. 'My name's Hilary and this is Clint. And no, we are in no way related to Hillary Clinton.'

'Righto. Nice to meet you. Again. Properly though, this time.'

Clint looked over from the TV. 'Are we going to yours now, Eliot? Are you still in that poky little place?'

'Yep,' said Eliot, his voice already beginning to fray. Cleo couldn't subject him to a whole Christmas of this on his own. A problem shared and all ...

'I think you should all just stay here,' Cleo said in her best decision-making voice. 'It's really snowing hard out there now, and the light will be fading soon as well. Just stay here and let's all have Christmas together.' She looked right at Eliot for the last two words, silently imploring.

'OK, um—' her mum started, but Cleo cut her off.

'Wait. I mean, wait, please. Sorry, Mum. I think you're going to say, where will everyone sleep? But I've worked it all out.' She hadn't. 'Eliot's grandparents could take where he slept last night, the spare room. Gloria can take my room. Stuart and Charlie can take Gabriela's room, if you don't mind sharing?'

'I don't mind.' Charlie shrugged. Thank God he was such a chilled kid. He'd always been that way.

'Gabriela, you can bunk in with Mum and Dad.'

'No thanks,' she replied.

'On an air mattress on the floor.'

'I'll take the office,' she sighed.

'I don't think the air mattress would fit in there ... '

'I'll make it work.'

Cleo counted on her fingers. 'Is that everyone?'

'You two?' Stuart said with a smile.

'We could sleep here, in the living room,' Cleo offered, and then to Eliot added, 'If that's OK? We could each take an end of the sofa.' She pointed at the big corner sofa, which had an equal number of seats on each side. 'I've slept on it before when Macaroni had the squits and I needed to keep letting him outside throughout the night. It's quite comfy.'

Eliot laughed. 'Sold. Count me in.'

'Are you sure?' Cleo asked. 'If you'd rather go home to

your own bed for Christmas I'll shut up and stop being so demanding?'

'I want to stay,' he replied, his voice low.

'Thank you, Cleo, all of you,' Stuart said. 'We really appreciate you putting us up, and I'm sorry we haven't come bearing gifts or food or booze or anything, but we owe you all big time.'

'We have alcohol.' Hilary turned away from the window and to the group, her back straight. 'And yes, thank you, Cleo, and Cleo's family, we are very grateful. What did we bring from home, Clint?'

Clint was already rummaging in a shopping bag at his feet. 'Bourbon, port, that Baileys stuff you like, Eliot, and half a bottle of tonic water.'

'Did you buy that for me, Grandpa?' Eliot asked, touched.

'Well, we knew you'd be stopping by at some point,' Clint said, with a refusal to admit the kind gesture.

'Actually, that's good, because I couldn't get your whisky, Stuart,' Cleo said apologetically. 'Nor your book, Gloria. None of the stuff, actually.'

Gloria waved a hand in the air. 'Not a bother, my dear, I see you have quite the Agatha Christie collection if you don't mind me devouring one or two during our stay.'

'And actually,' Stuart added, a smile creeping over his face, 'I've just had an email from the Merry Murder Mystery hotel ... due to the cancellation, they've emailed over instructions for an at-home version of the game we can all play over the coming days. We can each play a role, so get ready for a little mystery!'

Charlie looked completely chuffed and Gloria did an excited shimmy. Cleo's mum and dad, and Cleo and Eliot, were good sports and all said it sounded wonderful and great fun.

Clint said, 'For goodness' sake.'

Hilary added, 'Not my cup of tea!'

Gabriela rose from her chair and went over to Clint's alcohol stash, pulling out the bourbon and tonic water. 'Guess I'm hanging with you two this Christmas.'

Chapter 25

'Here are the rules,' Stuart said, when everyone had a drink in their hand and a place to sit. Outside, the snow contin- ued dropping, but inside there was a warm, Christmas Eve merriment sizzling through the group. 'There are ten of us, which means one murderer, one murder victim, and eight bystanders-come-detectives.'

'How do we know who's the murderer?' asked Gabriela.

'Well, thanks to your mum's double-sided printer, we've got ten cards – or pieces of paper, strictly – and we're all going to take one. One card says "murderer", one card says "victim", the other cards say "whodunnit". Don't show anyone your card. On the other side of your card is a shape, like a triangle, a diamond, a square, et cetera. Once you've read your card, you then hold it up with the shape-side showing the group. The murderer's card will have a shape printed below the word 'murderer', and that's also the shape on the back of the victim's card. So the murderer can identify the victim, but nobody else knows who anyone is.'

'Does that mean you already know because you printed it and cut them all?' Gabriela asked, quite affronted, and getting quite into the game. Cleo smiled.

Stuart shook his head. 'Nope, I promise. The email was very clear about opening the attachment and pressing print without looking at page two of the PDF – the "word" side, and then cutting them out without flipping the paper over.'

'Does the victim know who the murderer is?' Hilary asked.

'No.'

'Will the victim be murdered at the beginning of the game? Is that how things get started?' asked Cleo's mum.

'Can I be the victim?' asked Clint, one eye on the TV.

'No, and no, well, maybe, Clint. It depends on your card. But no, the victim can be killed anytime in the game, because a big part is the characters getting to know each other and their backgrounds and who they may or may not know in the group.'

Hilary tutted. 'I don't know any of you.'

'You know me, Gran.' Eliot laughed. 'And Felicity and Bryce, and the girls.'

'Well, that was a long time ago,' she replied.

After a moment's pause, Stuart continued. 'You'll each be given a character sheet with a description, a reason you might die, and a motive to kill. So, I suggest you read them and study them this evening.'

'I love studying on Christmas Eve.' Charlie sniggered.

'All right, everybody picks a card,' Stuart instructed.

Cleo reached across Eliot for one of the cards spread out on the table, pulling it close to her, and peeking at the word.

Victim! She was going to be getting the chop. Ah, man, she might have liked to have been able to play at being a detective, but never mind. At least she could plan a perfectly Oscar-worthy dying scene.

She peered around at the others to try and see if she could read their poker faces, but all were keeping shtum. Except Gloria, who was wiggling one eyebrow in excited anticipation, but whether that meant she was the murderer or just thrilled to be getting the game started was anyone's guess.

'All right, now here's the character info that goes with the shape you're holding up.' Stuart handed those out.

'I would love it *so* if you could all throw your full weight into this and dress up,' Gloria suggested.

'Well, not everyone has costumes with them,' Felicity said.

'Improvisation is the key to individuality!' Gloria declared.

'Oh, right.'

'While we're doing that,' Cleo stood up, 'does anyone need another drink?'

They all did, and she topped everybody up, and then they all went to separate corners of the room or parts of the house to learn their characters, find costumes, 'get a bit of damned peace and quiet' as Clint put it, or whatever else.

Cleo folded her paper and put it in her pocket. It wasn't quite how she'd envisaged her Christmas Eve, but actually, she was quite looking forward to this.

'Not doing an in-depth character study right now?' Eliot asked, following her to the kitchen.

215

'I'm playing the kitchen hand, naturally, with the Cinderella complex and a thing for stealing shoes. So I'm sort of me, mixed with Macaroni. Character study done. How about you?'

'Dashing Duke Danglybits, at your service, ma'am.'

Cleo laughed. 'Well, pleased to meet you, sir.' She curtsied. 'My name is Nicola Nickedyershoes.' She put her hands on her hips and surveyed the kitchen. 'Speaking of nicking things, can you see anything we can repurpose as presents?'

'For who?' Eliot asked, picking up a jug in the shape of a cow where the milk got poured out of its nose. 'Can I have this?'

'For everyone,' she said. 'I mean, you have a gift here from me, and my parents and Gabriela still have their gifts for each other and from me, but I want to be able to give something to Uncle Stu, Charlie, Gloria, your grandparents.'

'You don't need to worry about that; nobody is expecting anything.'

'I know, but tomorrow's Christmas,' Cleo said. *Tomorrow was Christmas*. According to this self-imposed deadline – which, if she didn't uphold now, would she ever? – she was nearly out of time. 'Speaking of . . . ' she started. In a house crammed with guests, the fact she and Eliot were standing alone in a room together might be an opportunity that didn't come around again. 'Do you, shall we just . . . can I talk to you a minute? If you aren't busy?'

'Of course,' he said. 'You want to go for a walk?'

'Yes! That would be—'

'Cleeeeeeo,' whined a voice from the living room.

'Yes?' Cleo yelled back to her sister.

'I know it's only Christmas Eve but I'm opening my present from you,' Gabriela called.

'What?'

'I'm opening my present from you.'

'OK.' And then Cleo remembered what she'd got for her sister. 'Shit, shit, shit, Gab – don't open that.' She raced into the living room just as Gabriela ripped open the paper, revealing, in large, smiling, glory, the romantic photo of her and Derek.

The room went silent.

'I'm so sorry, it completely slipped my mind,' Cleo said apologetically, blushing in front of the whole room. 'I should have changed the photo. The frame was the gift really. If you give it to me, I'll take the picture out—'

'No, it's fine,' Gabriela said, shaking her head and meeting Cleo's eyes. An understanding passed between them, the one that they'd always had, whether they were bickering or snuggling close, that said, *It'll always be OK*. Her voice was smaller than usual, however, as she said, 'I'll sort it out later. Thank you. The frame is beautiful.'

It wasn't like Gabriela to go the disappointed-not-angry route, but Cleo felt all the worse because of it.

Then, Gabriela slapped on a smile. 'Will you make me some of those gingerbread biscuits you used to make?'

She was clearly over that mishap and back to needing to be waited on. 'Erm, now?'

'Please? I feel so shit and I just want to comfort eat.'

Cleo nodded. 'Do you want some Quality Street?'

'No, I *want* my fiancé back, but that's not going to happen so please, Cleo, you're my sister, please help me feel better.'

'Jesus Christ,' Cleo muttered, flicking the oven on to warm. To Eliot she said, 'Let me just do this and then we'll go.'

'You made them into hearts?!' Gabriela cried when Cleo presented her with a plate of cookies less than half an hour later.

'Sorry, it was the only cookie cutter Mum had. I didn't think.'

'I'm not sure if I can eat these,' Gabriela said, stuffing the first one in her mouth. 'Actually, yes I can, these are delicious, thanks, Cleo.'

Cleo wiped a floury hand across her forehead. OK, where was Eliot . . .

'Cleo.' Her mum stepped in front of her. 'I was thinking about tomorrow's Christmas dinner.'

'Don't, Mum, I'm hosting. It's fine,' Cleo said, firmly.

'But your dad and I can help.'

'I know, but you were hoping to just be the guests this Christmas. I've got this, leave it to me. Have you seen Eliot?'

'In here,' he called, where he was in the kitchen, washing up the cooking equipment. 'I've been thinking,' he said when Cleo entered the room and poured herself a tumbler of port. 'My grandparents don't like *stuff*, so why don't we give them that posh cracker selection box you bought?'

'I can't give your grandparents a box of cheese biscuits for Christmas.'

'They'll love it. Wheel out the block of Stilton at the same

218

time and job done. Besides, my grandpa has been known, in his time, to win cream cracker eating competitions.'

'What, when you have to eat a load in a certain time without having a drink?' Cleo laughed.

'Yep. Strange but true.'

'OK,' Cleo said, too tired to argue. 'The cracker selection box is for your grandparents. We could tell Gloria to help herself to one of our Agatha Christie's?'

'And what about a bottle of wine for Stuart?'

'And the Toblerone for Charlie? It's that or a bag of sprouts at this stage.'

'He'll love it. You're a good person, Cleo.'

'I'm a pushover,' she replied instantly. 'But listen, I was saying earlier—'

'. . . So this is Cleo, my niece, and her friend Eliot.' Stuart walked into the kitchen talking at his phone screen. 'You guys, this is Kaleb.' He turned the phone around and Cleo saw a handsome guy she'd seen in many photos, with a big smile, bright eyes, blond hair and a smart shirt on.

'Hi, you two,' Kaleb said, his voice crackly with bad reception, but cheerful. 'Sorry about the shirt, I've been on Zoom calls all day, I'm shattered. Thanks so much for putting my Stu and Charlie up, and what do you think of my mum?'

'Your mum?' Eliot asked, standing close to Cleo to get into the frame.

'Gloria is my mum; didn't Stuart tell you?' He laughed. 'He never tells people that because he thinks it's funny for them to form opinions on their own.'

Behind the phone Stuart shrugged and nodded.

219

'It's our pleasure,' Cleo said. 'We're lucky to have them all here, and it's so nice to finally meet you.'

'You too. Don't put up with any bollocks from my mum, OK? She tends to plant herself into the centre of everybody's universe whether they like it or not.'

'Is that my Kaleb's voice?' Gloria boomed, entering the kitchen and shoving herself between Cleo and Eliot until they had been bumped clean out of the way. She took the phone out of Stuart's hand and wandered off with it, chatting loudly.

Stuart laughed then turned to Eliot. 'Your gran wants you to help her figure out her character, mate.'

Eliot faced Cleo. 'Duty calls. Can we chat a bit later?'

'Of course,' she said.

'I want us to talk as well,' he said.

'We will.'

Stuart raised his eyebrows at her when Eliot left the room.

'Don't you start,' she warned him.

'I wasn't going to breathe a word ... about your massive crush on Eliot.'

He scuttled out of the room and Cleo took another swig of port, and then picked up a gingerbread heart offcut and squeezed her fist around it until the spiced crumbs fell into the sink, softening in the water.

Chapter 26

Cleo's eyelids were drooping to the point she would close one to give it a break, then swap and close the other.

There was once a time, many years ago, that the excitement of Christmas would keep her wide awake for hours. The anticipation of what was to come, the excitement of waiting for Father Christmas. Now she was gagging to go to bed – or go to the sofa – and get a good night's sleep. That was being a grown-up, she guessed.

Gloria had already taken her leave, with a peppermint tea (from a bag, after Cleo had shuffled about in the snow, in the dark, locating her mum's mint plant, because Gloria only really liked fresh mint tea, only to find it lacking in leaves) and an Agatha Christie book. Cleo had grabbed her PJs, some fresh clothes for the morning and her toiletries from her room beforehand, and they were now in a bag in the corner of the living room.

Gabriela had taken three of the cushions from the armchairs and made a makeshift bed on the floor of the office. She'd also taken Cleo's favourite thick, fluffy blanket to sleep under, that Cleo had brought from her flat because she wanted something nice for her and Eliot to curl up under if they spent any time outside over Christmas.

'Right, I'm going to bed, night, everyone,' Gabriela announced, and left the room before anyone tried to make any more small talk with her.

'Which one is the bathroom again?' Hilary asked.

'I'll show you,' said Eliot.

'I'm going to bed anyway.' Clint yawned with gusto.

Cleo could hear Clint and Hilary grumbling to each other as they ascended the stairs about how in their hotel they would have had a balcony off their room. Eliot mouthed a '*sorry*' at Cleo, and followed them up.

'Maybe we'll go to bed too, all right with you, Charlie?' said Stuart, who then stopped Cleo before she could say anything. 'That's OK, we don't need any more drinks or snacks or pillows fluffing, and we know the way. Night, Cleo.' He gave her a hug and a kiss on the cheek, and the two of them went upstairs also.

But thirty seconds later, Stuart called down, 'Sorry, all, don't suppose you could spare one more pillow, could you? Gabriela's taken one of the two off her bed, totally fair enough, of course.'

'I'll grab one,' Cleo said to her dad who began to rise from his seat. She needed to keep moving anyway, otherwise she'd fall asleep standing up.

Finding the last pillow in the upstairs airing cupboard she passed it in to Stuart and said goodnight.

'Ooh, not that one, Clint.' She stopped him opening the office door.

'Where's the bloody bathroom then?'

'Next one over.' Cleo pointed. She listened for a second at Gabriela's door, leaning over Macaroni who had gone to sleep in front of it in a protective manner, to the soft sound of her sister crying, and her heart broke for her. She put up such a front but she must be a wreck – anyone would be after having their world turned upside down like this. Even grumpy bitches like Gabriela.

'Gabriela, don't cry,' Cleo said in a quiet voice, opening the door to the room.

'I'm not,' she sniffled.

'. . . OK.'

'It's just . . . I don't think I'm very likeable some-times, Cleo.'

Cleo went to her sister's side. 'That's not true,' she soothed with a half-truth. It was never that her sister turned mean, it was more like taking herself away from the coast had just altered a part of her. Taken away the playful side.

'I hate that I'm being like this because of some stupid boy.'

'It was a big relationship; you're allowed to mourn it. Even if he was a knob who never came back to the beach with you.'

Gabriela snorted, a snot bubble popping under her nostril. 'Major red flag.'

'Right?'

'But it's not even just that – it's . . . my whole life is tied up in his. We work together. We live together. Cambridge is *ours*. You know, to us. What do I do now?'

'Now? Now, you get some sleep, and you rest that brain, and you listen to the waves.'

Gabriela sniffed again in the dark, a deep, snotty snuffle. 'OK. Night, Clee.'

Cleo closed the door. *Wash him out of your system with those tears, sis. Clean him away and you might just see yourself again.*

Back downstairs, Eliot, her mum and her dad were clearing up plates.

'Sorry about my grandparents.' Eliot apologised. 'They're finding it a bit tough being back here, I think. They were really sad to leave the house next door, all those years ago. That, and . . . my parents really disappointed them back in the day so they aren't used to so much family time.'

Felicity put an arm around his shoulders. 'Totally understandable, say no more. Shall we watch something to wind down?' she suggested. 'What about a Christmas *Vicar of Dibley* or something?'

The threat of tears made an unexpected appearance behind Cleo's eyes. She really, really wanted to crash out but the living room was her bedroom now and she couldn't kick her own parents out of their own living room. 'Um, sure . . . ' she said in a small voice.

She saw Eliot looking at her with concern, and he stepped in, saying, 'Actually, I wonder—'

There was a tapping at the door, so small that although it stopped the conversation, nobody was sure if they'd quite heard it. Even Rhubarb, who had been fast asleep in the centre of the floor, did little more than raise his large head.

When it happened again, and Macaroni appeared at the top of the stairs and grinned with an impending woof, Cleo hightailed to the front door.

Unlocking it, convinced it was going to be nothing more than snow dropping in thuds onto the step, she couldn't have been more surprised at who was on the other side.

'What are you doing here?' Cleo said in surprise, forgetting to use her hushed voice.

Standing with her feet deep in the snow, more falling from the sky, the slow-falling flakes illuminated by the security light above the front door, with puffs of icy air coming from her panting mouth, was a red-cheeked, wet-haired Rosa. With giant bags under her eyes and in her hands, she said, 'Merry Christmas.'

Cleo blinked, then pulled herself together. 'Come in out of the snow.' She bundled her friend inside, taking her bags and putting them on the floor, hanging up her jacket, brushing the snow from her hair. Eliot began rubbing the tops of Rosa's arms to warm her up while Bryce went to the kitchen to make her a hot cup of tea.

'I'm so sorry to barge in,' Rosa said, her lips blue. 'I should have gone home but ... '

'Of course you shouldn't have,' Cleo said, leading Rosa into the living room, plonking her on the sofa and kneeling down before her. 'Unless you mean home: New Zealand. In which case, yes. Why aren't you in New Zealand?'

'My flight was cancelled because of the snow, and then so was the next one, and the next one, and it got to the point that I realised I would have missed Christmas by the time I got there, and I didn't want to spend Christmas hanging about in an airport, so I came back. But there were loads of train delays, then half of *them* were cancelled too – oh, thank you so much.' She took the mug of tea from Bryce and cradled her hands around it. 'So, it's been a bit of a journey, really. Then I got to Exeter and met a nice lady who was driving towards Lyme Regis and she said she knew someone with a Land Rover who could maybe come and pick me up from the top of town, because she didn't want to risk coming down these roads, and that person turned out to be your neighbour.' She pointed in the vague direction of the house next door, then looked at Cleo with sorry eyes. 'I didn't want to have to ask any more of them so said they could drop me here, because I saw your message and you said your parents and sister had come home so at least it wouldn't be interrupting . . . '

She trailed off, widening her eyes at Cleo and tilting her head ever so slightly in the direction of Eliot, and Cleo understood perfectly what she was silently saying.

'You did totally the right thing,' Cleo said hastily, and gave an almost imperceptible shake of her head. *No, I haven't said anything to him yet.*

'I'll go back to mine in the morning.'

'No, you won't.'

'Who's that?' came Hilary's voice from the door of the living room. 'Clint said he could hear the front door. Who's she?'

'Gran, this is our friend Rosa,' Eliot explained. 'She's going to be spending Christmas with us too.'

'It's like the stable in Bethlehem here,' Hilary muttered

and went back upstairs, as if she wasn't just as much to blame for that feeling.

'Who was that?' Rosa asked.

'I'll introduce you to everyone in the morning, it's turned into quite a full house,' said Cleo. 'Speaking of which ... ' She looked around. Where was Rosa going to sleep?

Eliot seemed to read her thoughts and said, 'Why don't I take the air mattress and sleep in the kitchen, and the two of you can share the sofa instead of us?'

Rosa visibly perked up, giving a small, excited kick to Cleo's leg. 'No, no, definitely don't let me change any sleeping arrangements, I can take the kitchen, you two share the sofa.'

'Nobody can sleep in the kitchen,' Felicity said. 'It'll be far too cold. Cleo, why don't you come and sleep in our room on the air mattress, like Gabriela was going to do, and Eliot and Rosa can share?'

'Can I sleep upstairs with you?' Rosa jumped in.

'In our bedroom?' Felicity clarified.

Rosa nodded. 'Um, yes please. I don't like to sleep downstairs because ... because ... I'm afraid of being the first person that would get murdered in a break-in.'

They all had a moment of looking at each other, and then a yawn that Cleo had been stifling escaped into the silence. 'I'm happy with that plan if you all are,' she admitted.

'Let's go for it,' said Eliot.

'We can always shuffle around tomorrow,' Felicity agreed, and headed upstairs with Bryce to pump the air mattress and put out a sleeping bag.

Rosa faced Cleo again. 'Sorry to be such a party crasher.'

'Not at all, you're very welcome. Believe me. Now, can I get you anything?' She handed Rosa a throw cushion. 'We're out of proper pillows, I'm afraid.'

'This will be heavenly; I've been sleeping on my back-pack for the past two nights. Three? I don't know, I've lost track. Thanks, Clee.'

'Don't mention it.'

'Will I wake ... whoever else is up there ... up if I have a super-quick shower?' Rosa asked.

At that point, the *squeak-squeak-squeak* of the foot pump started ringing through the house.

'I think you'll be fine,' Cleo laughed.

'All right, night night, mate.' Rosa stood with a grunt and, leaving her huge bag in the hallway, ascended the stairs with her holdall.

Alone at last, Cleo looked at Eliot, and did another huge yawn. She didn't think she could launch into a big confessional right now if she tried.

As they moved about, taking mugs and glasses into the kitchen, clearing discarded jumpers and magazines from the sofa, turning off lights, locking doors, refilling water bowls for the animals, above them, the creaks and talking lessened into silence.

Finally, back in the living room, Cleo leaned a sleepy head on Eliot's shoulder as they surveyed the corner sofa.

'Feet to feet or head to head?' she asked.

'I guess feet to feet,' Eliot replied. 'I don't want to have to listen to you snoring all night.'

'I don't snore,' she laughed.

'Don't you?' His voice had a teasing tone to it, which made her laugh more and then cover her mouth so as not to wake the household. She didn't think she could face making another bedtime drink for someone or showing them which room was the bathroom for the fourteenth time.

'All right, feet to feet it is then. I'm going to go and put my PJs on.' Cleo left the room, taking her bag into the downstairs cloakroom, where she got undressed and redressed in haste and then took a moment to take five breaths like the Headspace app recommended.

I am not 'sleeping with' Eliot, Cleo reminded herself. *I am sleeping next to him. Feet to feet. That's all. No need to lie awake all night thinking about it.*

When she returned to the living room, Eliot had set up some throw-cushion pillows for each of them at either end of the sofa, and had laid a soft, fleecy blanket down for her, the one her mum kept on the back of the sofa. He was tucked in under a woollen throw from the trunk in the hallway, and curled up on his stomach was Blueberry the cat, fast asleep.

'You two make a cute couple,' she commented and climbed in with an '*Ahhhhhh*' as soon as she lay down. Her socked feet bumped against Eliot's.

'Are you playing footsie with me?' he said, trapping her under his own feet.

'Yours are nice and warm,' she said with her eyes closed, enjoying the weight of him. He didn't move them, and the two of them grew silent.

'Night, Cleo,' he whispered into the dark. 'Merry Christmas.'

'Merry Christmas, Eliot,' she murmured back, and then fell into dreamland.

Chapter 27

~ Then ~

Winter 2018

He'd come back, just like he'd promised, that first winter. Would he always come back?

Things had changed over the summer. A small shift that looked like nothing but affected everything. As well as Eliot being gone, Cleo had accepted another change. Her twin wasn't coming home.

Gabriela hadn't made any promises, not since before uni, but she had always peppered conversations with 'one day when I'm living back there', and there'd been a noticeable shift over August. Now she was talking about buying a house with Derek, who Cleo still hadn't met. It was great that she was so happy. It was great that Eliot was doing so well in San Francisco.

Especially since she'd overheard her parents talking about the future of the Wavebreak Bay branch of Coacean, and just how financially viable it was proving to be at the moment.

In that moment, Cleo put the brakes on the train of thought running through her mind about what she wanted, how she wanted to grow, and switched the tracks to one focus: *I am needed here.*

She was happy with that decision. She actively sought being the unofficial 'second in command' after Lucy, because this business wasn't just her parents', it was hers too.

Despite the increase in hours she was putting in now, Cleo and Eliot had been inseparable since his return, but never had they crossed the friendship line as close as they had tonight.

That December late-afternoon they'd swum in the ocean before their shifts had started. It was one of those picture-perfect winter days, where the sea was still and glassy, the sun pooling yellow over the whole vista, and it was the first time he'd dipped into the Atlantic since coming back, and the first time she'd been in since he'd left. Before now, she just hadn't had the motivation – it was like it had flown away with him.

But now, their hair dry but still salty, they were finishing up their shifts in Coacean, after a party made up of friends and locals had given them all one of the busiest but most fun nights in a long time.

Cleo couldn't stop thinking about Eliot and, from the way he kept catching her eye, she was wondering if he felt the same. Something about going in the water had invigorated her, made her find herself again, and like a wave it was pushing her to take action.

'Guess what?' Asha, one of the summer staff Lucy had hired who had stayed on over the winter, caught her arm and hissed at her, an excited smile on her pretty face.

Cleo smiled back; Asha had an infectious way of causing people to mirror her. 'What?'

'Lucy said we can have a sleepover in the restaurant, because this party can't drive home. The kitchen and bar would be closed but they all have their own bottles of bubbly with them anyway, so the party can carry on.'

Cleo's smile twitched a little on one side, but she didn't let it slip. 'I don't know, maybe ... '

'You two aren't together, are you?'

'No,' Cleo said quickly. 'No, we're just friends. God, Eliot, gross.'

'I kinda fancy him,' Asha confessed, her eyes twinkling like the fairy lights scattered around the restaurant. 'Why do you think he's gross?'

'Oh just, you know, that ... face.' *I don't mean it, Eliot, I love your face.*

'You don't like his face? What's not to like?' Asha laughed.

Cleo shrugged. 'Oh, you know ... ' She gestured towards the centre of her own face. 'His ... nose is ... very, very standard.'

Asha blinked at her. 'He's gross because he has a standard nose?'

'Yeah, you know. Good luck picking him out of a line-up!'

'OK ... '

'Um, anyway,' Cleo said. 'That ... great that you like him. Yeah, I mean he's not gross at all, I suppose, if I think about it. Maybe I will try it on with him HAHAHA.'

'Haha.' Asha's chuckle didn't quite sound realistic. 'Don't you dare! He's just so yummy, and he lives in California for half the year, I mean … come on … '

'I know,' Cleo said, her heart growing heavy.

If only she'd stepped in, said something, not put someone else's happiness before her own, maybe she really would have taken her chance that night.

As she, Eliot, Asha and the diners eventually hunkered down on blankets on the floor of the restaurant, Asha sticking close to his side, Cleo felt like she'd betrayed herself.

But in the night, when Eliot rolled onto his side, and flopped a muscled arm over her while she faced away, wide awake, she didn't move away. There, in the dark, she simply closed her eyes and, just for once, let herself imagine things were different, and he was hers, and she was his, and distance and time didn't mean a thing.

Chapter 28

~ Now ~

Christmas Day

At one fifteen in the morning, Cleo checked the time on her phone. *How* was she this wide awake when she'd only dropped off to sleep an hour or so ago? Was her body deciding that all she needed was power naps, now?

As quietly as she could, she army-rolled off the sofa and tiptoed her way to the window. Eliot's breathing remained deep and stable where he slept, and all around her the house hummed with the sound of nothingness.

Outside, the sky was dark but the ground glowed an eerie white, snowflakes still silently falling. It was Christmas Day, and it was snowing. Magical.

Cleo watched, mesmerised, for a while, the tune of 'Silent Night' floating through her mind. The clouds were broken overhead, and a bright moon shone above the sea, spilling a pool of light on the midnight blue water.

There was a creak behind her and she turned her head, expecting Eliot to be up, but the shape of him was still on the sofa.

The living-room door opened with slow precision, and a shadowed arm holding the light on a phone screen as a makeshift torch before it entered the room.

Cleo held her breath. *Damn, Rosa* has *avoided being murdered by sleeping upstairs!*

The rest of the body stepped inside the door and crept towards the bookshelf, the phone screen aloft, and Cleo realised who it was.

What on earth did Gloria think she was doing creeping about at this hour? Could she not wait until morning to get another novel?

Cleo stayed still, not wanting to make a sound and startle the woman, nor wanting to wake up Eliot, who looked so delish asleep, with the moonlight on his face.

Gloria took her time perusing the shelves, reading the spine of every Agatha Christie before selecting three and tiptoeing out of the room again.

Shaking her head, Cleo returned to the sofa, leaving the curtains open.

'Hello,' whispered a sleepy voice.

'Oh no, did I wake you?' Cleo replied, propping up on her elbows.

'No, the reverse Santa Claus did when she came in and nicked things from your shelf.'

Cleo stifled a giggle. 'I was by the window. I thought, if she sees me all of a sudden, I might give her a heart attack.'

'Have you been awake for long?' Eliot propped himself up too, running a hand over his dishevelled hair.

'A little while, but I'm ready to go back to sleep now.'

'All right then.' He lay back down. 'Night. See you when the next library customer comes in.'

'Sweet dreams.'

Cleo lay back, a smile on her face and a warm feeling surrounding her despite the thick snow piling on the window sill. All right, sleep time.

Alllllll right then. Off to sleep. Time to fall asleep.

Ten minutes later, Cleo whispered, 'Eliot?'

'Yeah?'

'Do you want some nachos?'

He sat up, stretched, stood, and held his hand out to pull her up. 'Yep.'

Cleo and Eliot were as silent as assassins as they made their way to the kitchen and clicked the door shut behind them.

'We have to be so quiet,' she whispered. 'So many sounds in this old house travel through the floorboards and the pipes, and I don't want to end up having to make eleven portions of nachos.'

'Plus, my grandpa's hearing is wildly good right now.'

Cleo switched on the kitchen light and dimmed the bulbs immediately.

'I'm glad I'm not sleeping in here,' Eliot said, still speaking in a whisper. 'It's freezing on these tiles.'

Nodding, Cleo reached into a cupboard for a bag of tortilla chips and opened the plastic wrapper so slowly and quietly that she wouldn't have blamed Eliot if he'd given up and gone back to bed.

With Cleo directing him with elaborate hand gestures, Eliot found a baking tray and put the grill on, then set to work grating some cheese.

'It's Christmas Day!' he said with a sudden smile. 'Merry Christmas.'

'Merry Christmas!' She gasped. 'I'm going swimming today!'

'Now?'

'No ... ' She thought for a moment. 'No, not now. But later. I promised myself that this Christmas I would get back in the sea and—' Cleo clamped a hand over her mouth, scattering grated cheese on the floor that Rhubarb sensed and came nudging his way through the door to hoover up.

'And what?' asked Eliot.

'And ... nothing else, really. Just, you know, have a really good time doing so.'

'It sounds like a plan. I'll join you? It's been a while since we've had a splash about, huh?'

'Too long.' She nodded. 'When did we stop?' As if she didn't know.

Eliot shrugged. 'And why? Let's break that today. A new beginning, and all that.'

Cleo did a small happy dance then got back to her nachos prep. 'I think that's enough cheese.'

'Oops, haha, we might be having weird dreams later.'

Cleo used her thumb and forefinger to squeeze her lips together so she didn't laugh.

They were church-mice quiet as they crept around each other to load the nachos with other tasty toppings, and then slide the tray under the grill.

Cleo was giving a silent high-five to Eliot when she smelled smoke, which was coming off the electrical components of the little-used grill. *Crap.* The last thing they wanted was for a smoke alarm to start blaring.

She rushed to the back door, which led off the kitchen, and, with a little tugging to release the snow, managed to pull it wide open, sprinkling her PJ top with snow that quickly melted into a wet patch.

The kitchen filled with frosty air, and Cleo and Eliot huddled in front of the grill to keep warm.

There was something magical about the dark, still night-time and the ice that drifted in and explored the room. Eliot reached out and pulled Cleo into his toasty arms. She kept her eye on the grill but felt her heart boom. Without them saying any words, she was able to take in the rise and fall of his toasty chest beneath his T-shirt, the sound of his breathing.

Cleo turned a fraction, her eyes tracing his neck, the line of his jaw and up to his eyes, where he took his gaze away from the grill and met hers. They breathed in sync, breath becoming cloudy in the cold air.

Eliot moved one of his arms, taking his time, like he was testing the waters. He brought his hand up her arm until it lifted off her shoulder and he sighed out another cold exhale just as he placed his hand on the side of her head. Her cheek moved towards the warmth of his hand like a magnet and her eyes closed for a second.

If the snow wanted to come inside and coat them, freezing them in this moment in time, that would be all right with her. She probably wouldn't even feel it.

But not all her senses had disappeared, and her eyes fluttered open as the smoke smell returned.

Eliot dropped his arms from around her and grabbed an oven glove, pulling the tray from under the grill. 'Anyone for nachos with charred edges?' he whispered.

Cleo metaphorically put all of the parts of herself back together again and remembered how to function as a human, grabbed a serving bowl, and closed the back door.

'Let's take these back into the living room,' she said, keen to leave the cold now that she wasn't tucked into Eliot's warmth.

While Cleo switched off the grill and the lights, Eliot carried their midnight feast through to the living room, the two of them taking extra care with their footsteps when they passed the bottom of the stairs. Cleo had to jam her pyjama sleeve into her mouth to stop laughing, but they made it to the sofa without encountering another soul.

Cleo turned the lights of the Christmas tree on, the bulbs' firefly glows warming the atmosphere in the room. Eliot placed the bowl between them, and they reached in at the same time.

Crunch. Crunch-crunch-crunch.

Cleo put her hand over her mouth. 'We picked the loudest snack possible,' she chuckled in as hushed tones as she could manage.

'They're good, though,' Eliot chuckled, reaching for another.

240

'Very cheesy.'

'*You* are.'

'Don't make me laugh.' Cleo shook a tortilla chip at him.

'Is your sleeve still wet?' He took her wrist and turned it, exposing the large snow patch on her forearm.

'I think I'll make it through,' she said, caring not a bit because his fingers were on her skin again.

'Take my T-shirt,' he said, moving away and pulling off his T-shirt like it was nothing.

'No, I couldn't ... ' Cleo semi-protested at the same time as reaching out to take it, the fabric soft and tumble-drier toasty.

'Take it, you can't sleep in a wet top, you'll catch a cold.'

'All right, Granny,' she joked. 'Turn around.'

Eliot obliged, grabbing a nacho to take with him, and she turned too, removing her pyjama top and pulling on his T-shirt.

Do not smell it, you creepy weirdo, she scolded herself.

'Don't you look nice?' Eliot said when they'd both turned back to the nachos.

'Stop it, I look like a stereotype from a college movie who's borrowed her boyfriend's T-shirt.' Cleo clamped her mouth closed. *Nice one.*

Eliot smiled and looked down, and they ate some more of the snack in silence, until he said, 'I think I've had enough melted cheese for one night.'

'Good call.' She moved the bowl to the sideboard on the other side of the room, and returned to the sofa, lying back down in her place. 'Are you sleepy?' she whispered. On the

241

ceiling, the Christmas tree lights were causing shadows of branches, as if they were lying under a canopy in an enchanted forest.

'Say that again?' he whispered back.

'I said, are you sleepy now?'

'A little. Are you?'

'Huh?'

Eliot propped himself back up. 'I can't hear you very well from over here. Shall we just sleep head-to-head?'

'Really? What about my snoring?'

'I'll cope,' he said, picking up his throw cushions and swinging around on the sofa.

Cleo did the same, and they arranged their makeshift pillows in the corner of the sofa, and lay with their heads together, their feet stretching away.

'Do you think it'll snow in San Francisco this winter?' Cleo asked through a yawn.

'I don't know, I've never been there over winter.'

'Hmm,' she replied, her eyes closing.

She should stay awake, tell him, now would be perfect. If it weren't for the house full of people. Wasn't she supposed to give him space to think, anyway . . . ?

In time with each other, Cleo and Eliot's breathing slowed and steadied. Just before she sank into sleep, Cleo moved her arm to rest on the pillow above her head. Minutes later, Eliot did the same. Neither realised their fingers were only millimetres from touching. Or perhaps they did.

Chapter 29

Cleo awoke at first light. She didn't know if it was the comfortable sofa, the proximity of Eliot's gentle breathing, or the heavy cheese in her stomach, but she'd slept soundly the rest of the night.

Moving her head to the side, she smiled at Eliot, who faced her, though was still asleep.

Something had happened last night. This wasn't her wishful thinking or reading into the number of kisses he left on a text message. It was real, it was *almost*.

'Eliot?' she whispered. It was time.

Before any of the nine other people in the house began to demand her attention.

His eyelashes twitched, and from under his blanket Blueberry emerged, stretched, and hopped down onto the floor, padding over to the sideboard to sniff up at the discarded nacho bowl.

'Eliot,' she whispered again, her words fluttering the strands of hair at the front of his forehead.

With a deep inhale, he opened his eyes, meeting hers instantly, and said in a raspy voice, 'You haven't been staring at me all night, have you?'

She laughed. 'No.'

'Is anyone else up yet?'

With that, a toilet flushed on the floor above them.

'How long do we have, do you think?' Eliot asked.

Could he mean what she hoped he meant? 'What for?'

He gave that side smile that made her weak.

There was a thump on the living-room door. Cleo's eyes didn't leave Eliot's. 'Let's ignore it.'

'All right.'

The thump came again. *No*, Cleo thought, her moment with Eliot slipping away. She tried to ignore the noise and to focus on him and what she needed to say, but now all she could think about was who was thumping on the door.

One final thump and the door gave way, and in shot Macaroni in a whirlwind of wagging tail and happy panting, with Rhubarb lumbering close behind, both ignoring all sense of personal space to stick their snouts as close as possible to Eliot and Cleo's faces.

'Morning, boys,' Cleo sighed, and sat upright before her face was thoroughly licked clean.

'Merry Christmas!' Rosa said, entering the room and looking far more like her usual self in a clean jumper over her pyjamas and a good night's sleep evident in her skin. 'I came down to make a coffee – do either of you want one?'

'I'd take a tea, please,' Eliot replied, sitting up as well, the blanket dropping to his waist.

'Tea for me too,' Cleo said.

Before leaving to put the kettle on, Rosa used her foot to nudge at the book-shaped gift she'd given Cleo. 'Open it!'

Cleo picked the gift up from under the tree and tore open the paper, inside finding a recent festive romance novel – one she'd been dying to read – all festooned with snowflakes and swirling red lettering. She gave her friend a hug and a heartfelt thank you, and thought, *She does know me, quite well.*

Rosa backed out of the room, then said, 'Hello, I'm Rosa, Cleo's friend. Fancy a cuppa?'

'Hello, Rosa,' came Clint's gruff voice. 'Very kind of you. I take my tea strong with a dash of milk, thank you.'

'On it. Merry Chrimbo.'

'Yes ... Merry Christmas.'

Clint entered the living room, frowning, and walked over to the armchair, grabbed the remote and turned on the TV.

'Merry Christmas, Grandpa,' Eliot said.

Clint seemed to register his grandson and Cleo for the first time, saying, 'Merry Christmas. You're up early.'

'Barely, to be honest. Could you watch TV a bit later?'

'I just want to see what the weather's like.'

Cleo saw Eliot glance at the window, but he let it slide.

Rosa's head poked back into the room. 'Cleo, where's your tea? And coffee? And mugs? And milk?'

'Coming.' Cleo stood up, rolling her shoulders, and padded towards the kitchen where Rosa met her with a smirk on her face.

'Did you pull the "I'm so cold, lend me your top" line on Eliot?'

'Would you shush,' Cleo hissed, taking over the teas and coffees rather than making her friend do it.

Rosa sat down on a bar stool. 'Has it happened yet? Have you told him?'

Cleo shook her head, but couldn't say any more because Charlie walked in the room.

'Merry Christmas, I'm Rosa.' Rosa waved.

'Merry Christmas, I'm Charlie.'

'Rosa's my friend from the restaurant,' Cleo explained. 'She arrived late last night after her flight to New Zealand for Christmas was cancelled. She's spending the holidays with us too, now.'

'Nice one,' Charlie replied, then said, 'Do you have a character yet? Or is Rosa your character? Are you actually from New Zealand? It's probably against the rules to ask that.'

'What a strange line of questioning,' Rosa said, tilting her head to the side.

Cleo poured Rosa's coffee. 'Oh, I forgot to mention that – we're playing this murder mystery game over Christmas because ... ' she yawned, '... I'll explain why when I'm more awake but in short, we all got our characters given to us last night, so let me speak to my uncle Stuart whose game it is and I'm sure we'll find somebody for you to be. And, Charlie, Rosa is her real name.'

'OK. Cleo, do you have any juice?'

Cleo moved to the fridge and looked inside. 'One bottle

of orange. Do you mind having a small glass so there's enough to go around?'

'Course not,' he said, accepting a tumbler from her and taking a seat beside Rosa.

'Have you seen the snow?' Cleo asked as she re-boiled the kettle, anticipating more house guests to drift in at any moment, given that nobody was trying to be quiet any more. From the window above the counter, she could see that the blizzard had died down and the sky was lightening to a nearly clear baby blue, with just light clouds dropping small, sprinkling snowflakes atop the duvets of snow that lay over the clifftops, the town and the beach. The ocean was a pale silver, its surface calm and the waves lapping a salty curve onto the snow-dusted shore.

'Pretty cool, isn't it?' Gabriela said, entering the kitchen. 'Rosa, right?'

'Morning! Merry Christmas.'

'Happy Christmas.'

'Does anyone want to go down to the beach?' Cleo asked, an urge to get out there. 'We could take the dogs out; we could even go for a swim?'

They all laughed, but Cleo hadn't actually been joking. It was OK, she'd get down there at some point today, come hell or high water. Except, maybe not if it was too high.

She also would talk to Eliot today. She would, she would, she would.

'A happy Christmas morning to you all,' boomed a voice that entered the room before its owner. Gloria followed, dressed in a floor-length jade velvet dressing gown with jade faux-fur trim. She had a full face of make-up, victory rolls in her hair, and a long cigarette holder dangling between her fingers. 'I am Countess Formaldehyde of Agamemnon. I have travelled here on the QE2 with my lady-in-waiting, Sheryl, who I assume is around here somewhere.'

'I think Mum picked a Sheryl from the deck,' Gabriela said, ducking out of the way of the gesticulating, but empty, cigarette holder.

'Tea, Gloria? Um, Countess?' Cleo asked.

'I could *murder* a slice of toast,' she said in reply, then leaned over to Rosa. '*Murder*, do you get it? Did we meet yesterday?'

Eliot entered the kitchen, a navy Christmas sweater adorned with a 3D snowman above his red plaid PJ bottoms. 'Merry Christmas, everyone.'

The group chorused a reply but he kept his eyes on Cleo, who handed him a mug.

'Let's do breakfast when everyone's up?' Cleo suggested to Gloria. 'I mean, unless you're hungry now, then I can make you toast. I'll make you some toast.'

The mention of toast brought Rhubarb into the kitchen. He leaned his bulky body against Cleo, his nose upturned, and fixed her with ginormous puppy eyes.

Needless to say, one slice of toast for Gloria turned into nine different breakfast orders, from various egg-styles to a colour-chart of teas and four different thicknesses of porridge. Eliot was on hand for it all, taking over on the eggs when Cleo dropped one of the remaining few onto the floor, taking plates and cups and glasses between the kitchen and living room and coming back with empties. Cleo felt her blood boil like the kettle more than once but kept as cool as the snow outside. Everybody was here because their Christmas plans had been ruined; making sure they had a good time was the least she could do.

Finally, the kitchen quietened with the last houseguest having departed to the living room, or back upstairs to queue for the shower. One by one, hobs, the grill, the oven, the fan, were switched off.

Eliot poured Cleo a third cup of tea after she'd had to throw away the first two because they'd gone cold.

'No milk.' She stopped him. 'I don't know how long that'll last with all these people, so I'll go without.'

'Black tea?' He made a vomiting face. 'Don't you hate black tea?'

Cleo shrugged, and he sloshed milk into her mug.

'Hey—'

'Drink your tea,' he said, handing it over. 'We can borrow some milk from the restaurant, I'm sure.'

Cleo slumped and looked at the clock. 'Ugh, after all that, I'd forgotten I hadn't even started my shift yet.'

'I don't think it'll be too busy,' he said.

'You don't? I do.'

'Yeah, I do too, actually.'

The back door opened and Felicity walked in, snow over her boots, followed by two wet and happy dogs and one wet and grumpy sister.

'You did the dog walk already?' Cleo asked, unable to keep the disappointment from her voice. 'I thought maybe we could take them down to the beach.'

Gabriela shrugged. 'I didn't think you were serious about that.'

'I am serious. I really want to go down to the beach today, and it would be lovely if some of you could come with me.' In actual fact, in normal circumstances she'd happily go off on her own to the beach. But it was pretty freezing out there and, safety first, she shouldn't really take herself off into the sea without anyone else nearby to keep an eye on her.

'All right, we'll go later.' Gabriela huffed.

'I need to get ready for work,' Cleo said. 'Gloria, mind if I use my room for a bit?'

'Before you go, dear, could you have another check for some fresh mint out in the garden? And just FYI, I'll only be answering to Countess Formaldehyde today.'

Chapter 30

'We did it.' Eliot high-fived Cleo as they left the restaurant to a cloudless blue sky. It had been a busy shift for them both, the seafood Christmas brunch proving more popular than they'd imagined with the lure of seeing the glittering snow coating the cliffs and beach in front of Coacean.

'It's still so cold out here!' she said, pulling her coat around her. 'Gorgeous, though.'

'Are you still going to go swimming?'

'Oh, shitters!' she cried. 'Yes. I meant to bring my wetsuit down and have a quick dip after the shift before heading back, but I forgot.'

'Could you go in without?'

Cleo laughed. 'I've told myself I *am* going in the sea again this Christmas, but even putting on a brave front doesn't extend to skinny-dipping right now.' She gazed out at the big, beautiful sea, and mentally figured that if the turkey had gone into the oven while they were out, as she'd asked, then she should be able to finish cooking and make it down before the sun set after four. 'I'll come back down when we've finished our Christmas lunch.'

'Does it have to be today?'

'I want it to be today,' she stated, only half talking about the swimming.

Eliot's eyes moved up the hill. 'All right, I'll go up and get your suit, you wait here.'

'No, Eliot.' She took his hand as he began to walk away. 'I need to . . . can we talk a minute?'

Cleo's hand shook in his, not from the cold. She might be about to lose everything.

Her phone began to ring in her pocket.

'Ignore it,' Eliot said, and she did. 'I—' Eliot's phone started.

They dropped hands and Cleo said, 'We'd better check who it is.'

Taking out his phone, Eliot blew out a puff of air that steamed in the cold. 'It's Rosa.'

'We should answer.' Cleo nodded.

'Hi, Rosa,' Eliot said. 'Oh, hi, Gabriela. Yeah, she's here.'

Eliot handed the phone to Cleo, their fingers touching again, and at the cold of her skin, he pulled her into him under his coat.

Cleo spoke into the phone, pressed into Eliot's chest, and right now, if Gabriela fancied a long chat, that would be fine. She wanted to savour this.

'You OK, Gabriela?'

'Hi, sis,' Gabriela's voice came down the phone. 'What temperature did you say the turkey needed to go in on?'

Cleo groaned into Eliot. 'I don't remember, doesn't it say on the packet? But didn't I say it needed to go on around twelve or something?'

'Yeah . . . we forgot. We were watching Christmas movies. It's a tiny turkey, by the way.'

'I know, sorry.' Cleo gritted her teeth, feeling herself tense, but then Eliot's hand came up and held the back of her head, a gentle moment of calm. 'Can you ask Mum or Dad?' she asked. She hadn't wanted to rope them in – they'd been looking forward to a Christmas 'off', and Cleo had insisted they didn't get involved, but . . . she'd never cooked a turkey before. 'Or just leave it, I'll be back in a mo.'

After they'd hung up, Cleo pulled back from Eliot. But although she looked up into his kind, smiling face, she couldn't help anxious little threads of thoughts from racing into pockets of her mind about the Christmas dinner prep she needed to do, and how she was going to scale up from a two-person menu to an eleven-person menu. Lucky she was standing beside a restaurant manager, really.

'Will you help me with Christmas lunch?' Cleo asked Eliot.

'I will,' he said, nodding. And even though their moment had passed, again, Eliot took her hand and together, with a fair amount of sliding about and four soggy socks later, they made their way up to the top of the snow-covered hill.

*

Back at the house, the murder mystery game was in full swing. While Cleo and Eliot toiled in the kitchen, various members of the party kept entering to talk nonsense at them.

Cleo calculated how many carrot batons each person could have out of the two carrots that greedy Rhubarb had left her with after she'd stupidly left him alone with them, when Stuart came in and asked, "'Ello, where d'you two like to holiday during the summer?'

Cleo tried to remember her character's name. Nicola Shoe-Nicker or something. She slapped on a smile and answered, 'Wherever there are lots of people and I can get lost in a crowd.'

Eliot, Duke Danglybits, added in, 'My favourite type of summer holiday is when everyone else goes on theirs.'

'Very good.' Stuart, a 'stable boy with a dark past', nodded, and left the kitchen. 'Very good indeed. Sir, madam.'

Cleo crouched in front of the freezer. 'All right, I think that turkey could stretch to six, or even eight, if people have a really small amount.' She pulled out a bag of frozen chicken breasts. 'So, we're going to add these into the mix. How many do you reckon?'

'Maybe all of them?' Eliot said. He crouched next to her and whispered, 'You OK?'

'Yep,' she said, her voice tense.

'I want you to have a Merry Christmas.'

'I am, sorry.' She leaned her head against the freezer drawer for a second to cool it down in the hot kitchen. 'It just feels like I'm on a triple shift this Christmas, you know?'

'A quadruple shift,' he agreed. 'Why don't you go and

relax, open some presents with your family or play the game, and leave this to me?'

'No, really, we're nearly there now. Just promise me you'll come with me to the beach later? If I even get the chance to go?'

'I promise.'

'Can somebody just die already?' Gabriela sighed, chewing on a piece of sliced chicken breast.

It was a modest meal, to say the least. The chicken breast slices had been hidden in with the turkey so nobody could hog too much of one of them. The sprouts were rationed to three per person, the pigs in blankets were one each, much to Gloria's horror. Luckily the restaurant had an absolute abundance of spare potatoes, so those Cleo and Eliot had brought home, and they'd created a mountain of roasties.

Cleo rather agreed with her sister. If she could hurry up and be murdered, she might be allowed a lie-down.

'So, who's coming to the beach with me after we've eaten?'

'You're not going to have a lot of light left, love,' Bryce said, peering out of the window from his spot eating on a beanbag on the kitchen floor.

'It should be fine for another hour or so, don't you think?' Cleo's heart sank. It must have got later than she realised, because there was a definite indigo hue appearing overhead.

Charlie passed her the yellow paper crown. 'Your turn, Nicola Knickerless.'

'It's Nicola Nickedyershoes,' she replied, blushing. Great. Just what she wanted to be called in front of her dad. She forced the sadness out of her voice. They were sharing four cracker crowns between them, and when Cleo put it on it ripped and fell off into her dinner.

It's Christmas. It's Christmas. It's Christmas.

Felicity put her knife and fork down. 'I couldn't eat another bite. Thank you, Cleo and Eliot.'

'Don't thank me, it was all Cleo,' he protested.

'Thank you,' everybody chorused.

'Shall we do presents, now, and I'll clear up later?' she suggested. There was nothing like sitting around as a family, opening thoughtful gifts and everyone hugging and smiling.

'Good idea,' they all said.

No, Cleo, we'll clear up later, you relax, she thought with bitterness that she shook away as quickly as she could.

In the kerfuffle of the houseguests rising, moving chairs, removing hats, stealing one last potato, grabbing drinks and lumbering out of the kitchen and into the living room, Cleo came face to face with Charlie. He met her eyes, gave an excited smile, and then, in a way nobody could see, made a stabbing motion at her stomach.

'Oh!' she said. 'Did you just ... '

'Shh.' He grinned, and wove himself back into the throng.

Cleo gave him a beat before grabbing a red tea towel, holding it to her stomach like it was oozing blood, and crying out, 'I've been stabbed! I've been stabbed and I am dying and who will clean these floors if I go?' She collapsed onto the kitchen floor as everybody came running back in.

'What lovely shoes you all have, I can see them so well

down here,' she wailed, and as she closed her eyes, she heard the sound of Eliot's chuckle.

Cleo let out an elongated moan, adding in a bit of gurgling, and then flopped, motionless. She lay with her cheek against the kitchen floor, wishing Charlie had picked the living room to bump her off.

Gloria let out a scream for effect, and Cleo relished the fact she was able to lie down and close her eyes for a couple of minutes, while they all fussed about in character.

'Let's retire to the drawing room to discuss our next moves!' suggested Stuart, and with murmurs of agreements, steps began to retreat. Cleo opened her eyes and stood up, brushing crumbs off her body.

'No, no, darling, you can't move!' Gloria squawked, re-entering the kitchen. 'We might need to inspect the body.'

'I don't think I need to be lying—'

'Oh, do play along, dear,' Gloria begged. 'I had been so looking forward to our Merry Murder Mystery weekend.'

Cleo held her tongue and got back on the floor.

Chapter 31

~ The Groundhog Years ~

Summer 2019–Summer 2022

Her life didn't revolve around Eliot. Cleo's waiting for him to come back, year after year, was more of a symptom than a cause.

It started out with what seemed like such a small thing. After he'd left at the end of the winter, Cleo had taken a final swim of the season by herself. It had been cold that day, unseasonably, for March, and she was fully expecting the water to be icy.

There were very few people on the beach as she changed into her wetsuit. White tips leaped on the seawater, and the wind made it all the colder as it snuck in under the neoprene of her suit while she pulled it over her legs and arms. There were no large waves, but the water pulsed with the high tide moving quickly over the steep incline of pebbles that had built up.

Cleo shuffled in, gasping at the temperature, but knowing

she'd acclimatise in a minute or so. Treading water, despite not being out far, her breathing was rapid and her heart pulsed, the current pulling and pushing at her.

And then she froze. Not literally. But mentally. All of a sudden it hit her, how alone she was, how she had no real aims and goals any more. Eliot was having this great adventure, moving up in his career, moving on. Her twin was settling down, had found a place she wanted to call home that wasn't here, and she'd grown more distant, less herself, she visited less, she called less. The seasonal staff Cleo made friends with came and went. And what was she doing? Where was she going?

It was overwhelming, and Cleo felt herself shaking, there in the water. She needed to get moving, it was too cold to be staying still, but her mind was flooding with thoughts.

The ocean, the place she always went to think, in all weathers, was betraying her in this moment, making her think *too* much.

Cleo shook herself from her daze when her panting began to make her feel dizzy. She felt that wooziness, that confusion, just like the time she'd hit her head with the surfboard all those years ago, moments before she'd passed out. The feeling of losing control. No, no, she couldn't faint again, she was alone out here this time.

Cleo struggled back up the pebbles onto the beach, gasping in air, choking in some saltwater en route, clawing on the stones until she was lying back on them, cold and wet and hard against the back of her head. That was the last time she'd gone into the sea.

Her motivation dried along with her wetsuit that summer. Instead of doing something about those thoughts, she buried her head in the metaphorical sand.

Rather, she threw herself into work. It was so busy in the summer anyway, and her parents were semi-retired now, so she felt a responsibility to the family to always be on hand. Besides, she liked working at Coacean.

She met someone who she tried to give her heart to – an Italian backpacker over in the UK to work for the summer – but when it was time for him to leave neither of them felt a strong enough pull to try and stay in touch. Looking back, he had never appreciated her ongoing friendship with Eliot very much, albeit over FaceTime and postcards, and she hadn't appreciated him trying to curtail it.

Then the winters came and went, and they brought Eliot home with them, and each year she wanted to make the most of him being around, wanted to find the spark in herself again. But Cleo could feel that, ever so slowly, as the years passed, she was falling into a cycle of losing that drive, then putting everything into him returning, like he was the key to kickstarting her motivation.

When the waves were visiting Wavebreak Bay over the winters, and Eliot would take his surfboard down to the shore, Cleo would watch, finding excuses not to go in.

Sometimes she nearly plucked up the nerve to ask for his help getting in the water again, but then she'd tell herself it was nothing, she didn't need help, she just needed the right moment.

But although she loved her time with him back here, she

still found herself prioritising work, and others, and the fact he was often at work too meant she didn't even realise the winter had passed by so quickly until he was getting back on the plane.

Sometimes she caught herself on summer evenings watching the surfers from the restaurant decking.

But she'd stopped prioritising her love of the ocean, even though in her more rational moments she knew that the happy times outweighed that one time a million to one.

Now it was like a spinning wheel of excuses – *It's too cold today, too choppy, the weather looks like it's going to turn, I don't have time to wash and dry my hair today, I'll wait until someone fancies coming with me, I'll wait until Eliot is free, I'll wait until Gabriela comes back down, I'll wait until next year . . .*

Like with everything else, it was safer to stay in a stasis. If she didn't let anything change, if she didn't make a fuss at work, if she didn't confess her feelings to Eliot when he came home, if she didn't bug her sister to come back before she was ready, if she just kept everyone happy then she wouldn't rock the boat, she could hang on to the half-life she had, and wouldn't risk everything crumbling.

Now she didn't even go in the sea any more, not even for a swim.

She was a seashell, empty, dulled, and so, bringing it back to Eliot, she convinced herself that he wouldn't want to be anything more than her friend. Not when he was so adventurous and driven.

On the outside, Cleo was sunny. On the inside, she was stuck in this rut, and she knew nobody could drag her out of it if she didn't dig her claws in and pull for herself.

Chapter 32

~ Now ~

Cleo lay on the kitchen floor, her cheek on the tiles, scrolling celebrity gossip on her phone. What a Christmas.

In the living room she could hear laughter and raised voices as everybody tried to act over each other, giddy with the action that had recently taken place.

Eliot's voice came in behind her. 'Sorry, Cleo, my grandparents just need me to fix that creak on their bed then I'll be down to hang out with you.'

Without turning her head – she didn't want to disturb the evidence after all – Cleo called back, 'No, I'm fine, you go for it.'

From her position on the floor, Cleo could see through the window. It had darkened now, and she was looking up into the night sky. The moon was massive, as bright white as the snow that still coated the window panes in an arc, and it bathed the whole kitchen in a pale blue glow. She could see stars, clear and in their millions.

What a beautiful night it must be out there, the beach covered in snow, all of it glittering under the moonlight.

Beautiful, and fleeting. She might never get the chance to see something like that again, to be in this moment again, and she was missing it.

Because she was lying on the kitchen floor. Because that was what everyone else wanted her to do.

She'd done it again. She was so weak. It took nothing for her to slip back into her tried and tested ways of living her life to make others happy. And why wouldn't she have slipped back? Because she'd wanted to confess to Eliot, she'd thought she'd be a changed woman? How about she stopped being a pushover? How about she did what made her happy for a change?

Cleo sat up.

Two things. Two gifts she'd vowed she would do for herself this Christmas: move forward with Eliot, one way or another, and go in the ocean.

Just two things, out of the hundreds of things every day she did for others.

Cleo stood, brushing crumbs from her Christmas outfit.

It wasn't too late. Christmas wasn't over yet.

Moving to the window, Cleo looked down at the beach. The tide was low, and the moon highlighted the snow-white pebbles and wide stretch of sand as if it were daytime. It was breathtaking, just like she'd imagined it would be. And it was peaceful.

Cleo tiptoed out of the kitchen, past the door to the living room, and up the stairs. She opened the airing-cupboard door and began pulling out whatever she could find that would work. Spare blankets, a camping gas stove, a lantern with a working bulb (and another without), the pop-up tent.

She went into her parents' room and took the air mattress from under Rosa's things.

She was about to head back downstairs when Hilary called out, 'She's buggered off!'

'I'm right here,' Cleo called from the top of the staircase.

'Are you alive again or is it part of the game that somebody moves the body?'

Eliot came out of the spare room to see her arms full of equipment and a double blow-up mattress. 'Hello, what are you doing with all that?'

Other members of the party were crowding into the hall-way now to observe Cleo's incredible walking-dead moment.

'I'm still dead, I'm just . . . ' She looked from her extended family to Eliot. 'I'm out of the game.'

'What?' Gloria demanded.

'Come on, Cleo,' Gabriela whined.

'Do you want to make yourself a cup of tea, love?' asked Bryce. 'Then come back in the game afterwards?'

Cleo shook her head. 'No,' she said firmly. 'No, I don't want to spend any more of my Christmas lying on the ffff-*bloody* kitchen floor.'

She'd raised her voice at the end, something she probably hadn't done in years, and for a moment they all looked at her with wide eyes.

'I'm just . . . ' she continued.

Stop talking, calm down, keep the peace, said her head.

Tell them how you feel, stand up for yourself, said her heart.

What if they hate me? What if it ruins everyone's Christmas? her head answered.

Then wrecking ball the shit out of it all, cried her heart, over-dramatically. But it had a point, her Christmas had already been ruined.

'I'm just . . . I accepted that I was going to spend Christmas on my own, and I made plans with my friend. Then I accepted that things changed, and I adapted, and tried my hardest. But none of you noticed how it might feel for me, you just took me for granted.' Cleo looked around the group. 'I feel like I'm taken for granted all of the time, actually, and it's my fault because I always say yes to everything, but that doesn't mean it doesn't hurt when everyone here, apart from Eliot, is only spending Christmas with me because of a blizzard.'

'Sweetheart, I thought you didn't mind—' Felicity started.

'Yeah, I thought you liked being the one in control of everything,' added Gabriela, her eyes round with surprise. 'You always volunteer. You practically grab the reins.'

'I'm sorry, love,' Bryce added. 'Please know you can always speak up if you aren't happy about something. I'm sorry if we didn't raise you to realise that.'

Cleo looked at the faces of those around her. Oh God, it was true. She never let anyone else help out. She always slapped the smile on. How could she expect people to know the real her when she was so automatically inauthentic with them?

Cleo tried to steady her breath. 'No, I don't mind looking after the animals, I was here anyway, and I said yes, but . . . it still sucked. Things can still feel crappy even if you've brought them on yourself.'

She turned to her twin, who was standing dumbly in the

living-room door, her face giving the *it's going to be OK* vibe but her mouth hanging open.

'Gabriela, this was going to be our first Christmas apart. I know you probably think this is really pathetic, but that was a big deal to me. You didn't even invite me to spend it with you. Even if you knew I'd stay here and work, you could have *asked* me. It's like you don't even care about being around me any more.'

She was sure that Gabriela was about to put up an argument, but she simply said, 'Sorry, Clee.'

Cleo took a deep breath. 'I don't need apologies right now. The point is, I've cooked, and shopped, and found presents for you all, and worked, and entertained, and played along, and tried to make this an amazing Christmas for everyone else but I'm so ffff-*bloody* tired and I don't want to have to sleep on the sofa, with people coming in to watch TV or Gloria on a midnight prowl for another mystery novel.'

Gloria turned to study a painting in the hall as if she hadn't heard and was nothing to do with any of this.

'There were only two things I wanted to do over this Christmas. And one was for everyone to go swimming with me, because I haven't been in for a long time and I'm a bit scared actually, and I thought we could do it together. But you were always too busy, or too busy letting me do things for you. And I appreciate not everyone would want to go in the sea in this weather but you could have come to the beach with me, for support, but you didn't even hear me. Nobody ... ' She quietened for a moment. 'Nobody hears me.'

'What's the other thing?' Charlie spoke up after a minute, while the others all looked at their shoes or each other, wondering what to say.

'What?' Cleo sighed.

'What's the other thing you wanted to do over Christmas?'

'It was . . . something else. It doesn't matter.'

'These are all really fair points, love,' Bryce said. 'Come on down and join us in the living room.'

'Actually,' Cleo replied. 'I'm going to the beach.'

'No, you're not,' Gabriela snorted.

'I am.'

'You've still got pressies here, Clee, do you want to come in and open them?'

They didn't get it. 'No, Mum, really. I don't want to stop the party and have more attention; I just really want to do something I've been trying to do all day. I just want to do something . . . for me.'

Cleo faced Eliot again, and handed him the air mattress. 'I'm going to sleep on the beach. I want to be right there, no excuses, ready to get in the ocean when the sun's risen. Are you coming?'

'Cleo, you'll freeze,' Uncle Stuart said.

'I won't, I've camped in snow before, I know the tricks of the trade.'

'When have you camped in the snow?' Gabriela asked. Did Cleo detect a mild (very mild) hint of admiration?

'I used to be quite outdoorsy, you know,' Cleo told her.

'So did I . . . I guess I'd forgotten,' her sister commented.

'Me too,' said Cleo.

Bryce stepped forward. 'But, Clee, just go and see the sea, don't stay out all night.'

'I want to do this.' She hesitated and corrected herself. 'I'm doing this.'

Chapter 33

'Then I am too.'

Cleo couldn't hold back a smile from spreading across her face. For the first time that day, everything felt just as it should. 'You are?'

Eliot took some of the items from her arms. 'Sure, I promised, didn't I? Does anyone have any extra socks I can borrow?'

For the next few minutes, Cleo raced about, packing up layers, her wetsuit, some supplies, swapping bedding around so they had the thickest options, then swapping the air mattress for some camping mats because it was all a bit much, checking everyone had everything they needed but backing away when the requests for after-dinner tipples started coming her way.

As she and Eliot stepped out of the front door into the crunch of the snow, she called back, 'Merry Christmas, all, you're on your own now. Oh, and Rosa, you can take the sofa tonight.'

'Are you sure you want to do this?' Eliot asked as they took three steps along the coast path and Cleo slid, bouncing against the circular disc of tent that Eliot held under his arm.

The air was icy but although Cleo's heart was beating fast, it only revved her up. The moonlight reflecting off the snow gave them more than enough illumination to find their way down the hill and onto the beach.

As soon as she walked onto the pebbles, feeling the roll of them as they displaced under her feet, Cleo felt herself relax. The waves moved on a gentle loop in and out of the shore. This was her beach: quiet, wintery, still hers.

'Where do you want to set up?' Eliot asked. His voice sounded crystal clear out here in the silent night.

'Back here,' Cleo instructed, heading to a flattish patch tucked against the bottom of the hill, out of any wind.

'We won't get any cliffs falling on us in the night, will we?'

'Not here.' She grinned. 'Just a few pebbles in the back, but I brought camping mats.'

They worked quietly, popping the tent in place and placing pebbles in the corners to keep it sturdy, then filling it with their belongings.

'Want to go swimming?' Cleo asked.

Eliot hesitated. 'Er ... OK ... '

'I'm joking. We'll go in the morning.' As desperate as she was now to get back in the water, to prove she still could, it would be safer to wait until daylight. Besides, there was something else she couldn't put off any longer.

Climbing in the tent together, Eliot and she wrapped themselves in blankets and duvets, leaving the hatch open so they could see the glow of the ocean.

He put an arm around her, bringing her close to him, and, even though there was nothing but a thin piece of canvas between them and the fallen snow, she couldn't have been warmer.

'When did you last go in the sea, Clee?' he asked her.

It was honesty time, wasn't it? And Cleo was tired of hiding her true self at this point. Including hiding herself away from something that had made her so happy for so long. She'd thought finding herself would take too much effort. Until now she hadn't realised how much effort it was taking to keep beating herself up.

'I haven't gone in for years now. Maybe three?'

Eliot looked concerned. 'Has it been that long?'

'Time keeps slipping by. I don't know how.'

Cleo turned her head to the side, and looked up at Eliot, memorising his features, watching that smile spread onto his face. She knew that smile so well that even when he was on a different continent, she could picture it when she closed her eyes.

Sometimes, she would spend summer evenings watching the water and imagining that smile, and wonder if he was smiling too at that moment, whatever he was doing.

More than anything, Cleo hoped that smile didn't fade or change for her after she came clean.

'I want to tell you something,' she said, her words coming out quieter than she'd expected, as they found their way through the cold air from her to him.

In the dim light, she saw his smile relax just a little, but it was still there. He waited.

'Eliot, I . . . ' Cleo closed her eyes, just for a second, just to collect those thoughts that had been zooming around her mind like bumper cars over the past years. 'You and I have been friends for so long.'

She opened her eyes again and met his. He nodded.

Cleo continued, her voice dropping lower. She was almost terrified of the words coming out too loud, like she could pretend they didn't happen if nobody noticed them. 'I can't be your friend any more.'

'You can't?' he asked, a frown line appearing on his forehead.

'I mean, I will be, if you want, but . . . I'm not saying the right thing.' Cleo swallowed, her throat dry. 'I should have told you sooner, and it's OK if you don't feel the same way, it's really OK, but I've got to tell you how I feel or I'm going to . . . fade.'

That was it, the truth of it. Her authentic self was fading. She needed to be real, just to be seen again.

'How do you feel?' Eliot asked. His voice was low too, a raspy quality to it, and he shifted closer to Cleo, the arm around her pulling her further in towards him.

'I feel . . . ' Cleo was inches from his face now, intoxicated by the proximity, her eyes moving between his eyes and his lips, the world outside forgotten.

'Say it.'

She breathed in. 'I feel like I've fallen for you, and I can't just get back up and walk away.'

The last word was barely out of her lips when his own lips closed over it, kissing her, kissing her words. Eliot's hand moved up to her cheek, to her hair, and like a wave he swept over her, releasing her from the tension of holding this in for so long.

Cleo brought her own hand up, touching his neck, her fingertips running over his face in a way she'd longed to do. She was kissing Eliot. And it was as if shards of her being were coming back into focus.

A minute later she pulled back, breathless, and asked, 'So, how do you feel?'

A chuckle escaped his mouth. 'I can't stand you.'

'OK,' she laughed. 'Well, it's been nice knowing you, I'm just going to go and swim to France.'

Cleo began to get up but Eliot pulled her towards him and the two of them fell onto the makeshift bed.

'Oof,' said Eliot, shifting a large pebble from under his back.

Cleo, who lay beside him but with her chest up and resting on his, grew serious. She looked down at him. 'How *do* you feel, though? I need to know.'

He looked at her with his sea-grey eyes, and pushed a red curl back from her face. He made a soft exhalation and said, 'Cleo, why do you think I keep coming back every winter?'

She sank into him, pressing her forehead against his and kissing him again. 'But you keep going away again.'

'I know,' Eliot agreed, sounding as if his heart was heavy. 'The summers are long in California. I think about you all the time when I'm out there. Leaving you is the worst part of every year. But, it's part of me, it's something I can't leave behind for ever either. I don't know how to marry the two.'

'Slow down, pal, nobody's talking marriage,' Cleo joked.

'I've wanted to know how it felt to kiss you for so long.' Eliot smiled. 'It's not bad. A little wet, but—'

Cleo laughed, her voice ringing out into the night.

They fell into a silence again, Cleo resting her head on his shoulder. 'Why didn't you say anything sooner?' she asked him after a while.

'Why didn't you?' he countered.

'I didn't want to rock the boat,' she answered, honestly, too tired to be anything but. 'I didn't want to stop you living your California dreams. I was scared that if you didn't feel the same way, our friendship wouldn't be the same again. And it would become this forced, fake, inauthentic thing, and I need to be able to be real with you, you're the ... well I'm not very real with anyone else, just you. You know, aside from the whole hiding my secret crush on you for years.'

Eliot sighed. 'Even *if* I hadn't felt the same, nothing would ever change between us, Cleo. We could have a wild affair, elope, divorce, go through a bitter custody battle for our seven dogs and I'd still be here.'

'That's a big promise.'

'I can't help it, I'm just a really decent guy.' He smiled, then moved from under her so they both lay on their sides, face to face. 'I guess it's my turn to be honest, since you just braved it.'

Eliot wrapped his arm back around Cleo, pulling her close. 'I was afraid too, at least at first. That first year I left – it was 2018, I think – I felt like such a coward for letting so many years slip by without ever doing anything about it. And then it was too late, I was leaving. I swore I wouldn't let the opportunities pass us by again. But things kept getting in the way.'

Cleo gave a wry nod at that.

Eliot continued. 'But mainly, I came to believe that you deserved better than me.'

'What?'

'I'm away for half of every year. You shouldn't have to live like that, you should have somebody here, who gets to see you shining under the sun every day. Who can bring you tea in a flask when you come out of the sea. Who can stroke your feet after a long day at work. Who can watch *Selling Sunset* with you in the same room.'

'I liked it when we watched *Selling Sunset* together over Zoom,' Cleo interrupted, remembering a time over the summer when Eliot had dropped her a message saying it was an unusually rainy day in San Francisco Bay, and asking if she had any TV suggestions.

'It was a good day,' he agreed. 'But you deserve more than me. And I can't ask you to leave here, you love living in Wavebreak Bay. I don't know how we make this work.'

She did love living here. She'd forgotten, somewhat, but deep down this place felt more like home than anywhere else she could imagine. But would it ever really be home if he wouldn't stay here with her?

Just for tonight, just for Christmas, she was going to stop the worried thoughts from holding her back. Cleo closed the small gap between their bodies, pressing herself along the length of Eliot. 'I would like to stop trying to control whatever the future holds and just be here. Now. How does that sound to you?'

His eyes searched hers. 'That sounds ... yes. Yes, that sounds good.'

Their lips met again, stronger this time, bonding them together as if making up for the months they'd spent apart, for the time lost.

Eliot rolled Cleo onto her back, moving on top of her, without taking his lips off hers. She sucked in a gasp of air.

'Ouch!'

'What?' Eliot pulled his head away with concern.

'There's a really sharp stone under me,' Cleo replied, wriggling her back to move the pebbles beneath the camping mat. 'OK, where were we?' She slid a hand under his jumper and he flinched away from her touch.

'Sorry, automatic reaction, your hands feel like icebergs.'

'Oh, sorry,' Cleo said, withdrawing.

'It's fine, warm them up on me.' Eliot shifted so that her hands could rest on the bare skin of his sides. 'Christ, are you sure you're alive? They're freezing.'

He put his own hands on the sides of her face. They were warm, and combined with his kisses she could have sworn she was in the most luxurious of spas as opposed to out in the near-open air in the middle of the night. 'Do you want to … ' she breathed, in between kisses.

He pulled back, just a little. 'A million per cent. If you want to.'

'A million per cent. Maybe two,' she added, and she moved her hands around to his belt buckle. He tried to shift his hips up but got caught in the many folds of the blanket.

'Shit, sorry, hang on. What's going on with these blankets?' Eliot yanked and smacked his arm into the lantern, knocking it over, where the bulb gave a final sigh and then fizzed out, leaving them in the almost pitch black with the exception of the soft glow from the moonlight.

'It's romantic, at least,' Cleo said, her teeth chattering due to the removal of the blankets.

'Sorry.' Eliot moved back over her, pulling the blankets on top of her, and reached a hand underneath them. 'All right, there it is.' He kissed her on the tip of the nose and then she saw his eyes focus above her head like he was confused.

'What's up?' she asked. 'Or, what's wrong, rather?'

'How long is the fly on your jeans?' Eliot asked.

'I think that's the sleeping bag zipper.'

That did it for Cleo. Once she started snickering, she couldn't stop, until she'd fully got the giggles. Eliot rolled back off her, leaving one arm behind her head, laughing too, and covered them both with the blankets.

When Cleo could take a breath, she said, 'Maybe the kissing and the emotional outpouring is enough for tonight.'

'I think you're probably right,' he agreed. 'Are you tired, though?'

'No.'

'Shall I light a campfire?'

Cleo was about to say no, he didn't need to do that, or that she would do it, but she stopped herself. 'Yes please, that would be amazing.'

As she sat in the doorway of the tent, wrapped in all of the blankets, watching Eliot using his phone torch to find sticks and driftwood from the base of the cliff and then pile them up inside a dip he made within the pebbles, Cleo was reminded of that bonfire, a few years ago. The one she hadn't wanted him to leave early from. The one where she'd given in to herself and accepted how she felt, even though it was too late. Or so she'd thought.

Things had come full circle, because now he was building this for her, and though she still didn't want him to leave, he wasn't going anywhere tonight. And tonight, she was going to enjoy the moment.

With the fire lit, Eliot came back into the tent, sitting beside her. She opened up the blankets and let him in.

'Are you going to miss being just friends with me?' Cleo asked.

'No,' said Eliot. 'I haven't been just friends with you for a long time.'

That was a good answer. Cleo leant her head on his shoulder, and they watched the fire crackle, smoke curling into the air, while further down, the sugar-coated shoreline ebbed and flowed with the midnight waves.

Cleo's Christmas wishes had come true. Now she just had to hope they could last beyond the holidays.

'Merry Christmas,' she whispered to Eliot.

'Merry Christmas,' he replied.

Christmas night was coming to a close. The lights in Wavebreak Bay were being extinguished, the residents were full and merry and falling asleep, and on the beach, Cleo and Eliot's campfire was down to its last embers.

They'd talked and laughed, just like they always had, but Cleo felt closer to him than ever before.

'Oh, I have a gift for you!' she said, reaching to grab her backpack before the fire's light went out completely. She pulled out the tissue-wrapped parcel and gave it to him.

'I have something for you too,' Eliot said, handing her a small, blue box.

'Shall we open them together?' she suggested.

Eliot ripped into his and his eyes lit up in the low amber light. 'This is amazing, I've never seen anything like it before.' He turned the wooden luggage tag over in his hands, running his fingers over the resin wave. 'Thank you.'

'I thought you could put it on your luggage next time you leave,' she said, glossing over the whole 'him leaving' thing. 'And it might feel like you have a little bit of Wavebreak Bay, a little bit of me, going there with you.'

'I love it,' he said. 'I really love it.'

She smiled, pleased. 'My turn.'

Cleo opened the lid of the box and inside was another

square box, a jewellery box. She lifted the hinged lid of that, and—

'Eliot!'

'Don't run a mile, it's not an engagement ring or anything. Remember, I bought this before I knew how you felt. And before I told you how I felt. It's just, well, look ... '

Eliot pulled out the ring and held it up to show Cleo. It was a silvery band with a round stone the size of a pea in the centre. The stone, she saw when she looked carefully, was bright turquoise and transparent.

'It's seaglass,' he explained. 'From San Francisco. From a shop in Sausalito, to be exact – that place I told you about with the houseboats. I saw it and it made me think of you sitting here on the beach lobbing your pebbles into the water. And I thought ... ' He laughed. 'I thought that if you had this, it would be like I'd left a little bit of San Francisco, a little bit of me, here with *you*.'

'No way?' She laughed at how similar they were. 'Thank you so much, it's my favourite thing.'

A memory came back to her, of the seaglass necklace he'd left for her on the garden wall, over a decade ago, that she still had in her jewellery box. Back when they were new friends, she was only fifteen and he sixteen, and neither of them knew that time would pass and he'd one day give her another piece of seaglass, beside the same piece of sea.

'I think we should go in the tent now,' Eliot said, after she'd slipped the ring onto her right pinky finger.

'You do?'

'The fire's about to go, and it's getting cold.'

She nodded and made her way into the tent while he took a bottle down to the shoreline and collected some water to pour over the campfire.

He joined her a minute later and lay down beside her. She pulled the stack of blankets over them both and without any fear, without any worry about losing him, and without wanting to spend a second longer in her groundhog year, Cleo kissed Eliot.

Outside the tent, the waves bathed the shore, and pebbles moved under the tide, and under the stars the snow sparkled.

Chapter 34

Boxing Day

Cleo woke up, which in itself was a good thing because they hadn't frozen to death during the night. The fact that she woke up toasty warm, her skin against Eliot's, was a really good bonus.

She had no idea what time it was, but the canvas sides of the tent glowed with a low, peachy light that suggested it was dawn, and that the sun would be rising in the not-too-distant future.

In the dim light Cleo kissed Eliot's sleeping face and sat up, quietly unzipping the tent, and accidentally let out an 'Oooh,' at what she saw.

Before her, the sea was an arctic baby blue under a matching dome of sky, dark ripples breaking the silky surface. The horizon glowed with a melt of indigo into watermelon into peach into butter as the sun made its way up towards Wavebreak Bay.

The tide was heading back out again. It hadn't snowed

any more during the night, though the white powder still lay thick on the cliffs, and on the stones behind their tent.

Do it, do it, do it, her brain told her. *Do it before you think too much about it.*

Cleo's wetsuit was somewhere deep in the tent, but she had no idea where. She edged forward, poking her head out of the flap, letting the icy breeze kiss her cheeks, and she fluttered her eyes closed and inhaled the salty air.

She looked up towards the row of houses, but from where they were now, nobody could see down onto this bit of the beach unless they were at the edge of one of the gardens.

Cleo reached for her beach shoes, which she'd left beside the tent, and slipped them on.

'Are you loving me and leaving me?' came a sleepy voice from within the tent.

Cleo turned to look at a dishevelled and delicious Eliot. 'I'm going for a swim.'

'You're brave,' he yawned, sitting up.

'Yep,' she agreed.

'Are you just wearing that?'

Cleo looked down at her underwear and thermal vest she'd put back on in the night. 'Yep. Keep an eye on me, and put the kettle on,' she called behind her as she stood up.

With that, she took off, jumping over the pebbles, the cold dawn air running its fingers through her hair, and plunged into the waves.

The water hit her with such a blast of cold that her heart leapt upwards in surprise and she laughed out loud, yelping a swear word into the atmosphere.

She didn't stop, wading in without hesitation, the water so cold it made her skin tingle but not in the way she feared, the beauty of it making her feel alive.

It lapped over her knees, her thighs, made her shriek as it splashed over her bits. Lowering herself, she steadied her breathing as she kicked her legs and moved her arms under the surface. And after a minute, after the initial shock, she began to relax. Not warm up, but acclimatise to the cold, and she faced out to sea, the great big ocean stretching away in front of her eyes, and she felt both like she'd come home, but also incredibly lucky to be here, all at the same time.

The sky was turning a vibrant pink now, reflecting rose gold onto the water, and, as she watched, the bright glow of sunshine broke over the clifftops, turning the snow into glittering pearlescent, and a train of bright yellow appeared on the surface of the sea, a sun glitter just for her.

'Jeeeeeeesus,' came Eliot's voice, and when she moved in the water, she saw him wading in, wearing just his pants.

Cleo laughed. 'You've gotta take the plunge, believe me, it's worth it.'

'Are you sure?'

'Yes, come on in!'

Why did she ever stop this? Her heart was soaring, as high as the plane streaking in a slow arc overhead. While she waited for Eliot to reach her, it occurred to her that perhaps what she'd actually waited for all this time was this feeling, of coming back to *her* again. She lay back, feeling the water cradle her body, the coolness stroke her neck, and she floated for a moment, vowing to not give up on this again.

'This is incredible,' Eliot said, swimming up beside her.

Cleo circled upright and put her arms around him as they both trod water. 'I'm happy.'

'You are?'

'Aren't you?'

'I'm freezing, but yes, I'm very very happy.'

He wrapped his arms around her waist and they kissed, the morning sunlight shining right on them, and she remembered when they used to swim together as teenagers, back when they were just kids and had no idea what the future would hold beyond those ocean ripples. They still didn't.

'I'm going to start a Wavebreak Bay Christmas swim and make everyone do this every year,' Cleo joked, then wondered if it really needed to be a joke after all ...

'Why not?' said Eliot. 'But one thing at a time. I'm boiling some water on the camping stove. Do you want a tea yet or will you be staying in the ocean for a while?'

'I'll stay in a little while longer,' she said.

Eliot exited the water and stumbled back up the pebbles, grabbing a towel and a blanket to wrap himself with as he busied himself with the saucepan and the small bottle of decanted milk they'd brought from the house.

Cleo pushed her arms through the saltwater, swimming in a slow circle, enjoying the feel of her muscles waking up after far too long of being away from the water. Blissful.

Still. Very cold though. Next time she would definitely wear her trusty wetsuit. *Next time.* The thought made her smile to herself.

For now, her soggy knick-knacks and now see-through

vest had given up trying to keep her warm, and she was ready to snuggle up inside that blanket with her Eliot.

Cleo swam in towards the beach until her feet hit the pebbles and sand once again, and just as she was about to stand up in the remaining water, she heard a noise on the.cliff.

Looking up and shielding her eyes from the sunrise, she saw, like a trail of ants, a group of people following the coast path down to the beach. Down to the bit of beach they were on.

She heard the noise again, this time picking out two familiar sounds. One was Macaroni's overexcited woof, the high-pitched one he saved for when he was truly ecstatic about something or he was having a really great dream. And one was the sound of Gloria's voice extolling how beautiful it all was, and how they all should have come down to the beach yesterday. With Macaroni and Gloria were the whole gang, rapidly advancing down the steps to the beach.

'Bugger,' Cleo whispered, and waved to catch Eliot's attention, but he'd ducked back into the tent and didn't seem to notice her. She couldn't get out now, they'd all see her next-to-naked.

'Eliot?' she called.

'Good morning, sunshine!' Rosa called back, hopping down the last couple of steps and onto the beach.

Macaroni and Rhubarb shoved past her and ran to the water's edge to bark wildly at Cleo. Rhubarb wasn't a swimmer, in fact he hated getting anything higher than his paws soggy, so he seemed to be warning her that she was getting wet. Macaroni, on the other hand, dive-bombed into the ocean and doggy-paddled his way over, spinning in the water, splashing her face with salty water and hot kisses.

'Oh, hello, everyone.' Eliot came out of the tent holding two plastic mugs. He looked between them and Cleo, and then made a *whoops* face at her.

Gabriela marched through the throng, coming right over to the shoreline, a large parcel in her arm. 'I've got your Christmas present, Clee,' she declared.

'Thanks, Gabriela, I'll open it in a mo,' Cleo replied.

'I'm going to open it for you now,' Gabriela said.

'Oh, right.' Well, there wasn't much Cleo could do about it unless she strode out of the water in all her glory.

Gabriela tore into the wrapping paper and scrunched it up, throwing it in a ball back towards the tent. She then shook out the bundle, holding it aloft for Cleo to see. 'I thought you might like to have it now.'

'A changing robe?' Cleo cried, her eyes widening at the large, black changing robe with a lining as pink as the sky above them. 'You got me a changing robe?'

'You said you wanted one a few years ago, and I checked with Mum this year and she said you still didn't have one, so . . . ' Gabriela shrugged. 'Strictly it's from both Derek and me but he can do one.'

It was the most thoughtful gift, and Cleo thought that if she wouldn't be in danger of having them harden to icicles on her face, she might have shed a tear or two in this moment. Her twin *did* care. Her sister, in her own way, *did* hear her.

'Come on then, get out.' Gabriela stepped closer, the waves washing over her ankles and shoes, holding the robe up, shielding Cleo from the others. 'Didn't know you were a nudist,' she muttered when Cleo stepped from the water into the soft lining. Gabriela wrapped the changing robe around her sister, giving her a small hug as she did so.

'Thank you so much,' Cleo said, meaning it. She looked into her sister's eyes.

'Well, I knew you'd take up swimming again at some point,' she said.

'You did?'

'Of course. You were just having a blip. We all have those sometimes. I count Derek as a blip.'

Cleo smiled. 'I do too. I'm sorry again about the picture.'

'Don't be. Come on, we've got something else for you and Eliot.'

As they made their way up the beach towards the tent, which was now surrounded by everyone setting up seats and towels that they'd brought with them, Cleo whispered to her sister, 'Was it really obvious I wasn't wearing much in there?'

'Only to me. I let the dogs out for a wee shortly before we came down and I saw you from the garden. I'd know that lily-white bum anywhere – it's just like mine.'

Gabriela winked and stepped away from Cleo to help her dad unload something from his backpack.

'We brought bacon sandwiches,' Charlie cried as if he couldn't contain himself any more.

Rosa put her hands on her hips. 'You ruined the surprise!'

'Rosa and I made them,' he continued.

'Clint swapped his unopened bottle of port with your

neighbours so we could get some extra bacon and bread.' Stuart smiled, and Clint looked bashful and turned to face the cliff, but not before saying . . .

'Well, we all wanted to say we're sorry.'

The rest murmured in consent, while Cleo waved at them to stop.

'We bought flasks of tea and coffee down too, and hot chocolate,' said Cleo's mum, unzipping another bag.

Cleo hugged her changing robe around herself and watched the scene unfold, hardly believing what she was seeing. They were doing this for her, looking after *her*.

'Can I help—' she started.

'Nope.' Rosa cut her off. 'You eat one of these.' As she handed Cleo a tinfoil-wrapped sandwich, she murmured, 'Did you tell him?'

Cleo nodded.

'And?'

'We're just going to be friends . . .' Rosa's face fell.

'Whaaaaaat? Eliot!' Eliot, now wearing a sarong towel, a hoodie and a ski jacket, came over to them. 'You're just going to be friends. Do you even know what an amazing girl you have here, *throwing herself* at you?'

'I mean, I wasn't—'

'You told her we were just going to be friends?' Eliot smiled. 'Friends who do this?'

Eliot grabbed Cleo around the waist, one hand on the back of her neck, and dipped her backwards, giving her an elaborate, movie-style kiss and causing a surprised, '*Whooo!*' from their friends and families.

Rosa laughed. 'All right, all right, that's quite enough of that, actually. I take it back.'

'What's the time?' Cleo asked, suddenly. Rosa showed her her watch face. 'Oh sugar, I should really head back up soon and get in the shower, my shift starts in an hour.'

She was about to stand and start packing up the tent when Rosa grabbed the sleeve of her robe.

'No, it doesn't. *My* shift starts in an hour.'

'What do you mean?'

'I'm covering your shift; you now have the day off today. Perhaps still shower, but there's no rush.'

'Rosa, you don't have to do that, you're on holiday until January.'

She shrugged. 'It's the least I can do for you after you let me gatecrash your Christmas. Take the day off, spend Boxing Day with your family, or Eliot, or on your own. However you want.'

Cleo paused, guilt stabbing at her and telling her not to accept.

As if reading her mind, Rosa said, 'I'm not asking your permish, Cleo. Come on, let's go in the water, then I'll have a quick shower at the top of the beach, go to work, and afterwards I'll come and pick up the rest of my things.'

'Wait, what do you mean?' Cleo asked, confused.

'She means,' Gloria said, walking to the shore and flinging off her coat to reveal a purple, leopard-print one-piece swimming costume, 'that we've all come down here for a swim because you told us to, so are you in there, or are you a square?'

Gloria dived into the water like it was a plunge pool on a tropical island and not December in the Atlantic, but the others took their time, some very reluctantly, stripping to swimming costumes or trunks or wetsuits, or all of the above.

Cleo leapt into the tent and changed into her wetsuit in a flash, just like she used to do when she'd wake up and couldn't get to the beach quick enough. She emerged from the tent, put her beach shoes back on her feet, reached behind her and pulled up the zipper, and noticed her family were still huddled around, shivering.

Only Gabriela was striding out with confidence, though the expletives dripping from her mouth told them all exactly what she thought of the freezing water.

'Bugger it.' Eliot whooped, and ran back into the sea in his pants.

'Are you all OK?' Cleo asked, looking at her parents, Uncle Stu, Charlie and Rosa.

'Just plucking up some courage, love,' Bryce answered.

Uncle Stu nodded, wrapping his arms around his son. 'We're not as used to these Christmas swims as you guys are, we might need a moment.'

'You don't have to come in if you don't want,' Cleo stated. 'I love the gesture, but it is literally snowy out here.'

'We do want to,' cut in Felicity, looking at the others, who nodded. 'We just ... don't quite know how to take the plunge, as it were.'

'I can help with that.' Cleo smiled, taking the lead. She certainly got how they were feeling, and it was nice to know that, in a way, they were understanding her better too.

'There's actually no need to be scared, and even if that is what you feel, we've all got your back.'

She took Uncle Stu by the hand, since he seemed the most petrified and also the most unsteady on the pebbles, not being the owner of trusty beach shoes.

'It is going to be cold when you get in, but trust me, once you've acclimatised, it's the best feeling in the whole world, out there, in the water, the sunrise glowing against you.'

'Shiiiiiiit, though, Cleo,' Stu said as she led him into the sea and the tiny wave crest brushed over his shins. Suddenly he turned back and called, 'Bryce, get a photo of me. Kaleb will never believe this if I don't have proof.'

Cleo kept leading him in. 'Don't stop now, don't overthink it, just keep following me, keep breathing, keep going. We're heading out to where Gabriela is, OK, focus on her.' Her twin was lying on her back on the surface of the water, about ten metres away, hair pooling around her and pink light bathing her.

'OK,' said Stu, nodding, and grimacing, as he followed her into the water.

Once he was in, and she'd got him and the others breathing calmly and safely, she trod water and looked around, appreciating the sight. Her family and friends might be shrieking, splashing each other, cursing, and threatening to get out at any moment, but they were all here, with her, *seeing her*. She couldn't have asked for any more.

I did this, she thought. *I'm coming back to myself.*

As Cleo looked back at the view of her Bay from the ocean – with white blankets covering the town, the cliffs, the beach — the wispy clouds above began to sprinkle a gentle confetti of snowflakes on the swimmers. Tiny Christmas kisses.

'If I get out first, I'm taking that changing robe back!' shouted Gabriela, spitting out a gobful of seawater.

As Cleo swam back towards her extended family, offering her arms for balance, suggesting breathing tips for dealing with the shock of the cold, encouraging them, cheering with them when they too realised how damn good it could feel, she remembered a long-forgotten dream of wanting to be a part of a swimming club. She'd always loved the idea that the ocean was there for everyone, and that included her.

For the second time that morning, the second time of many more to come, Cleo was welcomed back into the sea.

Chapter 35

The snowfall over Wavebreak Bay was still lingering. Every other day it would appear to be melting under the winter sunrays, thinning in places, getting pockmarks on the surface, become less blanket-like and more blobby. And then a cloud would roll back over and sprinkle fresh powder over the Jurassic Coast and the excitement would start all over again.

The gritters had managed to get on top of things and over the last few days of December, the houseguests had managed to go on their merry ways.

Gloria, Stuart and Charlie had gone first, heading back up to Bath to reunite with Kaleb. Charlie was feeling chuffed with his performance as the murderer, and that nobody got it until Gabriela pounded on his and Stuart's bedroom door the morning of the twenty-seventh to say she'd figured out it was him.

Eliot's grandparents were now spending the rest of the

holidays and New Year's at the Wavebreak Views Hotel, much to their delight, after Lucy was able to pull a few strings with the owner on behalf of Eliot and get them a late cancellation room. Eliot had confirmed that they had a balcony in their room, and from there they could see if there was any change in the snowy weather, if they didn't fancy checking on the TV instead.

Cleo was back in her flat, leaving Gabriela to hang out in her childhood home and get a little space, something Cleo was enjoying having again, too. Although she was making the most of having Eliot around hers a lot more.

Business at Coacean continued to ebb and flow between Christmas and New Year. Merrily busy at times, blissfully quiet at others.

And in the quiet times, Cleo found herself lost in thought, gazing out at the ocean, but not with fear, not berating herself yet again for letting her hobby slide, but with a longing, an idea, some sparkles of excitement.

'Darling, what are your plans for New Year's?' Felicity asked Cleo on the twenty-ninth.

Cleo had practically finished the brunch shift when Felicity interrupted her thoughts. She was going to change in the loos and then head out for a swim, despite the cold, despite the fact a big part of her would like to go home, take a warm shower. In fact, the Cleo of the past few years would have found a million excuses – *I'm too tired, it's a bit overcast, I forgot to bring a towel* – but she knew she would love it once she was in, just like she was telling the others on Boxing Day. She just needed to keep that in mind.

'No big plans,' she answered. 'Just enjoying the night. How about you?'

'Well . . . ' her mum started, glancing at Lucy. The two of them were standing together beside the restaurant's laptop. 'We've just had a request for a huge booking. A Christmas party that wasn't able to happen because of the snow now wants a table for New Year's Eve instead.'

'Can you fit them in?' Cleo asked with trepidation.

'We caaaaaaaaan,' Lucy chimed in. 'But I'm going to need more staff, if you aren't doing anything?'

In a way, Cleo had been waiting for this moment. It had been weighing on her mind, when to broach what she wanted to say, and now seemed as good a time as any.

Cleo answered, 'Actually, could we speak on the decking for a moment?'

There was nobody sat outside at that time, and the three of them had the space to themselves. Cleo's hands were shaking, not from the cold. She wasn't used to asking for what she wanted. And in truth, she didn't know quite what it was that she wanted yet, but she knew it had something to do with the water.

'I don't want to work New Year's,' she declared.

'Oh. OK, that's fine.' Felicity laughed with relief.

'It's just that I do take on all the holidays and all the rubbish shifts, so this time, I want to . . . I want to say no.'

'Cleo, that's *fine*.' Lucy smiled. 'I thought you were about to quit! You can always say no. I'm sorry if I made you feel otherwise.'

'You didn't – I'm not blaming you for my problems. I'm a

grown-up and I should be able to say how I feel, but it would seem I am not very good at that. I'm working on it.'

Lucy nodded. 'Consider yourself crossed off the maybe list for New Year's.'

'Sorry.'

'You have nothing to apologise for.'

'OK.' Cleo had a little throat clear and then said, 'There is one more thing.'

'Let's hear it, get it all out there.' Lucy gave her a grin.

Cleo wanted to grab a handful of snow and eat it just to moisten her throat, but she didn't want to look weird.

'Right. OK. So here's the thing. Here it is. It's coming!' Cleo twirled a lock of her hair and then pulled her hand away, remembering that she'd heard you were supposed to project confidence in these situations, so she stretched her arms wide and said, 'I think I might want to go part time. At some point. Maybe.'

'Oh!' said Lucy.

'And you'd like a hug?' added her mum. 'What's happening?'

'No, sorry.' Cleo put her arms down by her sides. 'I've just been trying to have a really good think about what I want,' she said, adding, in her mind, *for a change*. 'I really, really liked getting back in the sea at Christmas, and I know it's early days, and that at the moment it's just a hobby, I suppose, but I was looking at courses last night about open-water safety and things like that.'

She looked down at her hands, her fingers having tangled themselves together, and continued, 'I don't know, I just thought maybe if I had a bit more time, I'd be able—' She stopped to correct herself from making it sound like time was the issue. It wasn't. It was her mindset. 'I'd *let myself* dedicate a bit more space for something like this.'

Cleo looked at her mum, worried she'd be offended that Cleo was wanting to step back – just a touch – from the family business. What was she thinking? She was so replaceable! Oh God, she was about to lose it all.

'I think it's a wonderful idea,' her mum said, and Lucy nodded.

Cleo blinked at them both. 'You do?'

'Yes. Can you give us a bit of time to see what we could offer you?'

'No way.' Cleo shook her head, and then briskly added, 'I'm joking, I'm completely joking, of course. Thank you. And I'll figure out exactly what *I* want, and come back to you.'

Lucy headed back inside, but Felicity held back, taking Cleo's arm. 'I actually need to ask you something, too, regarding what happened between you and, erm, Eliot, the other night.'

'Oh God.' Cleo felt a blush rising. 'Muuuuuum . . . '

'I don't need to know the details or anything, it's just, I thought you should know, I hadn't spoken to him yet about the second-branch-in-the-US idea we discussed a while back. But your dad and I have progressed with the business plan, and I was going to broach it with Eliot soon. But, how do you feel about that now? In respect to the two of you . . . you know . . . '

303

'Yep, yep, I know. Um . . . ' Cleo hesitated. 'To be honest, the thought of him not coming back every winter is, well . . . '

'I can imagine.'

'But I want him to be happy, so . . . '

'I can believe that, too.'

'You have to ask him, Mum,' Cleo said. 'It has to be his decision, not mine.'

Cleo always worked on New Year's Eve. Until this year. This year she'd said 'no', which hadn't been the disaster she'd expected; Lucy had just said, 'OK.'

And even better, Rosa and Eliot had also been able to wangle the night off. In all her years living in Wavebreak Bay, Cleo had never been to one of the New Year's soirées held jointly by the hotel and the youth hostel. It was the one night a year that the two businesses came together, knowing that neither could stop the other celebrating on the clifftop, so they joined forces.

Tonight, the Wavebreak Views Hotel would be hosting a formal dinner dance inside the ballroom, while the Oceanside Youth Hostel would be throwing a relaxed pizza party in their communal kitchen. Then, on the clifftop between the two venues, there would be a stage with a band playing a number of classic and modern songs intertwined, until midnight.

Because of it being the off-season, it was always a lot of fun but never riotous. You'd think that youth hostellers and fancy hotel patrons wouldn't mix all that well, but without fail, every year, guests came away saying how nice the whole thing was, how they got chatting to interesting people, how they didn't know they liked string covers of Bruno Mars songs so much until now.

Cleo knew this because she was usually working the brunch shift on New Year's Day as well, and people came in to eat kippers on toast and rave about the fun they'd had.

Tonight, there was a warm merriment inside Oceanside Youth Hostel, and Cleo was enjoying herself.

'I haven't been to one of these for years,' Gabriela commented to her as they went to grab some more pizza.

'Did you come for pizza or did you join in with the dinner dancing?' Cleo asked, her tone more accusatory than she'd intended.

'I don't remember, I think I got pissed on champagne.' She paused. 'No wait, I did dance actually. I recall tangoing with one of the barmen.'

Cleo practically dropped her plate. 'You don't tango!'

'No, I don't,' Gabriela agreed. 'I didn't know what I was doing.'

Her sister sashayed off with her plate of pizza and Cleo was left to gather her jaw up off the floor. Sometimes, Gabriela surprised her.

Following her back to the end of the long wooden table they were sitting at, Cleo tucked into her pizza, soon tuning in to the conversation next to them. A small group, three guys and two girls, all in their early twenties, Cleo guessed, and with a variety of global accents, were arguing about taking a New Year's Day dip in the sea.

'Come *onnnn*,' cried one of the women, the bangles on

her arm tinkling as she banged her fist on the table. 'So you can all skydive out of a plane but you can't face a bit of cold water?'

A man complete with man-bun laughed. 'It's an absolute no from me. You're not catching me freezing my ass off in the Atlantic in minus temperatures.'

'But look,' said Bangle Girl, shoving her phone at them, 'it'll be cold but so sunny tomorrow. Don't you think it would be an awesome way to start the year?'

'I think you're on your own,' the other woman said, glancing at the others. 'Sorry, hun.'

'But I don't want to go in on my own,' Bangle Girl sighed, and Cleo thought she knew how she felt.

When she was younger, she'd go in all the time on her own. Then she had started to feel like she couldn't go in without somebody with her, somebody to distract her from any difficult thoughts that came up if she stopped and was still for too long.

Now, Cleo was teaching herself that it was OK to do these things on your own again (safe conditions permitting, obvs). But she knew how this girl felt, just wanting someone else to be there to share the experience, to plunge into the water with her.

And so Cleo found herself leaning sideways, wiping mozzarella from her chin, and declaring to Bangle Girl, 'I'll go with you!'

Bangle Girl turned in her seat. 'What?'

'I'll go for a swim with you in the morning. Sorry to have eavesdropped.'

'That's OK,' Bangle Girl said, her pink-lipsticked smile spreading. 'That would be great. Are you staying in the hostel too?'

'Actually, I'm local,' Cleo said, immediately regretting saying the word 'local' in a creepy way. She pressed on. 'I used to swim on this beach all the time and I've just started up again. So I can go in with you, if you want to meet down on the beach in the morning?'

'Yesssss!' Bangle Girl cried, sliding across and throwing her arms around Cleo's neck, her bracelets quivering with excitement. 'See you tomorrow! Would ten work for you?'

'Ten sounds perfect,' Cleo said, and turned back to her group with a grin, stuffing the last of her pizza in her mouth. 'Shall we go outside and join the party on the clifftop?'

When they stepped out of the hostel, the winds plucked at tendrils of Cleo's hair, and she pulled it back into the hairband she was keeping on her wrist.

She was greeted with the scent of warm crêpes from a stand to her left, and the tinkles of laughter coming from the Prosecco bar on her right. Before them, a stage had been erected and it currently held a folky violinist duo who were really going for it, much to the whoops of the crowd. Pink lighting pooled on the pair, and reflected back on the faces of Cleo and her friends.

The hardy glass fencing that wrapped around the outer border of the hotel was encompassing the New Year guests, so there was no danger of anyone drunkenly tumbling over the side of the hill.

As she listened to the music, accepted a drink from Eliot,

and soaked it all in, Cleo thought about how much had changed over the past week. She'd done it, she'd unbroken the broken record of her life, braved up and told Eliot how she felt, taken the plunge back into the ocean. Could she keep it up? Could she find a way to not drift back into old patterns? Yes ... She wasn't sure how, but change had come, and it didn't need to stop there.

'Goodbye, old Cleo,' she whispered into the winds that were soon to be part of the year before.

And then she danced with her feet in the snow, and laughed, and drank, and when the countdown to midnight came, Cleo meant every syllable when she cried, 'Happy New Year!'

'What are you deep in thought about?' Rosa asked, as she and Cleo sat on top of a bench, the night sky above them, midnight behind them, and chocolatey crêpes in their hands, the snowfall having started up again and dropping flakes onto their heads.

'The future,' Cleo answered. 'What about you?'

'Also the future. I reckon everybody around the world tonight thinks about the future.'

'I'm also thinking about my crêpe.'

'Mmmm,' Rosa agreed, stuffing in the rest of hers.

Cleo did the same and then faced her friend. 'Tell me your New Year's wish.'

'I don't think I have *a* New Year's wish,' Rosa answered.

'Tell me one of them, then.'

Rosa fell into thought, and behind them the music played.

on, the colourful stage lights causing the grass by their feet to glow.

'I wish I could be truthful with myself.'

Cleo raised her eyebrows. 'What do you mean?'

'I mean that I tend to put off thinking about things because I'm worried about the conclusions I'll come to. Case in point: that girl I told you about back in New Zealand. I still think about her. But I never let myself think too hard because I don't want to close doors. Or realise I took the wrong one or something. You know?'

'I think that makes sense.' Cleo nodded. 'That was a solid answer. I thought we were going to say things like, "This year I wish to . . . " I don't know . . . "walk five miles on the coast path" or something.'

'God no, that sounds awful,' Rosa said with a laugh. 'What about you? You got your Christmas wish.' She nodded back towards Eliot who was with their other friends, chatting. Gabriela sat beside him, as if she felt more comfortable being in his vicinity. 'What's your wish for next year?'

'This year,' Cleo corrected.

Rosa laughed and raised her glass in the air. 'Yes, this year.'

'I suppose, if we're giving very philosophical answers like you did, I would say . . . ' She thought for a moment, looking down towards the tiny lights of Wavebreak Bay. At any other night during winter, with the exception of around Christmas, most of those lights would be dark, the beach town sleeping. But tonight it still twinkled with lights inside windows and the glow of a couple of campfires on the dark beaches.

If she looked out to sea, she could make out three, if not

309

four, boats on the inky horizon. One of them seemed large and with lights strung along the length of it, and Cleo suspected it was a cruise ship sailing silently past.

'I would say,' Cleo continued, 'that my New Year's wish would be to be more authentic. With everyone else but also with me.'

'You made a good start with it, with Eliot.'

'Yep,' she agreed. 'Let's just see if it can continue.'

'I think you'll do it,' Rosa said.

'Did someone say my name?' her sister barked from behind them, all of a sudden.

'No.' Cleo laughed. 'We're talking about New Year's wishes.'

Eliot came and stood beside her, and as the crowd broke out into another rousing rendition of 'Auld Lang Syne' – the third that night – he leaned over and said to her, 'Can I tell you my New Year's wish?'

'You absolutely have to tell me yours.' She smiled.

'I wish you'd come to San Francisco with me this summer.'

Chapter 36

January

Gabriela was in a funk. Not in the same way many people got the January blues. This was more like Gabriela's usual moodiness, topped with her heartbreak, sprinkled with lethargy and with a sprig of resentment jammed in the top.

She was still staying with their parents, working remotely, though since she shared an office job with Derek she seemed to spend most of her time marking herself as being 'in a meeting' and job hunting on the internet.

'He should leave, not me,' Gabriela grumbled when Cleo asked what kind of jobs she was going for.

'Have you told him that? Maybe he'd be happy to? Hasn't his dream always been to become a chef?'

Gabriela huffed out of her nose, then added, 'No, I want to be the one who gets an exciting new job.'

'Right.'

Her sister sighed. 'I'm fed up of offices anyway. I want to do something more active.'

Cleo nodded. 'OK. What like?'

'I don't know, Cleo, stop grilling me, I'm not made of cheese.'

Cleo laughed, but the look Gabriela shot her told her that wasn't intended as a joke, so she moved on. 'Is Mum or Dad here?'

'Probably,' Gabriela answered with classic vagueness.

Cleo left Gabriela to it, and wandered out of the kitchen. 'Hello, Bluebs, have you seen my mum or dad?' she asked the cat, who was asleep in a pool of sunshine. Blueberry ignored her, about as much help as her sister, so Cleo carried on her hunt. 'Mum?' she called.

'Up here, love,' came her mum's voice.

At the top of the stairs, she found her mum lying on her back in the middle of the room.

'Mum! Are you OK?'

'Yes, yes, fine,' Felicity said, sitting up. 'I've been doing some January yoga on YouTube and when it finished, I was so relaxed I didn't fancy getting up, so I just stayed here. What can I do for you?'

Cleo sat on the floor opposite her mum. 'Do you and Dad still have our kayaks in the garage?'

'Yes, I think so. Probably behind fifty thousand other things, but I do think they're still in there.'

'Mind if I get mine out? It's such a nice morning, I fancy heading out on the water.'

Felicity stood up and flexed her legs. 'My water baby is well and truly back, isn't she?'

'I think she just might be,' Cleo laughed.

'Oh, take your sister out with you, won't you?'

'I guarantee you Gabriela will have no interest in coming kayaking.'

'Ask her? She liked swimming with you on Boxing Day, and you used to go in together all the time.'

'Fiiiiine,' Cleo huffed, apparently having reverted to being a stroppy teenager. She went back downstairs to where Gabriela was looking at Derek's LinkedIn profile.

'I updated all of this for him,' she seethed. 'And I still have his login. Shall I make a few *new* updates?'

'Absolutely not,' Cleo said, shutting the laptop. 'Fancy coming kayaking with me?'

'I'm working, Cleo.'

'Are you, though? At this point you might as well just call in sick.'

Gabriela toyed with the idea for all of three seconds before opening her laptop back up and sending her manager a message to say she was taking the rest of the day off.

'Fine. Let's go kayaking.'

Cleo pulled open the door to the garage, the wood grating against the concrete and pushing the latest thin layer of snow aside.

'Could you give me a hand?' she called back to Gabriela, who was leaning against the wall opposite, looking the epitome of Instagram perfection in her teal full-length wetsuit.

She sighed and put her phone into her waterproof bag, then strode over to help shove the door out of the way.

'Thank you,' Cleo said. 'Hope it didn't get your wetsuit cobwebby.' She hoped nothing of the sort.

313

'It didn't,' Gabriela replied, and looked down to brush off any potential speck of grime.

Cleo stepped into the garage and pulled the light cord. An amber glow filled the space, barely adding any additional illumination to the sunlight that pooled in through the open doors and dusty windows.

'Ew,' Gabriela remarked under her breath, giving off further Alexis from *Schitt's Creek* vibes.

Among the tools and boxes and bikes it wasn't hard to spot the two large, orange kayaks, their bulky plastic frames bulbous in one corner of the garage.

Cleo stepped her way over to them, swatting at a cobweb or twelve en route, and smiled. *There you are.*

God, she'd missed kayaking, nearly as much as she'd missed swimming. Her dip with Bangle Girl – whose name was actually Flora – on the beach on New Year's Day had been such fun, and Cleo had felt so good being the one to encourage her into the water, that she wanted to be able to invite people kayaking, too. Even if it had to start with her reluctant twin.

Cleo clonked the kayaks out from where they were stacked, manoeuvring them towards her sister who begrudgingly dragged them out of the shed.

The sea was silky-smooth today. With the snow still sitting like icing upon the clifftops, it could almost be mistaken for a giant ice rink. The sun sparkled on it in a vast gold wake across the surface.

Gabriela and Cleo bump-bump-bumped the kayaks down the steps and onto the beach, navigating the pebbles in their beach shoes.

'When was the last time you went kayaking?' Gabriela asked as the two of them stood side by side on the shore.

Cleo tied her hair into a high ponytail, the curls lifting in the breeze. 'Gosh, years ago. Maybe five or six years? How about you?'

'Probably soon before I moved away for uni,' Gabriela answered.

'Are you nervous?'

'Am I, shit.'

'Right. Let's go then.'

Dragging the kayaks into the shallow water, Gabriela stepped in quickly, so that she could turn back and say to Cleo, 'Give me a shunt, would you?'

Cleo did so, pushing on the end of the kayak until it slid onto the surface of the sea, then climbed into her own while Gabriela adjusted herself for a selfie.

'Let's have a photo together,' she called, and on auto-pilot the twins got into the same position they always had in photos, with Gabriela holding up the phone – which once had been a waterproof camera – and Cleo grinning behind her.

Taking her seat and leaning back against the back rest, her knees bent, she used her oar to glide herself across the water towards her sister. It all came back to her, how to hold the paddle, what to do to make a turn, how delicious the feeling was when it dribbled cold dots onto your skin every time you lifted the paddle out of the water. Cleo couldn't help but smile to herself.

'What are you smiling about? Are you laughing at me?'

Gabriela demanded, her kayak drifting in a circle away from Cleo. Gabriela tried to turn in her seat to glare back at Cleo but caused it to wobble and gripped on tightly.

Cleo moved her own kayak alongside Gabriela's. 'Remember. Do this to make it stop,' she said. 'Then hold your paddle like this to move forward.'

Gabriela wobbled in her kayak again and then did what Cleo suggested. 'Thanks,' she murmured.

'Shall we go that way?' Cleo used her paddle to point down the coast in the direction of Seaton.

'OK,' Gabriela said, keeping her eyes on the water. 'Stay next to me, Cleo?'

'I will.'

They paddled forward for a couple of minutes, keeping it slow, until Gabriela looked up and to her left, letting out a 'Wow! Look, Cleo!'

They were alongside the cliff where their parents lived, and from this spot on the water they could see their dad waving down at them from the back garden.

Gabriela took her hand off her paddle to wave, then clamped it back on quickly. 'Look back at the town from here, isn't it weird?'

'What do you mean?' Cleo chuckled.

'You just ... don't often see it from this perspective, you know. It's been a while. It's quite pretty, really, our little bay.'

'Especially with the snow still on the ground.'

It was overcast that day, but with plump white clouds that brought no threat of rain, and it meant the morning frost was still coating the grass, giving the fields a sugared effect. The clifftops themselves still proudly wore a sheet of snow, hard and patchy, but hanging on.

The red sandstone cliffs shone brightly in contrast with the pale pastels of the sky, ground and sea, and since they were paused and dawdling, Cleo soaked in the view while her fingertips trailed in the water beside her.

Cleo tilted her head to the sky and closed her eyes. This felt so right, so *her*, to be back floating in her kayak, trickles of cool water dripping on her when she lifted the oar in and out of the ocean. All was calm, all was bright. She was an idiot for ever having stopped doing this.

That wasn't fair. Perhaps part of coming out of this rut was to stop beating herself up for things that were now in the past. At the time, she'd felt too busy to kayak. Then she'd felt too scared, or unmotivated, or down. And now she was, maybe, one stroke of the paddle at a time, moving again.

Cleo fluttered open her eyes and glanced at her sister, who also seemed mesmerised. 'Are you having a nice time?' she asked.

'It makes a change from job-hunting. Or trying not to check up on Derek.' She laughed. 'Or you know, working, which is what I was supposed to be doing. Thanks. For making me do this.'

It was rare, but nice, when Gabriela laughed at herself. She could be quite funny at times, and Cleo missed the silly side of her.

'Come on then,' Gabriela said, facing forward again. 'Let's keep going, I want to be back home before I need to wee.'

*

'Cleo, I need a wee,' Gabriela called an hour or so later.

'Already?' Cleo called back from her own kayak.

'Don't shame me, let's just take a break.' Gabriela reached her hand in the water and flicked a splash at Cleo.

Actually, Cleo was ready for a break anyway. They'd been moving slowly, very relaxed, but still. There were muscles in her shoulders and arms that were waking up after a long hibernation and were getting a little irate about the fact.

Cleo pointed at a cove with a small but deep pebble beach. It opened to a valley in the centre, so they could pull in there and move them and their kayaks back enough that they wouldn't risk being in the line of any cliff fall, which you did have to be careful of along the coast. 'Let's pull in there for a bit.'

'Do you see public toilets?' Gabriela squinted.

'I see public bushes,' replied Cleo.

They turned their kayaks carefully and paddled into the shore, Gabriela making Cleo hop out first so she could pull her in a bit before she stepped out.

'All right,' Cleo huffed as she walked backwards, pulling both kayaks away from the water's edge. 'Do you want to find somewhere to pee and I'll keep watch? Gabriela?'

She dropped the kayaks and turned round, just as Gabriela skipped back over. 'All done.'

'Already?'

'I'm a fast urinator. One of my many talents.' Gabriela sat down on the edge of the kayak and opened her waterproof bag. 'I brought snacks,' she said, tossing a bag of Haribo Tangfastics to Cleo.

'Good thinking,' Cleo said, sitting by her sister and pulling the bag open.

They sat for a while, catching their breaths, resting their muscles.

'I think you might be enjoying this,' Cleo commented.

'I am,' said Gabriela. 'It's surprisingly soothing. I'd forgotten.'

'I hope it's as soothing on the way back.'

'What do you mean?'

Cleo looked out at the sea. It wasn't choppy, per se, but the ripples were definitely more pronounced, now like the spiky top of a lemon meringue pie. 'I think the wind's picking up, which means we'll have to work harder on the way back, if it isn't going in our direction.'

'Might we drift out to sea?'

Cleo sensed worry in her usually cucumber-cool sister, and looked at her. 'I wouldn't have thought so.'

'You "wouldn't have thought so"? That's fine then! Let's go!' Gabriela got to her feet, dripping with remnants of seawater and sarcasm.

'Well, I can't say for sure, I'm not Triton.'

'What's that, an app?'

'The sea-ruler guy. The God.'

'The dad from *The Little Mermaid*?' Gabriela was getting visibly frustrated now.

Cleo stood up too. 'Look, never mind. I'm saying, I can't guarantee anything because the sea does what she wants, and I don't want to say it'll be fine just to make you feel better when I don't know.'

'I don't want to go back out on the kayak,' Gabriela stated, after they watched the sea for a few minutes, how it was turning rougher right in front of their eyes, and Cleo glanced at her sister, surprised to see she looked genuinely worried. 'It's been too long since I've been on one of these, Cleo. I feel a bit freaked out, to be honest.'

Cleo couldn't make her, so had to respect her decision. 'All right then.'

Gabriela pulled out her phone. 'Who shall we call to pick us up?'

'Mum's taken the car, she's gone to run some errands . . .' Cleo didn't really know anyone else with a car who she'd call for a lift if it wasn't an emergency. At least, nobody who wouldn't likely be at work right now.

'Why don't you have a car?' Gabriela asked.

'I don't know. I'd like one, but I just use public transport.'

'You should get one.'

'All right, one thing at a time. It's not like me having a car right now would solve anything.' Cleo checked the maps app on her phone. 'Look, we're only about five miles along the coast from Wavebreak Bay. Why don't we just walk it, along the coast path?'

'In our wetsuits? Do you enjoy chafing?'

'It'll be fine. We have trainers in our bags, and water, and sweets . . . some . . . a few left anyway.'

Gabriela pondered for a minute, looking between the kayaks, the path up the hill, and the water.

'How long do you think it would take?'

'Two or three hours? Ish?'

'You aren't thinking we drag the kayaks along with us, though?'

Cleo laughed. 'God, no. We'll leave them here, at the back of the beach. The tide won't reach them, and later today, when Mum's back, I'll borrow her car and drive back over to get them. You can come with me to help.'

'Or I could just wait here with them and you can pick us all up?' Gabriela sat back down and had another Haribo.

Cleo put her hands on her hips. 'How warm are you right now? Sitting there in a damp wetsuit, in the shade, with frost around you, and the wind picking up? Lovely and toasty?'

'No,' Gabriela said grudgingly.

'Maybe it would be better not to sit here another three hours then.'

'No, maybe not.' Standing, Gabriela let out a final dramatic sigh and then smiled. 'All right, sister, you've won me over. Let's take a lovely hike together on the great British coastal path.'

Chapter 37

After they'd switched their beach shoes for socks and trainers (not perfect for coast-path walking, but better), and pulled the kayaks to somewhere where it would easier to come and collect them from a nearby road later, Cleo and Gabriela set off, ascending the first of rather a lot of ups and downs that would be part of their hike that day.

In the cold weather, the lack of sunrays poking through the thick clouds had left the frost untouched into this mid-morning. Each grass blade was coated in sugary white, and the well-trampled slush underfoot had frozen hard, the women's trainers making soft thudding sounds as they walked.

Despite the beautiful conditions it was hard going, and by the top of the first hill, both were panting.

'Wetsuits . . .' Cleo said, 'are not . . . great . . . for hiking.'

'True story,' Gabriela agreed, reaching around to unzip the back of hers, letting in a flow of cold air. 'Ooo, that's it, cool Mama's sweat right off.'

Cleo laughed. 'Sorry I didn't check the weather before we went out.'

'I didn't check either,' her sister replied. 'You don't have to always assume all the responsibility.'

'I'm working on that, actually.'

'Good. That said, I couldn't have done this today without you.'

'Nah, you're a natural out there, you would have been fine.' Cleo brushed away the compliment.

'I know. But you're the one that motivated me away from that laptop. So thanks.'

They walked on, through a couple of fairly flat fields, Cleo turning over her sister's words. 'I'm thinking of ... I don't know ... looking into courses about water safety or open-water swimming or something.'

'But you know all that?'

'I do,' Cleo agreed. 'But it would be kinda cool to be able to share it with other people. Like you said, *motivate* them or whatever.'

'Like on Boxing Day? When you got everyone in the sea? That was pretty cool.'

'Yeah, like that.' Cleo's mind drifted, settling on the view. 'I don't think I'll ever get over the size of the sea, you know,' she said.

'The size of the sea?'

'You know, it just looks so ... ' She gesticulated to the

ocean that stretched beyond the horizon. 'So massive. It puts things in perspective. I like that.'

'Me too. Hey, you know what *I'm* working on?' Gabriela plucked at a dried, twiggy bush on the way past. 'Putting things in perspective.'

'You are?' Cleo asked. 'In what way? You've always been level-headed.'

'I have?'

Cleo thought about it. 'You can bring the flair at times, but you're quite … I don't know. I don't know why I'm trying to explain your own personality to you. Please, continue.'

'Thank you, sister.' Gabriela nodded. 'I suppose I'm just trying to be a bit more chill, now that everything has sunk in. And see it as a bit of an opportunity.'

'In what way?'

Gabriela was quiet for a minute, looking out to sea. 'I really did want to come home, you know, after uni. I never intended to just … not come back.' She looked at Cleo. 'Sorry for breaking my promise.'

'That's OK,' Cleo replied. 'We all grow up, it's OK that you changed your mind.'

'It was just so easy to stay there, and I got a good job, and I kept meaning to think about moving back, then I met Derek, who's never been much into the seaside and I just … '

'Got stuck in a rut?'

'Yeah.' Gabriela nodded. 'You know that feeling?'

'I have been in a Groundhog Year for the past who knows how long and am only just getting out of it now, so yes.'

'Well. Perhaps you've inspired me over the past week.'

Cleo laughed. 'Excuse me, I need to just fall down dead at the admittance that you, Gabriela Clearwater, would want to be more like me.'

'All right—'

'I'm sorry, are we walking through hell? Is that why it's frozen over up here?'

'I don't want to be like you, so get off your high horse,' Gabriela said, but her voice was teasing. 'I'm just saying, that maybe, lately, purely because I'm going through a bit of a tough time, you are a little, tiny, minutely amount . . . cool to me.'

'Did you hear that, world?' Cleo called out to sea. 'I am an *inspiration*.'

'I take it back, you're a dork.' Gabriela shook her head.

They moved to single file to take the steps down the other side of the hill, and were back to silently panting on the next ascent, so it wasn't until the top of the next hill, thirty-five minutes later, that the women spoke again.

'What are you going to do if Eliot goes back to San Francisco?' Gabriela asked.

'I don't think there's any "if" about it,' Cleo replied with a sigh. 'It's part of his life; I wouldn't ask him to change that.'

'Don't you think he'll want to change it though, now he's got together with you?'

'I don't know, Gab.' Cleo cut her off, the tone of her voice a little stronger than she intended. 'I don't know. We haven't talked about *us* in the wider concept yet. My choice, before you ask.' They continued a few steps before she asked, 'Did

Mum and Dad tell you about their plan to open a second branch in the US, and to ask Eliot to spearhead it?'

Gabriela nodded, eyes on her twin. 'Mmm-hmm. They told me on the drive back down here just before Christmas. I think they were trying to distract me.'

'What do you think?'

'Of the idea? It's good. I mean, great. In theory.' Gabriela shrugged.

Cleo could hear the hesitation in her sister's voice, the same hesitation as was in hers. 'Yeah. In theory.'

'It's just . . . ' Gabriela huffed suddenly, coming to a stop. 'I think I'm a little jealous.'

'Do *you* want to go to California?' asked Cleo, raising her eyebrows. Gabriela was impulsive and adventurous, but had never expressed much interest in taking off to work abroad before.

'I'm jealous *for you*,' she answered. 'I think Mum and Dad should send you out there for a change. Would you go to San Francisco? If Eliot asked?'

'Would you miss me if I did, dear sister?' She avoided the question, because she hadn't given an answer to Eliot yet. In fact, they hadn't yet chatted about his tipsy declaration that he wished she'd come with him. Maybe he hadn't meant it. Maybe he'd meant 'sometime', further down the line of their relationship. Not in two months' time.

But what if he had meant it . . . if he did want her to go with him . . . could she really do it?

Gabriela reached into her bag and pulled out the Haribo, of which there was only one remaining. She handed it over to Cleo. 'If you were feeling sad, I would miss the you that was happy, no matter where in the world you were.'

'Gabriela, that was a bit lovely.'

'Well, there you go. I win today's ray of sunshine award.'

They walked on, and Cleo pulled at the crotch of her wetsuit to ease the rubbing. 'Are you going to go back to Cambridge?'

Gabriela shrugged. 'I've been thinking about that a lot over the past few days. And ... I think it might be time to come home, at least for a while.'

Cleo stopped so suddenly she slid on a patch of iced-over snow and had to catch herself on her sister. 'You'd come home? Here?'

Gabriela nodded. 'Then we could be together again. What do you think?'

'When?'

'I guess as soon as I've collected my things. Maybe we could even live together? Wouldn't that be fun? Not in your crappy, tiny flat, but somewhere with separate bedrooms and maybe also separate bathrooms.'

'I ... I don't know what to say ... ' Cleo said. She'd wanted her sister back for so long; was this really happening? No more four-hour drives just to see her? No more catching up just on the odd holiday and long weekend? 'Don't say this impulsively though, Gabriela, and don't say it just because of me and my Christmas Day meltdown. You have to want this for yourself.'

'I know, I do,' said Gabriela. 'But if I come home, you'll be here, won't you? Because, I might not always act like it, but I really do care about being around you.'

Cleo remembered her words from Christmas Day, and nodded. 'Thank you.' They reached a stile between two fields. 'After you.'

'Can't I just go through the dog opening? My thighs can't take any more climbing.'

'Of course they can,' Cleo said, stepping to the top of the stile and reaching back to take her sister's hand. 'You're a tough cookie.'

'I am a tough cookie,' Gabriela repeated as if it were a mantra, and hauled herself over.

On the other side, the clifftop curled around and they saw a happy sight. The next hill over belonged to their parents' house – their childhood home. On this side, there was a break in the clouds, just a sliver, enough to let a series of sunrays down over the sea, causing a glitter on the water.

'Why have you always loved being in the ocean so much?' Gabriela asked, standing next to Cleo as they both drank in the view.

Cleo raised her arms above her head in a serene stretch. God, it was beautiful here, and something in her soul told her that she was going to do good things this coming summer. 'Because when you're out there, it's so quiet. Being in the sea gives you time to stop everything else and think. Or . . . stop thinking. Whichever you need, it provides that sanctuary.' She remembered speaking those words before, to Eliot, long ago.

Gabriela nodded. 'When you put it like that, I remember. Thanks for dragging me out this morning. I had a nice time. A very nice time, actually.'

'You did? Even with the big walk back?'

'Even with my poor blistered feet and chafed inner thighs. Thank you. And thanks for saving the day. You always were a safe pair of hands to hold on to when it came to all things watery.' Gabriela gave her a quick hug, then marched off down the final hill.

Cleo smiled to herself. Her twin didn't realise how much those words had meant to her.

Cleo had enjoyed this morning too. It might have been a frosty walk back, but it had warmed her that she and Gabriela were able to have some proper, real conversation. She felt closer to her twin sister than she had in a long time.

'Let's take a selfie,' Gabriela said.

Cleo struck a pose, and then realised her sister was waiting for her to be the one to take the picture. 'I'll be on camera-arm then,' Cleo said with a laugh.

She snapped a pic, one where the sun was on their faces, the frost in the background, and they were both grinning. They even looked a little alike in that slice of time.

Gabriela looked over Cleo's shoulder, then took the phone and zoomed in on her face. 'Yes.' She nodded. 'I like that one. Can you send it to me? I think I'll put it in my new frame. Right, first one back gets to have a long hot bath,' she called over her shoulder, having found a new drive to power-walk the rest of the way home.

Chapter 38

'Jesus, look at it out there,' Cleo said to herself later that same afternoon, after she'd emerged from her own hot bath at her parents' house, her legs rested but still weary, and rather chafed, from the hike.

The sunshine had disappeared behind a thick mulch of wet, grey clouds, that at that moment were unleashing large, sleeting raindrops onto the clifftop, pocking the remaining snow.

Her parents were holed away in their office having some kind of meeting with Lucy, and Gabriela had settled herself in front of the TV, grumbling about blisters.

Cleo dressed back into the clothes she'd been wearing when she'd come over that morning. It wasn't her ideal first-proper-date-with-Eliot outfit, but she was pretty sure he wouldn't care what she was wearing. Especially since she was going to have to cover it with her dad's biggest waterproof jacket anyway.

'Ugh, you aren't going out, are you?' Gabriela called from the sofa.

'I'm meeting Eliot. We have a date.'

'Oooooooo, kissy-kissy, *mmm, Eliot, I love yoooou.*'

'Shut up.' Cleo laughed and stepped out into the rain, which together with the wind was whipping itself into a frenzy.

Zooming down the hill, Cleo passed the back of Coacean, which seemed to be creaking on its stilts like it thought it was an old pirate ship out at sea or something, and ducked into the ice-cream parlour a little further along the seafront where she was meeting her man.

Eliot greeted her with a kiss, their rain-soaked foreheads pressing together. 'Hello, you. I nearly called to see if you wanted to cancel. If you wanted me to come to yours rather than get drenched.'

'Actually, I've been up at my parents' anyway – Gab and I had a bit of a surprise three-hour coast-path hike this afternoon so I came straight from there.'

Eliot nodded, his face clouding for a second.

'I love this place,' Cleo said as they chose a cherry-red booth beside the window of the near-empty fifties-style parlour. She and Eliot had come many times before as friends, never as boyfriend and girlfriend.

She wondered if he'd be up for sharing a milkshake with two straws.

'Milkshake with two straws to start things off?' Eliot suggested, and she could have snogged him right there and then.

'Hey, guys, how are you this evening?' Iris, the waitress, asked, all red lippy and curled hair.

Between them they ordered a strawberry milkshake to share, a bowl of butter pecan, butterscotch and honeycomb ice cream for Cleo, and a bowl of mint, peanut butter and Christmas pudding flavour ice cream for Eliot. With all the toppings they were allowed.

This right here was why she loved winter in Wavebreak Bay, times like this. In the summer, the ice-cream parlour was so crowded you often couldn't get a table, and had to eat your ices out on the beach under the watchful eyes of the gulls. In winter there was space, in all senses of the word.

'I need to talk to you about something,' Eliot said, that serious look on his face again after Iris had brought their ice creams.

Boom. Outside the window, a tall, churny wave splashed up and over the sea wall.

'A storm's a-coming,' Cleo said, grinning. Her grin dropped a little when Eliot didn't smile back.

'Your parents called me in for a meeting this morning,' he started. 'About opening up a new branch in America.'

The rain thundered down, slanted at an angle, stinging at the windows, and the streetlights illuminated the waves as the tide rolled high, the water tinged red with churned sand from the cliffs. And Cleo said, 'I know.'

'You know?'

'I knew they were going to ask you,' she explained. 'I didn't know it would be today.'

Boom. The sound of a huge crash further down the esplanade caught their attention just in time to see an enormous, foamy crest reach its claws high into the air.

'I don't know if I can do it,' Eliot said, before she had a chance to ask.

'Why not?' She held her breath.

'Because it would mean I wouldn't be able to come back for half of every year. At least not for a while. When I first opened the San Francisco branch, leaving six months in to come back here was a real struggle, business-wise.'

'Then why did you?'

'Because otherwise it would have been an even bigger struggle to not see you.'

Boom. Another wave followed, bigger than the first two, scattering pebbles over the road. She hoped Coacean would be all right down there. Luckily it was closed tonight.

'But you wanted to move forward, have something that was yours.'

He studied her. 'Have you thought about what I said at all? At New Year's?' Eliot asked, his eyes soft, his face hopeful. 'About coming to San Francisco with me this summer?'

Although Cleo had thought about it non-stop, she hadn't given herself the space she knew she needed to *really* think it through.

'I . . . '

At that moment, the lights flickered out, only further highlighting the white tips of the water leaping into the air across the road.

'Dammit, I knew that was coming,' came Iris's voice through the darkness, as a generator kicked on and the ice-cream counter buzzed to life again with a blue glow. 'Think

I'd better close up, you guys. Consider your ice creams on the house.'

'I'll give you an answer soon,' Cleo promised as they left the parlour, holding her coat hood on her head with one hand and shielding her eyes from the rain with the other.

Eliot nodded and grabbed for her hand, and they raced back up the town towards her flat, jumping over puddles and pressing themselves against shopfronts when cars drove past, spraying rainwater in all directions.

Not long after, as was the way with these things, the weather calmed down as quickly as it had turned. As they neared her home, the pounding rain slowed, steadied, and relaxed into a soft drizzle. The waves retreated. The wind ran out of puff.

From the top floor of her flat, while she towel-dried her hair, Cleo got a missed call from her mum, but she had an idea what it was about. When she and Eliot had run past, they'd both seen that Coacean was damaged.

'Thanks for coming over, Cleo,' Felicity addressed her daughters the following day, in the living room of the family home.

The Clearwater family nursed the teas and coffees that Bryce had served up, quiet, nobody quite knowing where to start.

Eventually, Cleo spoke. 'It doesn't look too bad to me.'

Gabriela snorted into her coffee and then cursed when it sploshed over the rim and onto her pale blue sweatshirt.

'Gabriela, don't say that word,' Bryce admonished.

'Dad, it's just a word.'

'Seriously though,' Cleo cut in, placing her mug down and walking to the window and looking down at the restaurant. Honestly, the weather today was as if butter couldn't melt in its mouth. It was a beautiful, mid-January day. The sea was completely flat, all waves ironed to perfection. There was neither a breeze nor a cloud in the crisp sky. The last of the snow had been washed away overnight, nearly a month after it first fell, and the grass glistened and stretched towards the rays. 'A couple of new windows, a lick of paint ... ' *An extensive bit of structural repair.*

Coacean was standing strong on its stilts, as always, but the storm had given her a battering last night. Subsequently, it was closed today, and their parents had asked them to come over to discuss a few things.

Felicity sighed. 'It's a little more work than that, but nothing we can't handle. I've asked a couple of building companies to come by this week and give us a quote, but I think we're going to have to be closed for about a month.'

'A month?' Cleo raised her eyebrows. She wouldn't be able to work for a month?

Bryce sighed. 'Luckily, we have good insurance so it won't affect us too badly, but still.'

'And there's something else,' Felicity said. 'Yesterday afternoon, Lucy asked to have a meeting with us, and unfortunately handed in her notice.'

'*WHAT?*' Cleo yelled in surprise.

'I know,' said Felicity.

'Which one is Lucy again?' asked Gabriela. 'Just kidding. That sucks. She's cool.'

'She is,' Felicity agreed. 'She applied to become the front-of-house manager at the hotel. And she got the job. They asked her to start ASAP, but she wanted to give us a month's notice.'

Bryce cut in. 'Though, with what happened last night and the fact we'll now be closed anyway, we've decided to let her go early.'

'Bloody hell ... ' Cleo leaned against the window. She couldn't believe her manager was leaving. After all these years. A stab in her heart reminded her that Eliot was considering leaving for good too.

Sure, he'd said he wouldn't, but how could she let him stay for her?

Go with him, a voice said in her mind.

Shut up, she told it. She didn't have time to think about that right now. It would be all hands on deck for Coacean at the moment. Cleo had never felt a stronger sense of duty to do whatever she could to save her family's business.

'Cleo, we wanted to talk to you about something, in light of Lucy leaving. About your role at the restaurant and what you might, if you're willing, be able to do to help out?'

Cleo lifted her eyes to her mum. 'Help out? I'll do anything to help out, you know that.'

'Brown-noser,' Gabriela snickered.

'Gabriela,' said Felicity. 'Would you stop joking around, this is serious.'

'Sorryyyyyy.'

'Mum, what do you need?' Cleo asked, pulling her mother's attention back. In her chest, her heart began beating fast. Her mouth felt like it had become dry. The clouds in her mind appeared to part a little and all of a sudden something she couldn't quite put her finger on felt like it was trying to tell her something. Something important. Something she wanted.

Felicity stood and faced her daughter. 'Firstly, about the part-time thing you asked about the other week—'

'Oh, Mum, don't worry about that for now, it's not important at all.' *God, Cleo, worst timing ever.*

'It *is* important. What you want *is important*,' Felicity stressed. 'And actually, I'd like to offer you more than that.'

'You do?' *Thud-thud-thud* went Cleo's heart.

'Nobody is more experienced than you, at Coacean. I remember your first day there, when you'd just turned sixteen.'

Cleo glanced to the mantelpiece, where an aged photo sat of her, grinning madly on her first day of work, arm in arm with her dad. She'd known on that day, that this was her future.

'We wanted to ask if … ' Felicity smiled at Bryce. 'Cleo, would you … would you apply to be the new Coacean manager?'

'Huh?'

'*Huh?*' echoed Gabriela. 'You want her to be manager? What about me?'

Cleo blinked.

Bryce slung an arm around her.

Felicity looked hopeful. 'Being a manager is quite a responsibility, but we think you'd be perfect to take that on.

And I know you wanted some space to do some courses, and I'm sure we can work out your new hours to fit in with that.'

Things were changing. This was what she wanted . . . right?

'What do you think?' pushed Bryce. 'We'll ask the rest of the team, of course, see if anyone's interested now. But no one's shown much interest in management, to be honest. At all.'

In any other circumstance, Cleo would rush in with a *yes of course*. A, *whatever you need*. But the words caught in her mouth. She needed a second, somewhere she could be still and think.

The one place she could always be still and think.

'Can I come back to you on that?' she asked, backing away, grabbing her wetsuit from where she'd left it hanging in the porch the day before. 'I'll be back soon.'

Chapter 39

Cleo drifted on her back on the big blue ocean, that big blue sky above her head. She breathed in the sea air deeply, her lungs allowing her to float on the surface, the cold water tickling the edges of her wetsuit. The sounds of seagulls, distant chatter, the thud of pebbles tumbling together as dogs ran along the beach; they all drifted in and out as Cleo's ears bobbed in and out of the ripples.

Her parents wanted her to take over as restaurant manager.

Her sister wanted to move back to Wavebreak Bay and live with her.

Eliot wanted her to go to San Francisco for the summer.

So, what did *she* want?

Cleo lifted her head and watched a couple of swimmers back on the beach, shivering and laughing together in towel robes as they poured small drinks from a flask. The morning sun was behind them, glinting off the metal, and, as she watched, one walked to the edge of the water again and stood with her feet in the seafoam, drinking, and closing her eyes.

She didn't want to let any of these people that she loved down. But she couldn't please everyone.

For the first time in a long time, she'd found her way back to herself, and she was going to put Cleo first.

Cleo raced back up the hill, thirty minutes later, her changing robe flapping behind her as she puffed up the incline.

Opening the porch door, she kicked off her beach shoes and crashed inside the house, leaving salty wet footprints in her wake.

Felicity, Bryce and Gabriela were in the kitchen, where Gabriela seemed to be reading to them from a cookery book, when Cleo appeared in the doorway.

'I KNOW WHAT I WANT,' she said with gusto.

'Hello, love, how was your swim?' Felicity asked.

'Mum, it was brilliant, and I've done some thinking, and I know what I want to do. About everything.'

Gabriela grabbed some bourbon biscuits from the cupboard and sat down, pushing the packet towards her twin. 'This sounds good. Spill.'

Cleo was fizzing inside. She felt like she'd cracked a code she'd been working on for a long time, one that she'd been slowly, slowly, making headway on. And now she knew what would truly break her out of the rut and let her move forward with her life. It was never *just* telling Eliot how she felt. It was never *just* getting back in the sea. It was never about her original dreams not being good enough. It was about all of it, all the pieces of her that existed in the past and the future, all of her authentic self.

'I love our restaurant, but I'm not the manager for you.' She said it quickly, like she might change her mind. Yet, for the first time, she wasn't thinking with a sense of obligation, but because this was what she wanted. 'But I know who is.'

'You do?' asked Bryce.

'I do.' She pointed at her twin. 'Gabriela should do it.'

Gabriela gasped and filled her gaping mouth with two more bourbons, before spitting them into her hand, jumping up and saying, 'Oi, what, what do you mean, why me?'

But the smile forming on her face betrayed her, so Cleo knew she wasn't dead against the idea.

'You're thinking of moving back. You have management experience, you're used to tough, busy environments and you have this wild streak of creativity and confidence that could be just what the place needs. It might have been a long time since you worked in Coacean, but you still grew up there. It's still just as much your business as the rest of ours. Besides,' Cleo faced her parents again, 'she's much bossier than me.'

'Shut your stupid face, I am not. Give me those bourbons.'

Felicity stepped forward. 'Gab, honey, if you'd like to do this, that would be a dream come true. We just always presumed you'd want to head off again rather than stay around here. We never wanted to pressure you into thinking you had to stay with the family business.'

'Well, I mean,' Gabriela looked at their faces, 'I *could*

do it.' She paused, chewing. 'I've never managed a restaurant though.'

'I'd still be around,' Cleo clarified. 'Maybe not as often, but I can help show you the ropes for anything you're unsure of. I think you'd be perfect, actually, to be honest.'

'But if you're hanging around, why don't you want to be manager?'

Cleo sat down, reaching for a biscuit. 'I do still want to be involved, but in a different way. I want to start a new venture, like a joint enterprise with Coacean, so I can create something I think I've been wanting to make for some time. I want to begin opening the restaurant for breakfast, daily, specifically to cater for a new swim club. Like, a "Coacean Swim Club" – but with a better name – where in the mornings people get together and I help them learn to love the water, and then we all have brekkie at the restaurant afterwards. I want to run it, take full responsibility for it. For the community. And for me.'

'That sounds wonderful,' said Felicity. 'That's what your courses would be useful for; I get it now.'

'Exactly,' Cleo said. 'I want to make a real go of it. It's going to take some time, and effort, but it's what I want.'

Bryce nodded. 'It's a great idea.'

And then Gabriela warmed her still-warming-back-up heart by reaching over, putting an arm around Cleo, and saying, 'What did I tell you? You're a safe pair of hands. People will be so lucky to have you.'

Cleo, once, had had a moment where she'd panicked in the water, frozen, and pushed aside thoughts of going in the sea again, let alone leading others into it. But she was so much more than that moment. And if she could motivate anyone else feeling that way too, then no one was suffering alone.

'And!' Cleo cut in. 'Since we're doing repairs, and there would be extra revenue from the breakfast takings, I want a changing area to be fitted so nobody – me – can make the excuse of not wanting to have to swim and then sit in soggy clothes during breakfast.'

She looked down at the puddle of water being created under the table by her feet, and wrapped her changing robe tighter around herself, before continuing. 'In fact, I want to be involved in the refurb. I want to be a decision-maker in the business now. Help turn it into the Coacean I want it to be. Because then, maybe, a year down the line, I'd like to join Eliot in California. I want to be a part of the new restaurant. I want to visit Alcatraz and take road trips and see the floating homes across the bay. And perhaps take my brekkie and swimming club over there. But first I want to do all this, here, for myself.'

She looked at her parents, who were looking at each other. She looked at Gabriela. Gabriela looked at her. There was a lot of looking, and not enough talking.

'Well?' asked Cleo. 'What do you think?'

Chapter 40

March

The spring sunshine kissed Cleo's skin, warm already, even at this time in the morning, as if it knew the summer season was on its way.

Standing with her feet in the shallow of the chilly, gentle waves, Cleo wriggled her toes, and threw her arms in the air to let out a cheer, releasing a rainbow of saltwater droplets from her wetsuit.

'That's amazing, Uncle Stu! Kaleb, hold that pose, I want a photo just like that.'

She held up her phone and snapped some more, quick, shots of the members of her 'Ocean & Orange Juice' swim club, who this morning had been joined by her uncle and his boyfriend who were down from Bath for a visit.

The bright pink, orange and turquoise rash vests she'd had made, with the club's logo that she'd designed, fresh from the printers only yesterday, looked gorgeous against the backdrop of teal ocean.

It was only the second week of her club's first season

of being up and running (and only the third week since Coacean reopened its doors following the storm damage).

She'd had a busy February, pouring all of her heart into planning the details of the Ocean & Orange Juice Club, advertising it on the town noticeboards and in the local paper, setting up social media pages, spreading the word, beginning her course on open-water safety and working with Coacean's super-fresh manager – her twin sister, thank you very much – on the new breakfast menu. Which, according to her handful (so far) of members, was absolutely delicious. And she had so many other ideas to bring in more new swimmers, new friends. Free pancakes for the star swimmer of the week? An O&OJ club trip? The possibilities were endless.

Cleo smiled at them now, splashing about, laughter rising towards the sunrise, and her soul felt happy, and blended in with the sand and the waves.

'Hey, you coming back in?' Rosa said, dragging herself up and out of the sea, squeezing out her hair, her cheeks flushed a healthy pink.

'Absolutely; just wanted to get some shots of you all having so much fun out there.'

Panting, Rosa put her hands on her hips and surveyed the scene alongside Cleo. 'It is fun. You've done a great thing, here, Clee. I'm going to miss this.'

After the restaurant closure, Rosa had broken the news that she was taking this as a sign and heading back to New Zealand. It was time to stop travelling, for now, and see once and for all about that Ms-Maybe back at home.

For a moment, Cleo had panicked. Another friend

leaving her! But she quickly remembered that that was OK. That people could come and go on their own journeys, and that didn't mean she had to put her own on hold. Her journey, her life, didn't have to be measured against or defined by other people's. Instead, they could simply be a part of each other's stories.

In her job, friends came and went. Cleo just had to remember that she did have people she could be real with, and maybe, down the line, she could be real with everyone, one day. Plus, she was building some new bonds and friendships now, thanks to her swim club, her own little community.

'You'll stay in touch, won't you?' Cleo hugged her tight. 'And you know there's always a place for you here.'

'Absolutely. I want to take a ride in that new van of yours. See a little more of the UK than just this place, as beautiful as it is, of course.' The two of them glanced up at the clifftop, to where Cleo's lemon-yellow VW campervan could just be seen, parked outside her parents' house since she'd bought it off Patrick, the fisherman moving to France, glinting under the morning sun.

In her spare time, she'd been sprucing it up, filling it with touches of who she was, favourite books, brand new notepads, photos of friends and family, postcards from Eliot. It was just what she'd always wanted.

'When are you taking her out on the road?' Rosa asked.

'In a few weeks, under Gabriela's orders.'

'She's going with you?'

'Oh yeah, this was all her idea. Technically, we split the

cost, and she hates the very idea of camping in any way, but she said if enforced minibreaks together was the only way to make sure I didn't get sucked into – her words – "a depressing pit of perfectionist people-pleasing", it was worth it.'

Rosa laughed, and then threw her arms around Cleo. 'Come on, one more swim, and then I'd better say goodbye, my friend.'

Cleo followed Rosa back into the ocean for their final swim together.

A little while later, when Rosa, Stuart, Kaleb, Iris from the diner, Amelie – Cleo's old schoolfriend – and the couple of new faces who had joined the club, all made their way up the beach to Coacean, Cleo pulled her wetsuit down to her waist and popped a hoodie over the top of her swimsuit, and packed up the club's remaining clobber.

And then …

'How was the ocean today?' came her favourite voice in the world.

Cleo smiled. 'She's amazing, as always.'

She turned around to face Eliot, and kissed him, his lips tasting of morning coffee and his skin as warm as Californian sunshine.

'Is it what you hoped it would be?' he asked, picking up a spare rash vest. 'And can I take one of these with me?'

'Very much so, and yes.' God, it felt good to be hopeful again, and not to be putting all her excitement onto Eliot and his schedule. Now, she was excited to do something for herself for a change.

Cleo was excited that, with her new role, she was able to

stay a part of the business, but in a way that let her be creative and true to what she really wanted, which was to work with, and in, the water.

She was excited about her swim group. She was excited every morning to get in the sea. And she was excited to keep trying, each day, to be authentically her.

She was excited that her twin sister had not only made the move back to Wavebreak Bay, but that she had taken on Coacean's manager position with her usual buzzy self-confidence. When their parents had questioned Gabriela on whether this was *really* what she wanted, considering it was quite a big change from her life in Cambridge, Gabriela had withered, 'No, Mum, Cambridge was a big change from my life *here*. Besides, I'm no more married to a life in office work than I am to that wanker Derek.' And so had begun a beautiful new road for Gabriela, who had come back home, and to herself again.

And Cleo was, of course, excited for Eliot to come home to her again in a few months' time, to spend the winter with her in Wavebreak Bay. He'd insisted. They were a team now.

And she was *very* excited that next summer she'd be heading back with him, for a dream Californian adventure, and to help build the new branch, perhaps taking Ocean & Orange Juice over to Cali.

'Are you all packed?' Cleo asked Eliot now. Spring was here, bringing with it promises of sunworshippers and holidaymakers, ice-cream enthusiasts and coast-path ramblers.

'Yep, all packed, keys returned. Next stop: San Francisco.'

'You're happy with your decision? Accepting the offer

from my parents, I mean. Is this truly what you want?' she asked. Just to be sure.

He laughed. 'Absolutely. It's perfect. I'm starting something new that's mine, and you're doing the same for you, and in no time at all we're going to be bringing those new things together. I think the rest of our lives just got pretty exciting.'

Cleo was going to miss him more than she ever had before, and from the way his face grew serious all of a sudden, she knew he felt the same.

'Don't fall in love with a California girl,' she said. 'Katy Perry made them sound really cool.'

'I'm already in love with someone just as cool,' Eliot replied.

'Who is she? I'll kill her.'

He laughed and pulled her in for a long, tight hug. Cleo pressed herself into him, as if she could fuse their hearts together once and for all. 'I'll miss you,' she said.

'I'll miss you too.'

'You'll still write me postcards, won't you? I know we'll FaceTime, but they're one of my favourite things about you over the summer.'

'I will write you a postcard for every week I'm away. And you'll do the same? I think you're going to have such an adventure this summer.'

Cleo grinned. 'Yes, every week.'

They were silent for a minute, imprinting each other's faces in their minds, although after fifteen years he still knew her better than anyone.

'Oh! We have something for you,' Eliot said all of a sudden, glancing back towards the restaurant, where Gabriela was pulling a bulky item from between the two flower-filled dinghies below the stilts.

'We?'

He raced over to Cleo's twin, just as Felicity and Bryce appeared too, and the four of them carried something large, shuffling and huddling to block it from her view.

'What are you all doing?' Cleo asked.

'Ta-dah!' Gabriela said, dropping the object onto the exposed sand with a thud, and standing to the side.

In the warm, spring breeze, Cleo's curls blew across her face. Strands of her hair were lightening due to the amount of time she was spending outdoors these days, and she pushed them out of her face to see what her family were gathered around.

A bright kayak, the minty-turquoise of sea foam, with the orange-pink swim club emblem on the top, stood tall, now propped up by Eliot's hands. It had a bow taped around it.

'Whose is that?' Cleo asked, her eyes wide. The kayak was beautiful.

'Yours, you idiot.' Gabriela came over and pulled her towards the board. 'But I might get a matching one because I'm jelly.'

'Mine?'

'From all of us,' Eliot explained. 'We thought it might come in useful for your club, so you can paddle about and keep an eye on everyone.'

'You all got this, for me?' Cleo was touched.

'You deserve to have something done for you, for a change,' Bryce explained, and Cleo felt tears prickle at her eyes at the thoughtfulness.

'I love it,' she said, stroking the gift. 'Thank you, all of you.'

'I need to get going,' Eliot said quietly, and Cleo's family filtered back into the house.

'Already? But it feels like winter's only just begun.'

'I'll always come home. You're my home.'

Eliot kissed Cleo in ways that surpassed all those kisses she'd had in her dreams. She savoured every second, running her fingers over his face, into his hair, and when he pulled away, she didn't let herself feel sad, because this winter one of her wishes had come true. And now she was finally being authentic with herself, and giving herself the space to follow her dreams, so many more were to follow.

Chapter 41

San Francisco, California
  15th May

Dear Cleo,
  How's the water? Have you tried out the new kayak
yet? Just think, next summer you'll be swimming in
the Pacific!
  San Francisco is as beautiful as ever, restaurant
doing well, saw a sea lion, reminded me of you.
  Wish you were here, but I'll always come back to you.
  Love, Eliot x

Newquay, Cornwall
1st June
Dear Eliot,
I'm on a minibreak! Gabriela is asleep on the beach and
I just had a swim in the sea, and tonight we're getting
takeout pizza because I'm refusing to be anywhere near
seafood on our holiday.

Guess who came to O&OJ last week? Alexis Alexander!
The surfer! She was in town, and she came to Coacean
and everything. I'm having the best summer I've had in a
long time.
I can't wait to spend next summer with you. It'll be like
old times, except better.
Wish you were here, but I'll always come back to you, too.
Love, Cleo x

ACKNOWLEDGEMENTS

Hi, my friends! Hope you liked *A Snowfall by the Sea*, and that it warmed you like a massive hot chocolate held in woollen mittens beside a fireplace.

A few words of thanks before I head back out to the beach . . .

Lovely Bec, my editor, thanks for your kindness, patience and oyster pearls of wisdom! You're awesome to work with, and to slosh back a couple of peach Bellinis with too. Darcy and Sophie, thanks a million for your insight and guidance, and for adding sun-sparkles to my words.

Thank you to all at Sphere and Little, Brown Book Group for everything you do. Thank you, Liz, Ben and Nithya, for your detailed eyes and friendly direction through the proofing process. Thank you, Natasha, for the peachy publicity, and Laura for the marvellous marketing. Thank you, Robyn and Bekki, for this wonderfully wintery and snow-dusted cover.

Thank you, Hannah, my ace literary agent, for being by my side and utterly brilliant, always. Love that I get to work with you. And an extended thanks to the amazing team at Hardman & Swainson: Nicole, Thérèse, Joanna and Caroline: you are all so appreciated.

Thanks to my family and friends who are the biggest cheerleaders and who put up with me when I fog over and disappear into the brains of my characters for a large part of each year. Extra clotted cream dollops go to my yummy Husband Phil, my other leading man Kodi, and my magnificent mum and dad. Heaps of thanks, too, to Emma for beta reading my books, which makes for *better* reading for everyone else.

Big love to the awesomely supportive author crowd, the beautiful bloggers, and my spectacular readers.

Without you all, these would just be a bunch of made-up stories floating about in my brain. Along with thoughts about what to eat next and wondering if I've told my dog that I love him enough times that day.

And a big thanks to my beloved Jurassic Coast, Devon, which inspired this novel, and my own seaside crew who live here, and are my year-round sunshine.

I'll let you go now, fellow bookworms. *Sea* ya later!

Isla xx

Escape to the mountains and fall in love this Christmas . . .

Alice Bright has a great life. She has a job she adores, a devoted family and friends she'd lay down her life for. But when tragedy strikes, she finds her whole world turned upside down.

Enter, Bear, a fluffy, lovable – and rapidly growing! – puppy searching for a home. Bear may be exactly what Alice needs to rekindle her spark, but a London flat is no place for a mountain dog, and soon Alice and Bear find themselves on a journey to the snow-topped mountains of Switzerland in search of a new beginning.

Amidst the warming log fires, cosy cafes and stunning views, Alice finds her heart slowly beginning to heal. But will new friends and a charming next door neighbour be enough to help Alice fall in love with life once more?

**'The most beautiful, heart-warming story.
Gorgeously cosy, uplifting . . . utterly lovely book'
Holly Martin**

Would you marry a stranger to live the life of your dreams?

August Anderson needs somewhere to live. Dumped by her boyfriend who would rather be alone than move in with her, she has almost given up on happiness. Until she notices that the beautiful Georgian townhouse she's long admired is seeking a new tenant, and suddenly things begin to look up ...

There's just one catch – the traditional, buttoned-up landlord is only willing to rent to a stable, married couple and August, quite frankly, is neither. Competition for the house is fierce and August knows she'll have to come up with a plan or risk losing her last shot at her happy ending.

Enter Flynn, the handsome, charming and somewhat unsuspecting gentleman who August accidentally spills her coffee over. Flynn is new to the area and is looking for somewhere to live, and August thinks she knows just the place, but only if he's willing to tell a little white lie ...

'Sunday afternoon bliss!' FABULOUS magazine

Will a magical winter in Lapland help
Myla fall in love with festive?

Myla is the UK's least-festive woman. Starting the year she
found out the truth about Santa Claus, everything bad that's
ever happened to her occurs around Christmas. Nowadays,
she wants nothing to do with this time of year, so of course
she would lose the bet with her sister and be forced to put
herself forward for a seasonal job in Lapland, welcoming
tourists to Santa's winter wonderland for the holidays.

Ten weeks, temperatures well below freezing, days that are
mostly dark, and the need to stay brimming with Christmas
spirit doesn't fill Myla with joy as she heads off to the arctic
circle for winter in Finland. But as she discovers that Lapland
is more than Santa Claus's Village, the very last person she
ever thought she'd fall for turns out to be a man who plays
an Elf, and who is bound to stay in character at all times.

Will a little love under the Northern Lights convince Myla
that her bad luck might finally have come to an end?

'A heart warmer' *Heat*